VOLUME

CW00839529

AXEL LENNART AND THE ICE WORLD

D.M.Z. Liyanage

AXEL LENNART AND THE ICE WORLD

Contents

Dedication

This book is dedicated to:

My family: Ella, Sebastian, Jessica and Ali, my mother Bridget and father Piyatissa, the Herons, the Vernons and the Jacksons, the Blakes, and my best friend, Sophie Shaw.

Friends: Jamie Gould, Amber, Lucy & Adam Smith, Tara Odesanya, Rolake Odesanya, Lottie & Ellie Hughes, Harper, Halle, Fay & Andy McEwan, Laura Humphrey, Tina Patel, Naomi Everett, Sarah Bayliss, Alli Salmon, Pauline Starkey, Alex Dawes, Elaine Li, Esther Caszo, Emma Swannack, Kas Graham, Sophia, Ruth and Gus Romano-Jackson, Jemima Warren, Rachel Tomlins, Lalitha Sundaram, Nino, Carolina, Mary & Mario Toraldo-King, Vic Howarth, Chris Leone, Greg Ellis, Oliver Brown, Karen Pryce, Nancy Baillie, Ben Parry, Justin Bamford, Graham Braithwaite, Emily Bradshaw, Tori (& William) Moss, Helen Jones, Lucy Reed, Amy Williams, Steffen Backer-Rowley, Will Gatford & Rose Schiowitz.

Bosses ☺: Malcolm Davidson, Matthew Dunn, John Munday, Robert Perry, Mark Sheehan, Stuart Fanti & Mike O'Dell...so many bosses!

Wonderful book reviewers: Jack & Scott Langley, Ed & Tim Medcalf, Hannah & Karina Rix, Asasila Igaga, Andrew Mace & daughter. Thank you for your kind reviews – they were a ray of light on dark days.

Escape and Capture

1.

The air was dry and smelt like burning. Through it, the alarms of the prison fortress blared, their high-pitched wail almost drowning out the thump of the Guards' boots as they hurried through a long corridor.

Within his cell, Convict-5257 stood, body crooked, his dirty fingers rigid and shaking with effort as they stretched out through the air towards the door. Despite the negative bleeps coming from it, the door had slid open slightly, and was now juddering as it desperately tried to close itself again. Renewing his efforts, the convict's fingertips started to glow with a red light. The door rattled violently against the strong magnetic lock that held it in place.

'VR-5, report,' The Head Guard barked as he entered the busy Control Room in the convict's sector.

'It *is* Prisoner-5257, sir,' Guard VR-5 replied, his face taut and pale. 'His powers – they must have returned!'

'Nonsense!' the Head Guard scoffed. 'It must be an equipment malfunction.'

He peered at the screen displaying a video feed of the corridor outside the convict's cell, as a troop of Unity Guards spilled into it, the crimson of their uniforms bright against the gloom. Blast visors pulled down over their faces, they waited, bodies tense. Shoulder's hunched and shaking, the convict gave a final push. With a loud cracking sound, his cell door broke apart. Shuddering from the exertion, the convict moved through the ragged opening, his movements jerky, limbs heavy with fatigue. The Head Guard, who had a thin face and watery blue eyes, pushed his lips into a narrow line. 'Shoot to kill,' he ordered.

The Unity Guards in the corridor complied. Blue fire raced through the darkness, burning through the air from the Guards' blast rifles, and filling the corridor with thick smoke. They continued firing until a few shots landed square in the convict's chest. Bird-like, he crumpled to the floor. As the smoke started to clear, the blood drained from the Guards' faces. The convict struggled to his feet, a crooked smile stretched across his mutilated face as he emerged from the hazy darkness and moved jaggedly towards them. The Head Guard's mouth dropped open in alarm.

'Lock down that sector. NOW!' he ordered.

With the push of the button, large blast doors came down on either side of the corridor, trapping the troop of Unity Guards in with the convict. Choking down their fear, the Guards fired again. The convict stumbled momentarily as more shots hit him, but with a murmur of words under his breath, the tips of his fingers started to glow again with red light. The gunfire stopped. For a moment there was quiet, disturbed only by the constant hum of the fortress air vents. Then, the Guards started to choke and gasp as water bubbled out from their open mouths. They dropped to their knees, rifles clattering to the floor as their hands reached uselessly up to their throats.

'What's happening to them?' the Head Guard asked.

'It looks like they're…*drowning*, sir,' Guard VR-5 replied.

As the Guards' bodies ceased to move, the convict came forward and placed his hand over a control panel in the wall. After a moment, the shield doors lifted smoothly, letting him pass through with ease.

'SHUT ALL THE SHIELD DOORS!' the Head Guard shouted.

'They're not responding, sir!' one of the other Guards cried.

With a low bleep and a quiet woosh, the doors to the Control Room opened and the convict appeared on the threshold.

'Fire! FIRE!' the Head Guard ordered.

Convict-5257 started to laugh. And with whispered words, everyone in the Control Room, save for the Head Guard, were suddenly lifted off their feet, as though invisible hands had wrapped themselves around their throats and pulled them upwards. They gasped for air helplessly, arms flailing in panic. With a glow in his fingertips, the Convict set the hanging men alight. Waving a hand with indifference, the Control Room doors slammed shut and emitted another bleep to indicate they were now locked.

The Head Guard pulled out a Persuader, but the gun melted in his hands as he pointed it at the convict. It ran through his fingers as a dark, reflective liquid, pooling on the floor in front of him. The Head Guard stumbled back in fear and alarm, his fingers slipping uselessly over the buttons of a nearby control desk as he tried to open the doors himself.

'Send more troops to Control, Prisoner-5257 has escaped!' the Head Guard said, into his communicator. 'Assistance is required. NOW!'

Smiling, the convict stretched his fingers out to point at the Head Guard's chest, until the sound of his heartbeat filled the room. His pulse started to quicken, and his breath turned to short, sharp gasps. The Head Guard's face grew red and flushed, his eyes large with terror.

'What – are –you – d-doing to me?' he gasped, a thin veil of sweat filming his face.

The convict's eyes gleamed with a strange red glow.

'Your heart is so…weak. So fragile…' the convict replied, with a crooked smile. Twisting his fingers, the air between them began to pulse with energy. *What is the code to access your ship?*

What could be seen of his face in the emergency lighting was cut and scarred, the bone of his jaw and skull visible in places. The Head Guard smiled a little and shook his head. 'You will *not* escape. The

Regime will *hunt* you down. You *will* be recaptured,' he said, smugly.

'No. All who serve the Regime will *die*. Defeated and afraid, just as *you* will,' the convict said, his fingertips beginning to glow red again.

'Stop this…W-wait…I will tell you. The code is 9…88-43…7. *Please*...let me live.'

Eyes glinting in the dark, the convict focused his mind on the Guard, who started to squirm uncomfortably as the beats of his heart grew quicker and quicker. His breath came in ragged gasps, as the pain in his chest increased.

'No…' the Head Guard cried. 'NO!'

*

Far away, on the blustery, ice world of Eleusis, Axel Lennart woke suddenly, his heart thumping in his chest. *Bad dreams*…he thought, as he blinked into the darkness. Pushing himself into a sitting position, he sat for a moment on the edge of his bed, frowning slightly. The dream of the prison fortress had felt so real; the feeling of it lingered upon him, like a dark cloud on a sunny day. And he could not explain it, but he felt strange, somehow. Like he was no longer alone – like someone was *watching* him. Casting a glance behind himself, he jolted slightly. But it was only his reflection in his bedroom window that had startled him.

'Ridiculous…' he murmured, scratching the back of his neck.

And yet…the feeling remained. *Was there someone there?* He frowned as he looked back into the semi-darkness beyond. Outside, the other huts of the Homestead were peaceful and quiet under a star-filled sky. The alarm on his Navwatch suddenly sounded in his ears, making him jump again. Rushing to slam it off, he groaned and rubbed his eyes wearily. He felt terrible.

As he grabbed his boots, the door of the bedroom slid open with a low bleep, and his tiny, battered old Chore Droid rumbled into the room. The droid, who was small enough for Axel to lift with one hand, looked like a silver rectangular box on wheels, his over-large eyes inquisitive and eager. He squeaked loudly and cheerily in greeting.

'Quiet, S-LO!' Axel hissed.

S-LO immediately froze.

'What're you trying to do? Wake up the whole Homestead with your *Good Morning!?* Axel said.

S-LO bleeped in annoyance and then let out a few much quieter, more inquisitive squeaks.

'Where am *I* going? Well, let's just say it's better that you don't know,' Axel whispered, pulling on his boots.

S-LO squeaked again.

'No, you *can't* come. Not safe for droids. Not even sure it's safe for *me*…Look, do me a favour, if Kolbjorn wakes up before I'm back, just tell him I went straight to Fosse junkyard to help Chuck, okay?'

S-LO bleeped negatively.

'What do you mean that it's against your programming to lie?'

The droid explained at length, in several haughty squeaks.

'*Hey*…I *do* have morals…' Axel interjected; a wounded look on his face.

A little while later he pushed his airbike down to the roadway as quietly as he could, wishing he could hush the crunch of the snow beneath his boots and the low hum of the airbike as it hovered above the ground. From here, he could see the vast roll of the Black Mountains in the distance and hear the frozen branches of the trees as they rattled in the wind, scattering snow through the cool, dark air.

This was Principality-5, the northernmost sector of Eleusis, and its capital, not that there was much of a population on this planet.

11

Most of the other Principalities were inhabited by nomadic tribes and were sparsely punctuated by a few trading posts - of the kind that made Principality-5 look like a bustling metropolis.

Axel's airbike was black and worn. Long handles stretched up from an engine concealed by metal casings that had seen better days. Third-hand and modified to the maximum, Axel had even installed a talk function and named her Sandra. Mounting his bike, he stole a glance back to the now distant huts of the Homestead, making certain all the windows were still dark, and no wisps of grey smoke curled into the air from the smoke holes.

Kolbjorn had better not find out where he was heading, or he'd really be in for it, Axel thought with a grimace as he started the engine. Kolbjorn hated rule breaking. Of any kind.

*

An hour later, Axel was starting to wish he had stayed in bed. Hearing the click and clatter of several blasters being readied to fire, he lifted his hands over his head in surrender.

'Okay, okay…take it easy, no need to get excited,' he said, as several threatening figures emerged from the murky gloom around him. 'I'm not armed. I've got a business proposition, for Balo Fuse.'

Unintelligible murmurs rose up around him as a small droid rumbled across the room and pressed a button. The unwelcome sound of several shield doors shutting behind Axel mingled with muted laughter. As his eyes adjusted to the lack of light, he could see that Balo's lair stood large and dark around him. The circular space seemed only to be lit by the control panels that punctuated the grey walls, their rectangular coloured buttons glowing faintly through the haze. Axel moved his feet and his boots crunched on something that sounded suspiciously like bone covered in gloop. He tried not to think on it.

As a greenish light appeared from an antechamber that led off from the room in which Axel stood, he could now see all the clearer the number of blasters pointed at his head. Balo's friends surrounded him. Nevertheless, Axel turned towards the source of the light, which was emanating from a kind of hovering throne that was moving slowly towards him. Balo Fuse - the waste of space Axel was here to see – lounged languidly on it.

'Business.......?' Balo drawled, feigning languid surprise. 'Proposition......?'

Balo Fuse was a moneylender and small-time crook. Originally from the distant planetary system of Olous, he had grey, scaled skin and large domed eyes. He was slight in figure, his shoulders constantly hunched, and a half-burnt smoke dart usually wedged firmly between his long fish-like lips.

'*Yes*. I'm here about my father's debts,' Axel prompted. 'You didn't reply to my message, so I thought I would come here and...'

'*Persuade* me?' Balo said, with a thick, guttural laugh, as the pink vapour of a smoke-dart poured out of his mouth and curled into the air around him.

'*Negotiate* with you,' Axel said, his patience wearing thin.

He knew he had a short temper, but he also knew that this was certainly not the time to lose it.

'You are referring, I suppose, to the debts of Kolbjorn Lennart - the man you *call* Father,' Balo sneered.

He surveyed Axel for a moment and considered what a tall and scrawny boy he was, mouse brown hair and olive skin – darker than usual for these parts – and bags under tired eyes, which were the colour of moss.

'On what desolate planet did he find you, again? Wasn't it Chalkis?'

Axel scowled. 'Yeah, what's it to you?'

'Just *curious*,' Balo said, an infuriating smile plastered across his face.

'Sounds like you know something - about me - where I come from?' Axel said, trying to hide the hope from his voice, immediately angry with himself for not being able to do so.

'Look at him…*So* eager to know where he comes from…To *belong*,' Balo said, laughing.

The others around them laughed too. Axel folded his arms and waited for them to stop. He should have known Balo was just toying with him.

'Balo. I *came* here to tell you that I can get you your money. I just need two days.'

'But payment is due today…'

'Come on Balo, if you'd just give me a chance -'

A sudden breeze whispered though the still close air of the lair, and Balo's large eyes drifted from the floor up to Axel with renewed interest, a new idea growing brighter in his mind. He licked his lips.

'What if I was to tell you that I no longer want money for Kolbjorn's debt?'

'Huh?'

'Well…I heard that the Regime have been finding all kinds of interesting things, out on the wastes. *Völvur* treasures, buried in the ice. Treasures with *special* powers.'

Axel laughed. 'Oh, come on, Balo - don't tell me you believe in all that Völvur nonsense? *Witches* and *Wizards*?!'

Balo puffed away, as a slow menacing grin spread across his moist face.

'What if I said I wanted *you* to go out there…into the wastes…and find me something? I have co-ordinates of an ice formation that is of some interest to me. I will send them to you.'

Axel processed this a moment. 'Look…I stopped doing that a while back, when the Regime started sending search parties out there. Do you know how many Patrols there are on the wastes right now? I'd most likely get caught before the fifth marker!'

'Bring me a Völvur object of value, and I will consider not only your *father's* debts cleared, but also those of your idiot friend, Chuck Bergo.'

'*Chuck's* debts?'

'Oh yes. His debts are almost as substantial as Kolbjorn's, I tell you. I will clear both debts if you bring me something today.'

'*Today?* That's impossible!' Axel said, wide eyed.

'Would you prefer I call in the debts? Make your *father* and your friend my slaves...' Balo interrupted greasily.

Axel paused, eyes narrowing as he considered the request.

'Alright. No problem. I'll bring you something. Something you've never seen before.'

The laughter of Balo and his friends filled the place again.

'Good...' Balo murmured, his thick lips spread tight across his shiny face. 'Be back in two hours with a *Völvur* object, or the deal is off.'

*

An hour later and Axel was far into the ice wastes, a scarf wrapped tight around his face, his whole body coated in a layer of snow. He was on foot now, his bike too loud to risk out here.

'Two hours?!' Axel grumbled to himself. 'What am I going to find in two hours? This is a joke.'

Holding his scanner to his eyes he picked out the unnaturally straight lines of a large ice formation through the blustery snow, some way ahead. Arms half outstretched like a fledgling bird, he hurried towards it, boots sliding over the ice of a frozen lake. As he grew near the formation, he found his feet slowing to a stop. There was *that* feeling again – like someone's eyes were on him, watching him. The wide sweep of the wastes stretched out in all directions, vast and empty, the white ground crisscrossed with the footprints of animals who had traversed it during the night, the only evidence of their mysterious presence fast disappearing under the thickly falling snow. Turning quickly, Axel saw that *this* time, his instincts had been correct.

'S-LO!' he groaned.

His little Chore Droid was rumbling along some way behind, but at Axel's tone he froze.

'S-LO, what are you doing here?!' Axel cried, stomping incredulously over to his droid.

S-LO emitted a few high-pitched squeaks.

'What do you mean, *I* need protection? From *what*?!'

S-LO bleeped that a strange man had been following Axel all the way from the Homestead. Frowning, Axel put his scanner to his eyes and looked around. 'What man?! There's no one in sight!' he grumbled.

S-LO continued to argue his point, with a series of technical sounding bleeps. Ignoring them, Axel rolled his eyes.

'Will you shut up? Or do you want to alert the whole Regime to the fact that you think I'm being followed? I don't believe this!' he said, stuffing his struggling droid under an arm before carrying on, back out into the blustery wastes.

'You'd better not get me caught! Rusty old bag of bolts...'

S-LO bleeped in indignance.

*

Balo's ice formation was at least three times Axel's height, made up of two large blocks leaning against each other, forming a narrow corridor between them. Stepping into the blue light of the corridor, Axel could see a squat, ancient-looking Autobot frozen within one of the smooth ice blocks, the silvery steel of his rectangular body untarnished and devoid of rust, his binocular shaped eyes tilted

16

upwards in an expression of eternal surprise.

'Sorry, friend, I haven't come to free you today,' Axel said, shooting the Autobot an apologetic wince.

Setting S-LO down, Axel watched the droid trundle down the corridor excitedly, cheered by the novelty of being outside of the hut. Axel followed, but with far less excitement. Just like the other spots he had already visited, it was clear that someone – most probably Unity Regime Guards - had been here already, as chunks of ice had been haphazardly melted away, presumably to retrieve items frozen within. With a sinking heart, Axel realised that the Guards were unlikely to have missed anything of worth. He did find an old metal tool half buried in the frozen ground. It had some writing printed onto it in the old language, which read '*WILSON TENNIS PRO 2000.*'

Axel scratched his head bemusedly as he inspected the tool. S-LO rumbled over and squeaked in query.

'*I* don't know what it's for, S-LO. Disciplining rogue Chore Droids, perhaps...?' Axel said, with an evil grin.

S-LO bleeped in irritation.

'Well, whatever it was for, I doubt it's the kind of *treasure* Balo's after,' Axel added, throwing it aside.

The end of the corridor came up against the sheer surface of an ice cliff, within which a starship had been frozen mid-flight. The name '*Celandine*' glimmered off the bow. It was strange – the name seemed familiar somehow, but Axel couldn't remember where he had heard it before. Pulling his gaze away from the ship, he leant heavily against one ice wall, staring sullenly into another. The ghost of his reflection stared back at him, dressed in a standard grey Regime bodysuit and cloak, his mouse-brown hair shorn close to his head on each side, exactly as per Regime regulations.

Ripping the wrapper off a Banth stick, he devoured half of it in one hopeless bite. His gaze drifted across the ice wall in front of him, his eye catching on something. Pausing mid-chew, he stuffed the rest of the stick into his pocket and moved closer to the wall. He couldn't be sure, but it looked like there was an object frozen deep within it. It was almost invisible against the shadows, but it looked small and rectangular – like a case of some kind.

'S-LO, buddy – come take a look at this!' he said, pulling a laser heating device from his belt.

S-LO hurried over and bleeped curiously as Axel melted the ice around the object. It was a small metal case, with the name *'ELEUSIS'* branded onto it.

'Huh,' Axel mused.

Hands slipping eagerly over the wet release buttons of the case, he pried it open. Shoulders slumping in disappointment, Axel shifted back onto his haunches. The case only contained a stack of small rectangular strips of grey metal, each of which emitted a small glow of white light that dimmed and brightened in a repetitive sequence.

'Oh, S-LO. They're just a bunch of info-chips, pre-regime from the looks of them,' Axel said.

Turning the chips over in his hands, he could see no identifying marks on them. Wondering what data they held, he looked back down the corridor, his eyes fixing on the permanently surprised Autobot.

'We...We...We're all d-d-doomed...' the ancient Autobot stuttered, once Axel had thawed him out.

Water ran through the joints in the droid's outer casings, causing sparks to flash up here and there. Axel winced, feeling sorry for the poor bot. He'd been right - everyone on this world had been doomed, the day the ice came, eighteen years ago.

'Hey old boy, do you think you could do me a favour and read these chips for me?' Axel said, knowing he did not have much time before this droid gave out for good, or before a troop of Unity Guards passed through the area.

The lights of the Autobot's eyes flashed momentarily before dimming.

'Y-yes…s-sir, h-happy to b-e of as-assistance,' he replied, after a long pause.

'Thanks,' Axel said, slotting one of the chips in.

A moment later, a large holographic image of buildings and roads splurged out into the air from the Autobot's projector.

'Maps…' Axel said, hurriedly taking the chip out and slotting another one in. 'They're just old maps of Eleusis - before it was frozen,' he grumbled, kicking the ground half-heartedly and slumping down next to the Autobot. 'No one'll want these! They're worthless.'

Glancing at his Navwatch, Axel's heart sunk further into his stomach. It was time to start on the return journey.

'We're all d-doomed…We…we're…were…' the Autobot said again, the hologram shutting off and the lights of his over-sized eyes dimming.

Axel shot the droid a sympathetic look. 'Got that right, friend,' he agreed, eyeing the tennis racket and useless info-chips dispiritedly. 'But don't worry, rest now.'

Standing slowly, he reached gently under the Autobot's head and pressed the button to power him down. S-LO let out a solitary, melancholic bleep. The loud rumble of something approaching roused them both from their momentary dip in spirits. The unmistakable hum of several Unity Regime Air Tractors grew louder and louder on the cool, snowy air. Axel groaned. Peering reluctantly around the edge of an ice outcrop, his suspicions were confirmed as he set eyes on a convoy of large grey vehicles hovering towards him.

'*Spacenuts*,' Axel swore, stuffing his hands into his pockets for inspiration, and coming up with only his half-eaten Banth stick. Windowless and tank-like, the smooth metal surface of the air tractors started to emerge through the snow, their gray outer-casings dull and pristine.

'Come on S-LO, we wouldn't want to outstay our welcome,' Axel said, stuffing the info-chips into his pocket, before grabbing his alarmed droid and, after a moment's hesitation, the metal tennis tool. Rushing out into the swirling snow, he took cover behind a rocky outcrop, praying that they hadn't been seen. The icy ground under him started to tremble as the air tractors grew nearer, and with a sinking sensation in the pit of his stomach, Axel heard them come to a stop somewhere behind the outcrop that was sheltering them from view. Heart clicking against his ribs, he flattened himself against the rocks as he heard the crunch of two sets of boots on snow and the sharp clatter of Snipe Rifles knocking against hard chest plates. Axel shot a worried glance at S-LO. They *were* doomed.

'Leave our airbikes and take the tractors back for refueling. We'll finish the sweep of Sector-3,' a harsh voice commanded, to whoever was driving the air tractors.

Through the crack in the rocks, Axel glimpsed a little of the Unity Guards as they waited for their airbikes to be unloaded, their crimson cloaks whipping in the wind. As the rumble of the tractors quietened, he could make out the quiet hum of the Guards' airbikes hovering a little way off the ground, on the other side of the rocks. The closest Guard was a fat man, whose belly strained at the waist of his uniform, his knuckles scabbed and red from a recent fight. An almost spent smoke-dart hung limply from his thick lips, encasing his wide, soft face in a halo of grey vapour. The name 'TQ-1' was emblazoned on his red bodysuit.

'TQ-1. C-Come in,' a message struggled through deep static onto his communicator.

'Control, this is TQ-1, do you read, copy?' the fat Guard replied.

Nothing but static returned.

'Bad signal out here - must be a storm coming,' the second Guard said, his sallow face thin and pinched under his visor, as he tried his own device. 'We'd better hurry and complete our sweep, and get that find back to base,' he said, motioning to a long dark case that was strapped to the back of one of the airbikes.

Axel eyed it curiously. Whatever it was might be of interest to Balo, he thought, wondering how he could swipe it from under the Guards' noses.

'Just let me finish my dart,' the fat Guard grunted.

'S-Search for Ob-bject X-06 upgraded, h-high priority,' a message from the Control Room crackled through to the Guards' communicators.

Axel listened with interest, wondering what this Object X-06 was, and why the Regime was so interested in it. But just then, a sudden, sharp pain in his head broke his chain of thought. A terrible headache. Holding a hand to his pounding head, he grimaced, feeling a bout of nausea bubble up through him. Shaking slightly, he turned back to the wastes behind him confusedly. Just as before, he could have sworn he was being watched. An approaching snowstorm was blowing in off the edges of the wastes, moving closer with every passing moment, but there was no one in sight. Setting S-LO down onto the thick snow, Axel's eyes were drawn upwards, to the tumultuous sky overhead.

For a moment, the swiftly moving clouds thinned and he could see the triple moons of Scarto, Upllox and Tocras, as they spun above the horizon, their pale outlines just visible in the daytime sky. As he looked at them, he felt that strange presence again - that puzzling familiarity. The feeling washed over him with renewed strength. It was as if he had just seen someone whose face he knew but could not place. Scanning the expanse, he could not see anything out of the ordinary, yet the presence remained heavy in the air. Like a magnet it drew him out of the safety of the rocks, closer to the moons beyond, towards the approaching snowstorm that had suddenly crept very close. From another hiding place not far away, a stranger watched, with bright blue eyes, large and full of dread. As his gaze drifted from Axel up to the moon of Scarto, he murmured under his breath, '*You found him.*'

Axel couldn't stop himself from taking another step, and then another, and another, until the fat Guard dropped his smoke dart and jabbed his companion in the chest. In one smooth motion, he pointed his Snipe Rifle at Axel's back and powered it up.

'HALT! YOU! STOP RIGHT THERE. DON'T MOVE!'

Axel was suddenly shaken back to reality. *What had just happened?!* He thought, realising he had just walked himself straight out of his cover and onto the ice of a frozen lake. He raised his hands above his head in a placating manner.

'Turn around and identify yourself,' the thin Guard ordered, a greasy smile spreading slowly across his face.

'IDENTIFY YOURSELF!' the fat Guard prompted.

The Stranger's Warning

2.

Axel lifted his shaking hands in surrender whilst weighing up his options…of which there seemed to be very few. The rocks he had hidden behind stood halfway between him and the Guards. If he could just get to them…well, maybe he could at least buy himself some time.

'TURN AROUND!' the thin-faced Guard shouted.

Deciding to try his luck, Axel sprinted towards the rocks. The Guards blinked for a moment in surprise, before opening fire. Blue shots rained around Axel as he ran, each one melting the ice with a violent hiss, one grazing the edge of his boot as he threw himself behind the rocks. With a disconcerting sound, the surface of the lake started to crack, and icy liquid bubbled out from beneath.

Grabbing a shuddering S-LO, Axel struggled through a narrow crevice in the rocks, forcing them both into a small space inside the outcrop. The Guards hurried over, circling the rocks with their Snipe Rifles raised. Momentarily confused by Axel's absence, the fat Guard grinned and jerked his head towards the rocks themselves, licking his lips with anticipation.

Forcing S-LO through a small opening in the other side of the rocks, Axel tried to push himself through. With rising panic, he realised he was stuck. Pointing their Snipe Rifles into a crevice in the outcrop, the Guards laughed as they lit it up with blue fire. A moment later, the thin-faced Guard ran a torch into the rocks.

'H-He's not in there!' the thin Guard said, his eye catching on the second opening in the rocks, just as the loud whirr of an airbike powering up vibrated across the wastes.

As the surface of the lake started to buckle and break up from the heat of the snipe fire, the Guards hurried back around the rocks and grimaced in shocked surprise, as Axel escaped on one of their airbikes.

'SO LONG, HOSERS!' he yelled at the Guards, with a smile and a wave.

A moment later, gunfire sparked off the handlebars, hitting the dark case that was attached to the back of the bike. Black smoke plumed out of the case, clearing just enough for Axel to see the fat Guard mounting the other airbike with surprising agility.

S-LO squeaked in terror. Axel's airbike started to bleep in distress and he noticed a second fresh bullet hole in the engine.

'Don't worry, S-LO…we're going to get out of this…'

S-LO bleeped an unconvinced tone. Axel shot another glance over his shoulder, just in time to see the Guard's bike miraculously short out and crash into the snow. The red-faced Guard shook his fist impotently at Axel, muttering expletives under his breath.

'Ha-HA! I *don't* believe it! Did you *see* that S-LO?! We're saved!' Axel cried.

They soared across the ice wastes, S-LO bleeping a jubilant song. Unfortunately, the airbike was not feeling so jubilant, and with a splutter and buck, it catapulted both Axel and S-LO into a large mound of snow.

'This had better be worth it,' Axel grumbled, as the airbike finally gave way and crashed to the ground in a blaze of smoke and flames in front of them.

Pulling the long case from the burning airbike, Axel laid it on the snow. As S-LO rumbled over, Axel opened the case, revealing a sword with a blade of black ice within. With tentative hands, he lifted it out of the case.

'A Völvur ice-sword…' he murmured thoughtfully. He didn't go in for the old stories about the Völvur, but he had to admit there was something strange about this sword. It vibrated slightly under his fingers, as though a great power ran through it. He grinned slowly.

'HA! Well, old pal, looks like our luck has finally come in!' Axel said.

Running his fingers along the blade, he reached the point at which the Guards' gunfire had hit it. With a sickening crack, the blade broke clean into two pieces. Axel shot a glum look at S-LO.

*

'I send you for treasure and *this* is what you bring back to me? A broken sword, some old maps, and *this*? What *is* this?' Balo said, his large, slimy eyeballs full of disgust as he held up the tennis tool.

'Look, you asked for a Völvur object – you didn't say that it couldn't be broken. Do you know what we went through, to get this stuff?' Axel said, taking back the tennis tool. 'We ran into a couple of Unity Guards…And they weren't exactly happy to see us. We're lucky to get back here in one piece!'

'This does not cover what is owed. Your *father*, Kolbjorn and your friend, Chuck, will have to *pay* as planned, and *you* will lose a hand for wasting my time.'

And with that, Balo started to move away, back into the darkness.

'Huh? No wait -' Axel said, as a large droid restrained him and started to sharpen a terrifying looking cutting tool.

'Balo - wait. I can *still* get you your money. If you'll *just* listen -' Balo laughed and continued moving away.

'Come on, Balo, let's just talk about this a minute, man to…man.'

The droid moved his cutting tool closer to Axel's hand. S-LO, who was being held and taunted by another droid, squirmed and shuddered in fear, but was unable to get free.

'Balo...You're making a mistake!' Axel cried in desperation.

The cutting tool came ever closer and was just about to make contact with Axel's wrist, when he said, 'I can get you fifteen thousand Kroner – that's *three* times what you're owed!'

Balo froze and turned back to face Axel. 'I'm listening.'

The droid's cutting tool powered down and Axel slumped backwards in relief.

'You must know that the Banren Run is taking place today. Well - Chuck and I intend to take part. And if we win, the prize money will be more than enough to clear *both* debts, and...*I*, well, *I* get to keep my hand, see? Everyone's happy.'

Balo's laughter filled the lair.

'You *can't* win,' he scoffed. 'Everyone knows the Banren Run is fixed. The Proxy's son will win.'

Axel winced. He knew this to be true. 'Look, I can do it. Just give us two more days, so we can compete. I mean, what have you got to lose?'

Balo cocked his head to one side, as he considered this proposal. '*You* shouldn't leave Eleusis right now...' he said.

'Huh? Why not?' Axel asked, mystified.

Balo was about to reply when there was a low bleep and a door shuddered open. Everyone looked to the shadowy doorway, where the hooded stranger from the wastes stood, his body thin, his overlarge blue eyes luminous in the gloom.

'Who is this?!' Balo growled.

'You not hurt boy!' the stranger ordered, moving forward quickly and pointing at Axel.

Balo's gaze travelled slickly from the stranger back to Axel, whose mouth had fallen open in surprise.

'You know this…*thing*?' Balo said.

Axel was about to reply when S-LO suddenly piped up, shuddering as he emitted a fast-flowing stream of bleeps. Axel raised his eyebrows as he turned towards the stranger.

'*Him?! He* was the one who was following me? Are you sure?' S-LO bleeped to the affirmative.

Balo's gaze snapped back to Axel. 'You *allowed* yourself to be followed?!'

'Hey look, I checked, alright? I couldn't see *anyone*!'

'You *compromised* the security of *my* lair?' Balo said evenly, severely unimpressed.

Axel groaned. *Forget about his hand - Balo would want his head for this.*

'Who are you?' Balo asked, his fish-like eyes on the stranger.

'I not important. You must let boy go.'

'Or what?' Balo challenged.

'I have powers,' the stranger replied. 'I use them on you."

Balo paused, curious. 'Alright, then…Go ahead,' he said, his large, bulbous eyes moist and dark.

Everyone stared at the stranger, who seemed suddenly cowed by all the attention. Taking a deep breath, he shut his eyes, and muttered strange words under his breath. His wizened hands started to shake violently with effort. But nothing happened. A moment later, the stranger dropped to his knees, exhausted and wheezing. The lair exploded into laughter. Struggling against the droid who was holding him, Axel was racking his brain for a way out of this, when his eye fell upon a loose wire that was poking out of the droid's arm. He strained his fingers towards it. But Axel was out of time.

'No, wait – DON'T!' Axel cried, as, upon Balo's nod, his men opened fire on the stranger.

As the smoke from the blasters cleared, Axel prepared himself for the worst, but the stranger was nowhere to be seen.

'FIND HIM!' Balo shouted to his men, who started to search the lair in earnest. A sudden crackling noise froze them in their footsteps, as a control panel in one of the walls sparked and blew up, and then another panel suffered the same fate and another and another, until the lair was pitch black – even the light of Balo's throne had gone out. Managing to reach the wires, Axel gave them an almighty yank, until the droid who had been holding him sparked and went offline. Struggling free of the droid's grasp, Axel crawled blindly across the gooey, bone-strewn floor, feeling his way through the slime over to S-LO.

'Come on buddy, time to go!' Axel whispered, stuffing his shuddering droid under his arm as dim emergency lighting came on.

'Stop them!' one of Balo's men cried, in an off-world language.

'THERE HE GOES!' another shouted, opening fire in the direction of Axel's fast-moving silhouette.

Stumbling down a corridor, in the direction of what he hoped was the way out, Axel tripped over a large bone and both he and S-LO hit the floor hard. Ahead of them, an exit hatch opened in the ceiling, letting a pale shaft of daylight and a mass of spiraling snowflakes into the lair. Axel pulled himself onto the hatch ladder one-handed, as blue gunfire rushed past them. S-LO bleeped in panic.

'Alright, S-LO, alright!' Axel said, climbing as fast as he could.

'I know what you really want, boy. To know where you come from…To find out who you are…' Balo's voice carried through the lair.

The silence grew loud as the gunfire stopped. Axel hesitated a moment.

'You should be careful what you wish for, *Lennart*…' Balo continued. 'Go to Scarto. Win the Banren Run and give your prize to me. Do this, and both debts will be cleared. Fail, and *you* will bear the consequences, along with your *father* and your friend.'

Axel swallowed and nodded.

'You won't regret it, Balo.'

'Perhaps. But *you* may...' Balo replied, as the laughter of his friends filled the lair once again.

Not wishing to hang around, Axel climbed the remaining rungs as fast as he could, and thrust S-LO through the open hatch, before pulling himself out into the snowy air. Inexplicably, the hatch door's electronics blew up as it shut behind them, and a thick black cloud of smoke billowed out from it.

'*What a morning*' Axel groaned exhaustedly, as S-LO let out a long bleep of relief.

'Hel-lo,' a voice wheezed, making Axel jump.

It was the stranger with the luminous blue eyes. He was slight and skinny in figure, his face heavily wrinkled, wisps of white hair sprouting at the base of a mainly bald head. He was panting slightly, as though he had just run a long way, and his body was slumped in the snow in an exhausted fashion.

'You! What were you thinking? You could have gotten us both killed down there!' Axel said.

'Oh, you want have only one hand? Twice I save you now,' the creature replied.

'Listen, mister – I don't know how you did what you did down there, but Balo *wouldn't* have taken my hand – I think. Anyway, no thanks to you, I just made a deal with that nightmare,' Axel said, huffily brushing some snow off of his bodysuit. 'So, are you at least going to tell me who you are, and what it is you want with me? And what do you mean, 'saved me twice'?'

The stranger nodded keenly; his bright, overlarge eyes creepy in the lightly falling snow. 'Once from crook here and once from Unity Guards. Broke their airbike, see? I help you get away.'

'Uh-huh,' Axel said, unconvinced.

'I Bodo. I came warn you. *He* has escaped. *He* already here…*watching*….*waiting*….' the stranger said, with a shudder.

'What? *Who's* escaped?'

'He…*Him*,' Bodo said, pointing a shaky finger at the sky.

Axel looked in the direction of Bodo's finger. All he could see were wispy clouds.

'Boy must not leave Eleusis. You safe here. *Protected.* Promise me you stay here.'

Axel shot an uncertain glance at S-LO. This guy was clearly some special kind of nutbag. 'I *can't* do that – don't you know it's the Banren Run today? It's a race that only comes round once a cycle, see, and I just promised Balo the winnings.'

Bodo moved forward, grabbing Axel's wrist with a firm grasp, the expression in his wide blue eyes desperate and earnest.

'*No!* You must listen me. *Please.* You *must* not go.'

'No, *you* listen to *me*, mister,' Axel said, shrugging the stranger off, despite the chill that he was feeling at these words. 'I *have* to go. I *have* to win that Run.'

*

Back on the wastes, the thin-faced Guard pushed the tip of his gun into a footprint in the snow, his gaze following a trail of them up to the ice block formation Axel had visited. Moving into the dark blue light of the corridor between the two ice blocks, his eye darted to the newly thawed Autobot, and then to the drip, drip, drip of water from a spot at the other end of the corridor, where the case that had held the maps lay open and empty as it floated gently on a large puddle. The name '*ELEUSIS*' was clearly visible on it. Reaching under the Autobot's head, the Guard powered the droid on.

'Doomed! D-D-D-Doomed…' the Autobot immediately stuttered, confusedly.

The Guard surveyed the droid coldly. 'The boy who was here today, what did he take from here?'

'M-m-maps…' the Autobot replied simply, before something within him crackled and his head blew up in a shower of white sparks.

Ban Huno

3.

The pale sun had crept overhead by the time Axel reached the spaceship junkyard of Fosse - a vast frozen basin covered in old wrecks as far as the eye could see. He spotted the robust form of his best friend - Chuck Bergo, welding the body of a large, crumbling wreck of a spaceship. It was an old pre-regime craft – a silver P-600 Sunrise that was covered in rust. All around him, the other Banren Run participants bustled about in barely controlled panic, readying old crafts for flight in preparation for the race.

'Ah finally. *He appears,*' Chuck grumbled, as he spotted Axel hurrying over from his airbike, a harried expression on his face.

'All right, all right, I'm here now, aren't I?'

Chuck raised his eyebrows. 'What happened to you? You look terrible,' he asked.

'I had a rough morning. What's your excuse?'

Chuck bundled a wrench into Axel's hand and pushed him in the direction of the P-600.

'For your information, women from at least three systems find *this* look irresistible,' Chuck said, motioning to himself.

'Love *is* blind!'

'For your sake, my friend, I hope it is.'

Chuck had a square, honest face that was covered with freckles, and a bulky frame, carefully honed through an overzealous love of space beans. Somehow, oil and dirt always seemed to find its way onto his bodysuit, much to the annoyance of his long-suffering mother – Binko - who still did his laundry. His sandy hair was much longer than the regulation length, not due to any particularly rebellious feeling but just because he constantly forgot to get it cut.

'So…where *have* you been?' Chuck probed, setting his welding gear down and wiping some dirt from his hands with an old rag.

Axel grimaced, folding his arms over his chest. 'I went to see Balo Fuse.'

'Fuse?! What did you want with that old crook?'

'Cut a deal with him. To clear my father's debts.' Axel shot Chuck a sideways glance. 'And yours too.'

'He *told* you? About my debts?'

'Why didn't you tell me? A problem shared and all that...'

Chuck's gaze dropped down to his feet, and his shoulders slumped.

'Look, I get it, brother. So, well…I told Balo we'd win this thing.'

'*What?!*'

'If we don't get the winnings to Balo in two days, we're all toast. You, your mother, my father and me. Oh – and probably your brother too. I always forget about him.'

'Yeah me too.' Chuck processed everything for a moment. 'But Axe - do you really think we could win…? In this heap of junk?' he said motioning to the decrepit P-600.

'We just *have* to, Chuck, we've got no choice,' Axel said, putting a hand on Chuck's shoulder and shaking him slightly. 'Listen, all we have to do is fix up this ship. Fly our torchbearer to Scarto. Be the first to light the beacon in the old Ban Huno fortress. We win. Easy. *I'll fly.*'

'*You fly?* You can barely fly a *functioning* craft, let alone *this*.'

*

'Have you finished with the intake manifold?' Chuck shouted to Axel a few hours later.

33

The sun now hung low in the crimson sky, turning the snow a fiery red. Once the sun touched the horizon, the Run would begin.

'Hours ago,' Axel replied, firing up his hair blower.

He pointed it at the sealant he had just applied to a large crack in the body of the P-600. Chuck stuck his head out of one of the windows of the craft, his face horror struck. 'I don't even want to know what you're doing,' he murmured, looking nauseous at the sight of the hair blower.

'You worry too much,' Axel chuckled, slapping one of the wings.

A large chunk of rusty metal came off in his hand. They both looked at it in alarm.

'*Do I?*' Chuck said.

'Look – Mork's got a CC-9, that's hardly better than a P-600,' Axel said, trying to shift Chuck's attention away from their dire situation.

Augustus Mork was a skinny fellow with skin the colour of ebony, who constantly seemed to be blighted with bad luck. As he waved at Axel excitedly, there was a loud cracking noise and a large section of his wing suddenly fell off, narrowly missing his head. His co-pilot, a short, permanently angry boy called Ludvig Bats, immediately came out and started shouting at him.

'Well, I suppose it could be worse - at least we're not travelling with Ludvig,' Chuck said, finally seeing the bright side, before disappearing back into the ship.

A few moments later there was the metallic clatter of something falling within the P-600, followed by a tiny, high-pitched scream.

'There are *Finkworms* living in here!' Chuck screeched. 'You know, I hate to break it to you Axe, but this ship isn't going to last another *hour* let alone the journey to Ban Huno.'

'Look, she'll get us there, okay?' Axel said, running his palm over the rusty surface of the ship. '*Please* get us there…' he added, to the ship.

The quiet rumbling of small wheels on snow alerted Axel to the presence of his Chore Droid behind him.

'Oh, S-LO, *not again*! Didn't I tell you to stay at home?'

S-LO bleeped pleadingly.

'I don't *care how* boring it is in the hut. You are *not* coming. Hear me? NO.'

*

Once the sealant was dry, Axel climbed on board and clicked the flight computer on. It took a while and some few well positioned slaps but eventually it roared to life. Brushing some dust and cobwebs off the intercom, he pushed the volume up to maximum.

'READY YET?' he asked Chuck's bottom, which was sticking in the air as he repaired something under the control desk.

Chuck hit his head on the desk in response. Axel chuckled to himself.

'Sure, now that I've got your ejector seat connected,' Chuck said darkly, crawling back out and strapping himself in.

He flicked a few switches and noticed a light on the control panel flickering uncertainly.

'Servicebot...What are you still doing over there?! Did you fix the aft reckoner?' Chuck asked his dowdy looking droid.

Servicebot bleeped sheepishly, before disappearing to the back of the ship to make the repair.

'Hang on...aren't we meant to have a torchbearer to carry the torch to this beacon?' Chuck asked.

'Yes,' Axel replied.

They were silent for a moment as they looked around the cabin, which was empty save for themselves and Chuck's fraught looking Servicebot. Looking back at the horizon, Axel registered that the sun was dropping dangerously close to the horizon. They exchanged anxious glances.

'Who's our torchbearer again?' Chuck asked.

'Blix Bo.'

'You mean the Control Room worker – that weirdo who lives out in the ice fields? The one you like?'

'Shut up, Chuck,' Axel grumbled, as he tapped his Navwatch. 'Blix Bo…? Blix are you there?'

Nothing but static returned. Axel and Chuck exchanged anxious glances.

'Here! I'm here!' a breathless voice called out behind them as Blix clambered on-board.

Her green eyes were bright from running in the cold wind, her usually pale skin flushed.

'Sorry, I forgot the torch! I've got it now, though - no need to panic,' she said, holding up a long smooth white stick, which was alight at one end with a small, flickering flame.

But Axel and Chuck weren't looking at the torch.

'Blix…What are you wearing?' Chuck asked.

She was sporting a heavily padded boiler suit, complete with a hood that fit a little too snugly round her head. Only one curl of her dark blonde hair had escaped the suit, which was an unfortunate shade of shiny brown.

'Look, it's warm, ok? I found it in one of the compartments at the back. I imagine it's cold in space? There are loads more in there if you want one.'

'I'd rather freeze to death, thanks,' Chuck said, starting up the engines.

'I…err…cleaned up this seat for you,' Axel said, motioning to a slightly less dusty perch next to him.

Chuck raised his eyebrows suggestively, a lazy grin stretched across this face. Axel narrowed his eyes and cleared his throat in annoyance.

'Thanks, Axel...At least *one* of you knows how to treat a lady,' Blix said, as she clambered over Chuck to get to her seat, almost setting him alight in the process.

'Ouch! WATCH IT!' Chuck screeched, patting down a few areas where his suit had started to smoulder.

Suddenly the radio crackled into life. 'BF-52 to AL-28, come in.'

Axel and Chuck exchanged glances. It was Berau Feovold – the son of the Proxy, who ruled Eleusis on behalf of the Regime. One day, Berau would be Proxy himself.

'Hi Berau, how's it all going?' Axel replied wearily.

'Good,' Berau said. 'I just wanted to wish you good luck.'

'How *nice* of you,' Axel said dryly.

In the background, Berau's co-pilot, Egil Skog and their torchbearer, Mari Slette, could be heard laughing.

'Good fortune, Blix,' Mari jeered. 'I hope you survive the journey!'

'I hope you don't,' Blix muttered in response.

'We got the T84 in the draw,' Berau bragged. 'Lucky, huh?'

'Yeah, *lucky*,' Chuck said, gripping the parking lever tightly in frustration as they all peered outside.

The shiny T84 looked pretty much new in comparison to the P-600.

'You remember, nine years ago, when *twelve* racers died during the Run?' Egil chipped in. 'I heard their ships were never found - the pieces were too small to locate.'

Chuck tensed. Servicebot let out a nervous bleep and scuttled off-board. Axel sighed. 'Yeah, Egil, we haven't forgotten. Safe travels.'

He clicked the radio off.

'Was it just me or did it sound like they were bidding us farewell?' Chuck asked.

'*I* think Berau *thinks* we haven't got a chance,' Axel replied.

'Well, that makes two of us,' Chuck murmured.

'Enough of that!' Blix said, poking Chuck with the torch. 'Be optimistic! And where's your sense of adventure?'

'Hmm, let's see, buried somewhere far beneath my fear of death,' Chuck replied.

With a jolt, Axel realised that the sun was starting to set. The Run was beginning. 'AL-28 to Control, starting checks complete, ready to take off,' Axel said into the radio.

'Noted, AL-28. Initial flight route over ice wastes only,' the response from the control station crackled back.

'Roger that, Control,' Axel said, as he gently pushed up the dusty ignition lever, slapping the flight computer a few times to keep it going. 'F-Flight c-com-omputer o-online,' the computer stuttered uncertainly.

For ten glorious seconds, everything powered up beautifully. Unfortunately for Axel, Chuck and Blix, the decrepit condition of the ship was not the only thing working against them. Standing just outside, concealed within the growing shadow of the P-600, was Bodo – the stranger from the wastes.

'Boy should *not* leave…Must *stay* here. Must *stay safe!*' Bodo muttered to himself, as he hurriedly pried open a rusty control panel in the side of the ship, pulled out several large wires, and cut them all.

Instantly, the P-600's main systems shut off.

'No, no, no, no!' Axel cried.

'We are going to *die* in this thing,' Chuck said, looking nauseous again.

In the junkyard around them, several other rusty spacecraft were taking off, gaining a head start on the race to Ban Huno. Berau's T84 was one of the first to leave. Amazingly, even Mork had somehow managed to get his wing stuck back on and the CC-9 was taxiing around, preparing to take off. Axel and Chuck flicked switches and hammered on buttons, but nothing seemed to work. Blix watched helplessly.

They were now the only ship left on the ground. The P-600 was a hulking, corroded craft that hadn't flown in over sixty years - any number of things could have caused it to fail, Axel thought to himself in despair, until he caught sight of Bodo's shadowy form running away from the ship. Scrambling outside, he found the cut wires, and groaned. Patching them up as quickly as he could, Axel got himself back on board, trying everything he could think of to get the ship up and running again, but nothing was working. The lights flickered and died. Axel looked at Blix, defeated and then kicked at the control desk in frustration.

'It's NO use!' he said his temper flaring.

Blix shook her head. 'Just give the ship a moment – don't lose hope,' she said, shutting her eyes briefly, as though concentrating on that thought.

Chuck looked at Blix and rolled his eyes. 'Hope? Sister, I think it will take more than us wishing on a star to get *this* ship going.'

And then, suddenly…magically…everything came back on.

'I don't believe it!' Axel exclaimed, relief pulsing through him.

Blix gasped in relief, already looking worn out. 'Looks like that wish came true…' she murmured, raising her eyebrows at Chuck.

'I guess so…' he said, his brows knitted together in confusion.

'P-p-pl-lease lay in a cour-course,' the flight computer said.

Axel punched in the co-ordinates of Scarto, and specifically the old fortress of Ban Huno. He pushed a lever up and without further ado, they blasted out of the junkyard, quickly rising above the cloud

39

layer, where the setting sun had tinted the sky pink and gold. The triple moons also came into view, their landscapes as icy as that of the world below them.

Somewhat surprisingly for a giant heap of rusting metal, the P-600 turned out to be pretty fast. Soon, they had caught up with the others, bringing up the rear of the strange convoy of flying rust buckets. An excited bleeping sounded from the back of the cockpit and Axel frowned.

'S-LO!' he exclaimed, shaking his head.

The Chore Droid bleeped nervously.

'I *don't believe* this!'

The ice wastes stretched out beneath them, the winds constantly blowing fresh snow here and there, giving the expanse a restless feel.

'Adjusting for the break through upper atmosphere,' Chuck said, gently turning some of the knobs and quelling the flashing lights on the control desk.

Axel pulled the nose of the P-600 up and they started to leave the airspace of Principality-5, which was now dizzyingly far beneath them. Picking up their speed, they overtook the other crafts with ease until they were neck and neck with the leader, Berau's T84. Spotting them, the T84 sped up.

'We need more power, Chuck,' Axel said as the stars beyond the atmospheric haze grew clearer.

'Ok, ok, I'll see what I can do,' Chuck said, disappearing somewhere in the back with his hover spanner.

Berau's T84 blasted ahead as more and more craft behind them dropped back down to the planet surface, unable to break through Eleusis' gravity field.

'We're losing speed!' Axel cried, as Blix used S-LO to extinguish several small fires on the control panel.

The craft jerked suddenly, causing Chuck to hit his head again.

'Ouch! Can you *learn* to fly?! How can you be a Patrol pilot and be *this* bad?'

Axel grinned to himself.

'Okay, okay - that's the best I can do,' Chuck said, after making some adjustments.

The ship jolted forward a little and they burst into space, the stars twinkling around them, the uninhabited moon of Scarto gleaming white some distance ahead.

'Amazing...' Blix murmured, her eyes wide with wonder.

They looked at each other and smiled, until an ominous rumbling sound drew their attention back to the ship. Axel tried to accelerate, but the P-600 was not co-operating. Axel groaned as they started to get sucked back into Eleusis' gravity field.

'Come on, *come on*...Oh no. Chuck - it's not enough!'

'Okay, okay,' Chuck said, scratching his head with the spanner. 'There's one more thing I can try,' he said, disappearing towards the back of the ship again.

Searching for anything of use, Blix noticed a holographic note, hovering over part of the control panel. It read, *'DO NOT USE – DANGER!'* in the old language that was used before the Regime. Clicking the note off revealed a lever beneath it marked *'Surge.'*

'I think...I think I can help!' she cried suddenly, unstrapping herself and diving under the control desk.

'Blix, I think that note was there for a reason,' Axel said nervously.

'Just need a minute!' she said, as Axel heard the worrying sound of a lot of wiring being pulled out and reconnected very fast.

'Right, try it now,' she said, strapping herself firmly back in, just as Chuck reappeared from a hatch in the side of the cockpit.

Axel's hand hovered hesitantly over the lever.

'Trust me,' Blix said.

'Huh? Wait, no don't -' Chuck said.

Axel pulled the lever down.

The Light in the Caves

4.

Everything went off again, came back on again and with a sudden surge of energy they rocketed forward at breakneck speed, catapulting S-LO into Blix's arms as she stumbled back into her chair.

'WOW, look at her go!' Chuck yelled.

Silence reigned as the P-600 surpassed all of their wildest expectations.

'We're passing the T84!' Axel said in disbelief. 'Blix - where did you learn how to do that? This ship must be a hundred years old!'

'Oh, you know, here and there,' Blix replied with a shrug.

The P-600 accelerated exponentially, going faster than any of the other ships had managed so far.

'I think...I think we're in the lead!' Chuck said breathlessly as their speed levelled out.

'You know, we might actually have a shot at winning this thing!' Axel cried.

They grinned at each other in wild amazement, just as a loud blasting noise emanated from the back of the craft. The P-600 shuddered violently.

'W-What was that?' Chuck said, his face pale.

'I-I-Incoming-ming fire f-f-from enemy ship,' the flight computer replied as another blast ripped a big hole in the hull.

'E-Emergency Airlock holding,' the computer said reassuringly.

'They're firing on us!' Axel said in disbelief, looking at a flickering image of Berau's craft through the flight computer.

'What?!' Chuck said.

'AL-28 to BF-52 - WHAT ARE YOU DOING?' Axel shouted through the radio.

'*Winning*,' Egil's voice crackled back.

Axel and Chuck exchanged glances.

'Brill...' Chuck said, dusting off the heavy zapper.

'Wait a minute!' Blix said, horrified. 'We can't fire on the Proxy's son! Who will rule Eleusis if we kill him?'

'Whoever it is, I *guarantee* they will be saner than Berau,' Chuck said.

S-LO bleeped in agreement.

'Wait - just stop and think a moment!' Blix reasoned.

Another blast shuddered through the P-600.

'Look, sister - a few more hits like that and we won't be thinking anything!' Chuck yelled back as he readied the zapper to fire.

Axel gripped the wheel uncertainly. 'Wait, let me try something. Hold on to something,' he said, taking a breath before rolling the large ship, as the next onslaught of fire came at them.

*

There was momentary quiet on board the T84.

'How did he do that? He missed every single shot!' Mari asked.

'His flying is so poor, our shots keep missing!' Egil replied.

A dark light filled Berau's eyes.

'Keep firing,' he said quietly, tightening his hold on the wheel.

'If we hit them again, there's no way they'll survive,' Mari said, a hint of concern behind her cold eyes.

Berau kept his eyes focused on the fast approaching ice moon. 'I know,' he replied evenly.

*

'CHUCK, WILL YOU *PLEASE* STOP SCREAMING?!' Axel yelled as the P-600 spun in the air, bits of wing breaking off as it went.

Managing to stabilise the craft, Axel took a deep breath of relief.

'S-Starting dd-descent into Scarto's atmosphere,' the flight computer said, finally getting it together in preparation for landing.

'SEE? Everything is under control,' Axel said.

Chuck stumbled over to a dark corner and threw up in it.

The uninhabited moon of Scarto was similar in landscape to Eleusis, in that it was covered in rocks filmed with ice and snow, but today, something about it was very different. Axel could not shake the feeling that a darkness lingered upon it. He shuddered slightly, wondering why he felt that way, his thoughts jumbled. As they cut through the clouds, the vast snowy landscape stretched out for kilopars beneath them. Another blast hit the ship, bringing Axel back out of himself.

'I'VE LOST CONTROL!' Axel cried, turning the wheel left and right to little effect.

'D-Deviation from course is occ-occurring,' the flight computer said, as the ship careered wildly off to the left.

Another round of heavy fire ripped through the P-600.

'HE'S TRYING TO KILL US!' Chuck yelled as some serious bleeping emanated from the control panel.

'NO - REALLY?!' Axel replied.

'D-D-Damage to h-hull. S-suggest land-landing immediately,' the flight computer despaired.

An almighty cracking noise followed another blast and the ship split in half, the rear end crashing into the rocky sea below with frightening force. Axel, Chuck and Blix stared in alarm at the gaping hole in the back of the ship. S-LO bleeped anxiously. 'Anti-Anti-Anti-crash system c-compromised,' the flight computer said. What was left of the P-600 spun into a nosedive, spiraling wildly towards a dark ocean below.

'EVERYTHING'S BROKEN!' Chuck yelled.

'WERE YOU BEING SERIOUS ABOUT THAT EJECTOR SEAT?' Axel asked.

'NO, YOU IDIOT, THAT WAS A JOKE,' Chuck replied.

'HAHAHAHA, WELL IT'S REALLY FUNNY *NOW*, ISN'T IT?'

'WILL YOU TWO SHUT UP A MINUTE?!' Blix yelled.

'C-Crash imminent…Crash imminent,' the flight computer said.

'Axel…There must be something we can do?' Blix asked, terror hanging undisguised in her eyes, as the P-600 fell almost vertically through the atmosphere, gaining speed as she went.

Axel frowned and shook his head. Blix nodded, squeezing her eyes shut as she hugged a shuddering S-LO hard to her chest. Axel looked back to the grey rocky sea they were fast approaching, the veins in his temple throbbing.

As they spiraled down to their doom, a strange feeling took hold of Axel. Familiarity mixed with dread. It was the same presence he had felt that morning, out on the wastes, and in his nightmares the night before. It was as if someone he had once known was here on Scarto. Someone he had long forgotten. He winced as the sharp throb of a headache clouded his thoughts.

'*We shouldn't have come here…*' he said, to no one but himself.

'I *KNOW*!' Chuck replied.

Barely hearing Chuck's response, Axel's fingers left the worn surface of the wheel and stretched into the air beyond the windscreen, as though he was expecting a helping hand to be there to meet his, to stop them from crashing. Oddly, it seemed to work.

Everything slowed down.

It felt like they were still falling, only very, very slowly. And then, the ship stopped moving altogether. 'What's going on?' Chuck said, peering out of the cockpit window. The P-600 was hanging just above the treacherous rocks and the charcoal surface of the sea. Then, it gently glided into the cool, dark water, as if a giant invisible hand had caught it and laid it carefully down.

It wasn't quite gentle enough for Chuck, however, who hit his head again and immediately passed out. Ice water gushed into the ship, which was also rapidly filling with thick black smoke and a couple of confused looking sea eels. The bleeping continued incessantly from the control panel.

'YOU OK?' Axel said, putting a hand on Blix's shoulder.

She nodded, unbuckling herself. Coughing, they waded across to where Chuck was lying unconscious, partially submerged in the freezing water. Axel shook Chuck vigorously and he woke up suddenly, a dazed look in his eyes.

'WE'RE STILL ALIVE,' Blix said to him loudly.

Chuck nodded and patted himself down, as if to make sure everything was still there, finding an eel in his lap. 'G-good! That's good n-news, I t-thik,' he slurred.

Making their way to the back of the craft, they saw that they had crashed just a little way out to sea. Strangely, the ship was resting on some very sharp looking rocks, which should have destroyed it on impact. They exchanged bemused glances. Chuck opened his mouth to speak, and then closed it again, his forehead creased in confusion.

'R-r-reactor leak, evacuate…evac…evac…' the flight computer gurgled, finally dying out as water flooded its systems.

'HURRY!' Axel cried, fishing an upside-down S-LO from out of the water and pushing Chuck and Blix towards the open end of the ship. 'WE HAVE TO GET OUT!'

They plunged into the icy sea, battling against the frothy waves, just as what was left of the P-600 exploded behind them. In the churn of the water, Blix disappeared beneath the surface, the weight of the wet boiler suit dragging her down.

'BLIX!' Axel cried, exchanging a panicked glance with Chuck.

Diving down, they tried to find her. For a moment, there was nothing but the heavy beat of the dark water against the rocks. Catching sight of her, Axel swum down towards the seabed, grabbing hold of Blix and pulling her back up to the surface. Spluttering, they dragged themselves out of the water onto the rocky shore, where Blix promptly fell onto Axel, winding him. For a moment they stared at each other, noses almost touching, eyes wide. Chuck, who had S-LO stuck under his arm, rolled his eyes at the droid and cleared his throat.

'Err, thanks - I – err, right. Well, thank-you…very much,' Blix gasped, as they both got up as fast as they could, with as much dignity as they could.

Dragging themselves further up the rocky beach, they collapsed onto the pebbles and watched as the remains of their ship drifted below the waves.

'Well, that was…odd,' Chuck said, shivering.

Axel stared at the water, lost to his thoughts.

'How did we survive that? Our speed, the rocks…It was like something…*caught* us.' Blix asked, shivering.

'Yeah. I mean, not that I'm complaining, but we should be dead,' Chuck said.

Blix nodded, staring wide-eyed at the crash site, where fire still danced on the surface of the churning water. Axel struggled to work it out, his eyes drifting on a point far beyond the wreckage of the P-600, where silver waves broke upon the curved hull of another old star ship. He wondered vaguely how many other forgotten ships lay hidden beneath the constantly moving waves.

'Oh no,' Blix said, standing suddenly and staring impotently into the water. 'I lost the torch!'

Chuck grinned smugly. 'No, you didn't,' he said, pulling it out from somewhere in the back of his trousers. He gave it a few sharp slaps and the flame reappeared. '*And*, it's still alight!'

'Where were you stowing that?' Blix asked, accepting the torch gingerly. 'Somewhere safe,' Chuck replied, with a nonchalant shrug.

There was that feeling again, Axel thought with a shudder - *that odd, pulsing familiarity. That silent threat, hanging heavy in the air.* Summoning the will to do it, he forced himself to look at the caves behind them.

'What is it?' Chuck asked.

'I just feel like...I don't know,' Axel shrugged, his eyes still on the caves. He pulled the wet collar of his bodysuit away from his neck and shivered. 'There's something strange about this place.'

The wind howled around them.

'Well, it's not exactly homely, I'm with you there,' Chuck said.

They were standing on a beach that was known as the Bay of Ruins, as all around them stood the remnants of an ancient city. 'Hey, look,' Blix said, pointing upwards. The black mountain of Loth towered above them, and the fortress of Ban Huno jutted out of one side of it, the beacon still unlit.

'We're so close,' Axel said, talking mostly to himself, Balo Fuse's threat hanging over him like a dark cloud.

'You know, I was really starting to believe it – that we might win this thing, I mean. Pay off our debts. Be free,' Chuck sighed.

'Debts?' Blix asked.

'Uh-huh. We owe Balo Fuse...well, a lot.'

'Balo Fuse? You two *are* in trouble,' Blix said, horrified.

Chuck rolled his eyes. 'Well thank you, genius – I think we'd already managed to work that out.'

Together, they looked at the almost vertical cliffs that stood between them and the mountain, with no discernible way up.

'Come on, we'd better start heading towards the meeting point, before it gets dark,' Chuck said, dropping his gaze to the ground.

But just as he turned away from the mountain, Blix caught his arm.

'Wait - did you see that?' she said, suddenly.

Axel shivered, his throat constricting at her words.

'Huh?' Chuck said, as they peered into the dark mouths of the caves that lined the base of the cliffs. 'See what?'

'I thought I saw something - over there – a light, in the caves.'

'Blix -'Axel murmured, his voice full of dread.

He had not seen the light, but the presence pounded loud in his mind, and he could have sworn that he'd just heard something – a melody of some kind.

'I can't see anything,' Chuck said.

'I...*saw* it,' Blix murmured, her eyes large and empty and fixed unflinchingly on the darkness.

Suddenly she moved towards it, her quick footsteps morphing into an uneasy run over the black pebbles of the beach.

'Blix - don't!' Axel said as he tried to grab her arm.

She slipped through his grasp. Sprinting full pelt into the cave, Blix was soon swallowed up by the darkness, stumbling near the entrance and falling hard onto the sandy ground within. She looked up slowly, the light of her torch brightening automatically in response to the darkness. Axel stopped just inside the entrance, his head pounding.

'You okay?' Axel asked, helping Blix up off the ground.

She shook her head a little, looking ashamed and embarrassed. Her skin was pale and clammy, her breaths short and shallow.

'Sorry. That was odd. Don't know what came over me.'

'It's okay,' Axel said, unnerved.

He leant back against the rocks for a moment, as he took in a few deep breaths to try to alleviate the pain in his head, as he registered the surprising beauty of the cave. It was incredibly large, stretching much further back than he ever would have imagined. All around were large green crystals that seemed to glow a little of their own accord.

'Why are we here?' Chuck wheezed, finally entering the cave.

'It's...well...I think...I'm not sure,' Blix said, confused.

'Then, can we go? Somehow, it's colder in here than it is outside,' Chuck said, hugging himself as he shivered, his breath clouding around his mouth.

'Well, maybe you should have put on one of these,' Blix said, motioning to her boiler suit.

Chuck scowled.

Taking the torch, Axel moved closer to the back of the cave. The wall here was too smooth to be natural, he thought as he ran his fingers over the stone, the pounding in his head worsening the closer he got.

'You're both crazy,' Chuck said, catching sight of Axel feeling the wall, and stopping as his fingertips made contact with a hard edge.

'There's something here,' he said, turning to look at Chuck and Blix.

As he pushed gently against it, a concealed casing jerkily slid back, to reveal a rusty control panel beneath. The display came to life as Axel touched it.

'That looks ancient,' Blix said, as she came over. 'Look at the markings.'

'Pre-regime?' Chuck said, his interest piqued.

'What do you think it does?' Blix asked.

'Well, let's find out,' Axel said, pushing a button.

The control panel spoke in the old language. 'Eight-digit access code required.'

The three of them exchanged glances.

'Try my birthday,' Chuck said.

'Well, for all *we* know, I guess it could be Chuck's birthday,' Axel said, shrugging. Blix grinned.

51

He keyed in the numbers, each digit making a different bleeping sound as he went. 'Incorrect. One attempt remaining,' the control panel replied.

'Well, this was fun…but can we go now? This place is giving me the creeps,' Chuck said, shivering again.

'Just one more try…' Axel murmured, remembering the melody he had heard earlier.

Concentrating, he keyed in the code that made that same sequence of sounds. For a moment nothing happened.

'Access granted,' the control panel finally said, and with a low grinding noise, a hidden door slid open in the back wall of the cave, to reveal a hazy, steam-filled darkness beyond.

'Axe…H-How…How did you get that door open?' Chuck said.

'I think I heard the sounds of the key-pad when Blix noticed the light,' Axel said, peering into the secret room.

'Which means, someone *was* here,' Blix said.

'But…*I* didn't *see* or *hear* anything,' Chuck said. 'And I was right next to you both!'

A chill wind blew through the mouth of the cave and whistled eerily through the open door. They all shivered.

'One way to find out…' Axel said, stepping through the door and into the darkness beyond.

'Now - I don't think *that's* a great idea!' Chuck said.

'Come on, now, don't be such a baby,' Blix said with a grin, as she followed Axel into the room beyond.

'Hey - *I* am *not* a baby!' Chuck exclaimed indignantly.

S-LO, who had been painfully navigating the pebbled beach, finally entered the cave. With an excited bleep, the little droid whizzed across the sand, straight into the secret room. Chuck sighed and followed.

The air smelt stale and was heavy with moisture, so much so that a low mist hung just above the floor, concealing it from view.

52

Droplets of water rained down from somewhere above, and streams of it also ran down some of the walls, over ancient looking control panels, the illuminated buttons of which now blinked alive. 'What is this place?' Chuck grimaced.

Wiping dirt off some buttons in the wall, Blix studied them.

'I think it's a lift,' she said, fascinated as S-LO cleaned a panel for her to inspect.

'Must lead to one of the old insurgent bases – one the Regime never found,' Blix replied.

Axel slumped back against a wall, closing his eyes a moment as the presence he could feel but not explain closed in on him, and the pounding in his head grew worse.

'Axe - you alright?' Chuck asked, concerned.

'Yeah, Yeah, I'm fine,' Axel replied, trying to shrug it off. 'Just a headache.'

A moment later, there was a loud groan and the door slid shut behind them with surprising speed. They exchanged panicked glances, and Blix pushed buttons, looking for any way to get it open again.

'We're trapped! The door release doesn't work!' she cried.

'Great. *Brilliant* idea, this was,' Chuck said.

The lift began to violently shake, knocking them all to the floor, before moving upwards at incredible speed.

'WHAT'S HAPPENING?!' Chuck cried.

A few moments later, the lift shuddered to a stop. With a slow grinding sound the door opened, revealing a long corridor beyond that melted into darkness. S-LO bumbled towards the door, but Blix stopped him just in time, a haunted look in her eyes as she stared into the seemingly endless corridor.

The pounding presence in Axel's head had become almost unbearable. He shut his eyes, grimacing in pain. Shivering, the sound of his breathing was suddenly very loud in his ears, hot perspiration streaming down his face. A sharp pain pierced his skull. He scrambled back against the wall, eyes wide and terrified, as though he had seen a ghost.

'What is it, Axe? What's wrong?' Chuck asked.

Blix eyed Axel anxiously, a strange look in her eyes, as though a suspicion she had long held had just been confirmed.

'Stop! M-make it stop. It hurts...*He's inside* my head,' Axel whispered.

The pain became a dull pounding, a sound like metal on metal, a clinking, black wings beating and then the harsh sound of a bird's cry pierced his mind. Then he saw fire and ice, and a box...a large black box that was whispering to him in a strange language, vibrating with such energy, pulsing louder and louder and LOUDER!

Axel lifted his hands to his head and started to scream.

'Right, that's enough of that,' Chuck said, banging on a control panel until the door shut. A moment later, the lift started to move upwards again. Axel passed out, his body slumping down onto the damp, dirty floor.

'Axel! Axel, wake up,' Chuck said, shaking him. 'What's wrong with him?'

'I-I don't know,' Blix said, her face drained of blood.

The lift juddered to a stop, and the door opened, revealing stone steps beyond.

'Come on,' Chuck said, grabbing one of Axel's arms, as Blix did the same. Together, they pulled him out of the lift and onto the steps.

'Buddy, you okay?' Chuck asked, shaking Axel's limp body.

Bleeping in concern, S-LO aimed a small tube at Axel's face and splashed him with soapy water. He groaned, his eyes opening slightly.

'W-what happened?' he murmured, groaning as he put a hand to his throbbing head.

'I don't know – it's like you started hallucinating or something…You were…screaming,' Chuck said.

'Screaming?' Axel said groggily. 'I – I don't remember.'

He blinked a few times rapidly in succession.

'And you two…you're okay?' he asked.

They nodded, faces pale and anxious. Axel noticed his hands were shaking. He could still feel the strange beat within his head, but it was receding.

'Weird…' he said, casting a fearful look back at the open mouth of the lift.

As if in response, the door to the lift closed behind them, and with a clanking noise they heard it returning down to the ground. Axel felt his body relax a little, rubbing the back of his neck he tried to make sense of it all. 'Must have been some bad space beans,' he said, smiling wanly. Chuck and Blix stared at him.

'Sure,' Blix nodded, unconvinced.

'Can we go home now?' Chuck sighed.

'W-where are we?' Axel wheezed.

At the top of the steps, daylight filtered through a metal grate. As they neared it, the grate slid away and with a low grinding noise, the top step started to rise, pushing them up to the level above.

S-LO bleeped in surprise.

Clouds suddenly snaked around their ankles and the vast sweep of the mountains stretched out before them. The Bay of Ruins was dizzyingly far beneath the stone tower they stood in.

'I don't believe it…' Chuck said, as they turned around and found themselves at the base of a large circle of cut firewood - the unlit beacon.

'We're in Ban Huno?!' Axel murmured incredulously.

'And the beacon's still unlit...' Blix said.

'Which means…' Chuck drifted off, a wonder-filled smile spreading across his face like sunlight breaking though rain clouds.

Blix casually threw the torch into the beacon. They stepped back as the wood caught fire with terrifying speed.

'We just made Balo a rich man,' Blix said.

'We're saved!' Chuck gasped.

'Well....that was easier than I thought...' Axel said, before his knees gave way below him and he hit the floor, the grey light of the day seamlessly dulling into black, behind his rapidly closing eyelids.

The Bright Darkness

5.

Axel woke with a start, to heat and red light. The air was dense with steam. He tried to lift his hand to wipe the perspiration off his face, but something was stopping him. He realised that he must be inside a recovery chamber, within which metal straps curved over his forehead, limbs and torso, holding him down. The glass lid of the chamber stretched over him, on which a cool layer of condensation formed before dripping uncomfortably onto his face.

Axel's dreams had been vivid and disturbing, full of a violent rainstorm, where heavy droplets hit the ground like bullets. Lightning split the sky and a starship was falling…falling, helplessly tumbling towards the wet ground…drawn towards his outstretched hand.

'You had quite a spell,' a voice cut through the quiet, still air. Axel tried to turn his head towards the sound and realised he couldn't do that either.

'B-Berau?' Axel said, recognising the voice as he strained towards it. 'That you?'

At the click of a button being pushed, the glass lid slid away with a hiss and the chamber slowly tilted into a vertical position. The steam from within rolled to the cold floor in thick white clouds as the chamber came to rest. As the air started to clear, the Proxy's son came into view, his eyes dark and tumultuous with fear. Medical equipment lights blinked at Axel through the hazy air, beyond which were rough stone walls.

'Where are we?'

'The cellars of the old fortress,' Berau replied.

'Ban Huno….?' Axel said, his recent memories jumbled and confused.

Someone had dressed him in a new, clean jumpsuit. Axel hoped that someone hadn't been Berau. Thankfully it did not seem likely.

'Listen, can't you let me out of this thing?' he said, squirming uncomfortably in the stretcher, his cuts and bruises from the crash pushing painfully against the metal straps.

Berau lounged close to the door, arms tightly crossed against his body, a bitten look souring his face, a golden circlet resting loose on his head. On his father's death, Berau would rule Eleusis on behalf of the Regime as the new Proxy. 'How did you do it?'

'Do what?'

'*Win. Cheat.* You lit the beacon, but your ship crashed so far from it.'

'We *won?* How?'

'That's what I'm asking you, idiot.'

Axel's gaze shifted to the floor, his clammy forehead creasing with the effort of recollection.

'I…I don't remember much past *you* shooting us out of the sky,' Axel said, pushing against his restraints. The edges of Berau's mouth curved upwards slightly, but his eyes stayed dark and humourless.

'How convenient.'

'It's true. Look - can't you let me out of this thing? Or am I your prisoner?'

Berau thought on this a moment, before reluctantly pushing another button. With a noisy clank, the restraints opened and Axel slid heavily to the damp floor.

'*Thank you,*' he said through gritted teeth.

Berau surveyed Axel a moment in silence. 'My father said *you* would win. You were always his favourite, even when we were children.'

'That's ridiculous. *You're* his son.'

58

A shadow passed across Bearu's face. He frowned slightly and then looked away. 'Forgive me. The way I have acted - I have not treated you like the brother you are to me.'

'Huh! *That's* an understatement. You could have killed us, *brother*,' Axel murmured, rubbing his head, hoping it would ease the dull thump of the presence he could still feel within it.

'Drink this – it will aid your healing,' Berau said, taking a glass vial from a nearby shelf and pushing it into Axel's shaking hands.

Eyeing the clear liquid with distrust, he looked at Berau.

'What is it?'

Axel took it wearily but did not drink.

Berau smiled. 'Afraid?' he asked, wryly.

Narrowing his eyes, Axel lifted the glass to his lips and drunk it whole. The liquid felt strange against his throat. A moment later a glorious warmth flooded his body. Raising his arm, he watched in amazement as the cuts and scrapes from the crash healed in moments.

'Gilead Water…' Axel murmured.

His father, Kolbjorn had spoken of this tonic before. It was rumoured to be powerful enough to revive the freshly dead, if only for a few moments. Axel shuddered at the thought of it.

'Now, what do you remember?'

'I remember the crash…and…and…' he stalled as he recollected the cave and the strange melody and thought he could remember the whisper of his name on the cold wind.

He grew pale and shuddered, his palms clammy.

'What?' Berau asked.

Axel shivered involuntarily. 'I don't remember anything more,' he said blankly.

Berau scowled, turning away in frustration. 'If my father had his way, *you* would succeed him in *all* things,' he said, hands trembling slightly.

Axel grinned widely. 'What you say is impossible, Berau. And even if it was – what makes you think *I'd* want to be Proxy? All I want to do is get to Chalkis – find out who my parents were...'

Berau smiled coldly and fixed his dark eyes on Axel's.

'I know there is little my father could ask of you that you would refuse.' Axel felt his brow furrow and he looked away.

Berau smiled humourlessly again. 'When I am Proxy, many things will change. My father rules with his heart. *I* will not.'

Axel's frown deepened. 'Look, however you want to rule this ice cube is up to you. You've got nothing to worry about from me.'

They were interrupted by the sound of a familiar irritated voice, panicked bleeping from a Medibot, followed by the sound of a scuffle, and a button being pushed. A moment later, the door opened and Chuck stumbled in, along with a very excited S-LO.

'Axel! Good - you're awake. You coming? They're waiting to put some kind of crown on that thick skull.'

*

In the light of the setting sun, Axel joined his friends on the steps in front of the beacon. Blix looked very beautiful - her shiny boiler suit had been banished, and she now wore a long white dress, her dark golden hair draped in shiny waves across her shoulders. S-LO had been polished and even Chuck looked cleaner than normal.

Beyond them stretched the snow-capped tops of the dark mountains, and wisps of sun-tinged cloud curled softly around their feet. Blix smiled warmly at Axel and kissed his cheek. He couldn't help but return a wide grin. Chuck rolled his eyes.

'Are you ok?' Blix asked. 'They wouldn't let us see you.'

'It would take a herd of hungry Batfnats to end me,' Axel said.

'Yeah, as long as you don't faint again,' Chuck said with a wry grin.

'What do you mean - faint?' Axel asked.

'You don't remember?' Blix said.

'Remember what?'

'*How* have you forgotten again?!' Blix said.

'You had...kind of...an episode...' Chuck said.

Axel frowned. 'An episode of what?'

Their conversation was interrupted by the start of the proceedings. The Proxy approached, his silver hair and beard bright in the dying light, and although there was the usual kindness in his eyes, there was a heaviness about him as he placed gold circlets on each of their heads and presented Blix with a torch that burned with a flame of molten gold. In the crowd gathered on the lower steps, Blix's little sister, Agnete waved excitedly. Blix grinned warmly in response.

'Well done, Axel Lennart, *Lightbearer,* I didn't doubt for a moment that it would be *you* standing here, a Victor,' the Proxy said, after he had congratulated Chuck and Blix.

'Perhaps you should have, sir,' Axel murmured.

He glanced at Berau, who was standing nearby, only a few steps down. His face was cold and hard, something far more disturbing than fear now present in the depths of his dark eyes. The Proxy's gaze shifted from his son to the floor, he shook his head slightly and looked back at Axel.

'Yes, perhaps.'

As the celebrations started, Axel's navwatch bleeped with an incoming transmission. A small hologram of Balo Fuse drifted into the air, a menacing smile spread over his fish-like lips. 'Well...Lennart, it seems I must *congratulate* you. Once I receive the winnings, you can consider your debts cleared.'

'Thanks, Balo!' Axel said, briefly shooting a glance at Chuck and Blix who were watching.

'Perhaps, you would be interested in placing another wager, or in taking out a loan?' Balo continued greasily.

'A wager?' Axel said, his interest piqued. 'Uh, what did you have in mind?'

'Goodbye, Balo,' Chuck said, quickly clicking off the transmission.

Axel's mouth dropped open in shock. 'Hey – that could have been a great deal!'

'Hmm,' Blix muttered, unconvinced.

Chuck nodded. 'For once I agree with ol' genius here. Look around. We've got everything we need.'

Axel rolled his eyes and nodded reluctantly. 'So, what do we do now that we've won the Run?'

'Uhh, well...' Chuck said, adjusting his gold circlet, which was slightly too large for his head. 'Just go back to our usual lives as Patrol Pilots for the Proxy and er...Control Room Workers,' he said, motioning to Blix.

'I think I need an Ice-Ale,' Axel grumbled.

*

After a great feast, a bonfire was lit in the centre of the courtyard and dancing started. Not everyone shared in the joy, however. From a dark corner, Protector-9, the Security Chief of Eleusis, watched Axel bitterly, his thin lips pressed firmly together into a hard line.

Protector-9, or Nine as he was commonly known, had hair that was a pale blond, cut exactly to the prescribed measurements of the Regime. The severity of the style exaggerated the angular contours of his body and the harsh features of his face. One of his eyes was missing, and a black visor rested over his empty eye socket, connected directly to his brain by wires. Small coloured lights lit up on it from time to time, making him look part-droid.

Unaware of Nine's scrutiny, Axel's gaze was on his adoptive father – Kolbjorn Lennart, who had just arrived. In contrast to Nine, Kolbjorn was broad shouldered - a great hulking mass of a man, with a dark beard and a face full of fire and force. An old and large scar ran down the left side of his face, through his eyebrow and onto his cheek, his skin weather-beaten and rough. Axel moved through the throng to meet his father with a wide grin of greeting, however this soon faded when he saw that Kolbjorn's expression was full of thunder.

'Axel....' Kolbjorn growled, grabbing him by the shoulder and pulling him into a quiet corner. 'What were you thinking?'

'Nice to see you too! Anyway, what do you mean?' Axel said, shrugging away from Kolbjorn's grasp.

Kolbjorn shook his head, agitated, anxious. 'Son, you shouldn't have won. This is all wrong.'

'Wrong? Why?'

'Don't you see what this looks like, Axel? Winning over the Regime's favourite?'

'Ah, come on...Berau will get over it.'

'*No*, he *won't*. And the Regime *won't* forgive it. How could you be so foolish?' Kolbjorn argued.

Axel stepped back, stung. 'I can't do anything right, can I?'

Kolbjorn frowned. 'That's not what this is about,' he said, casting a furtive glance at the Unity Guards posted along the parapet walls above them.

Axel followed Kolbjorn's gaze, his eyebrows furrowed.

'Don't you get it? They *see* you now.'

Axel's frown deepened, and he felt a chill run through him that was nothing to do with the faceless Guards but was more to do with something that had been on his mind for a long while. Something he couldn't quite understand and didn't want to. He thought of all the strange things that had occurred recently, and the odd presence he could feel even now. His gaze dropped to his hands, which were pale in the dimming light, as if they held the answers to the questions that troubled him. His fingertips tingled strangely.

He shook his head, trying to ignore the vat of anger that was bubbling within.

'Look, I did it for you, ok…? The debt to Balo has been paid off…' Axel said, moving away from Kolbjorn, whose expression immediately softened.

'What?! Axel - wait,' he called vainly after his son, who was fast disappearing into the throng.

*

With wistful enjoyment the Proxy watched the dancing and merry making of the celebrations from the safety of a stone columned portico that ran around the main courtyard. Beyond this, a few of the Proxy's personal Guard, the blue-cloaked Heimdall, stood watch. Inside, his only company was a squat silver Servicebot, who bleeped conversationally from time to time, patiently awaiting any orders his master might have. A small fire burnt brightly within a pit inside the portico, and as the Proxy moved closer to it, to warm himself, he caught sight of his shaking, wrinkled hands and he frowned, anxiety pulling at the corners of his eyes and mouth.

'Quite an interesting turn of events,' a harsh voice cut into his thoughts.

Protector-9 stood at the edge of the portico, his dark living eye somehow piercing in the gloom. He was leaning casually against a column, but his hard, muscular body was taut, tense, like a coiled spring. He wore a black cloak, as did the rest of the Protectors, and it merged seamlessly into the shadows, as if it had been made from them.

'Nine,' the Proxy said, turning to face him. 'I must say I was surprised to see you here. Won't you have a glass of smoke gin with me?'

Nine did not move. 'I came here to see if you had located the maps I asked for,' he said, after a long pause.

'Ahh, the old maps of the wastes,' the Proxy replied, trying to keep his tone casual. 'No, I'm afraid a copy has not yet been located.'

Nine said nothing for a moment, his face blank, and taut, barely containing the bubbling anger within. 'You *still* have not located them?'

'It would appear that most of them, if not all, were likely destroyed during the war the Regime waged to acquire Eleusis, or are buried in the ice that followed. I will continue looking, of course,' the Proxy said, returning Nine's strong glare with his own, kinder glance.

The Servicebot rolled towards Nine, offering him a small glass of smoke gin. It was a thick silvery liquid, from which smoke rose incessantly, as though it was on fire.

'What a primitive droid, you have,' Nine commented, kicking the Proxy's Servicebot. 'It looks as though it has been here as long as you have.'

Servicebot bleeped haughtily and shunted forward, spilling the drink over the bottom of Nine's cloak, causing smoke to billow from his hem. The Proxy suppressed a smile.

'My apologies, Protector, as you say, my old Servicebot might be in need of a few new circuits. Some say that as droids age, they start to develop the ability to feel. I think you may have hurt her feelings.'

Nine moved forward, closer to the Proxy's throne. As the golden light of the bonfire hit his skin, it glowed white with an unnatural, metallic sheen.

'It does seem strange, all this...*celebration*,' Nine remarked quietly. 'The Regime has been humiliated, and you *celebrate*.'

The Proxy looked up at his visitor, eyebrows raised. 'Humiliated?'

Nine gave the Proxy a small, tight smile.

'A Proxy should be *far* above his subjects. When the time comes, the people might start to think that Berau should not rule, when there are others close by with such *talents* as Axel Lennart possesses.'

The Proxy said nothing for a moment and then smiled a little.

'What would you have me do, Protector? Throw the boy in the Cylindric for winning a contest?'

'Interesting that you should call it a *contest*, rather than a race. That boy, that unworthy favourite of yours, should be *punished* for his arrogance. *Not* rewarded. Indeed, a collection of pre-regime maps were stolen from the wastes yesterday, by a boy who closely matches his description. It would not surprise me if *he* were the thief!'

A look of surprise flitted unchecked across the Proxy's face, his expression darkening under Nine's watchful gaze. 'I find that very unlikely, but I will talk to him myself. You will not touch him,' the Proxy ordered, his eyes steely.

Nine leant forward, his artificially sweetened breath polluting the air. 'I do not need to remind you, I think, of the importance of what we are searching for out there on the wastes, especially given recent circumstances. If Ragnar was to hear of any resistance...'

'I assure you, Protector, everything possible is being done to locate the maps you require,' the Proxy said, refusing to be intimidated by Nine's threat. 'There is nothing here that Ragnar, or the rest of the Regime need worry about.'

Nine turned to leave, frustration tautening his gleaming face.

'On the contrary, Proxy, I think that there is much here that would concern the Regime. *Find those maps, or I will have no choice but to take this further,*' he hissed, before walking away, the sound of his footsteps thunderous in the relative quiet of the portico.

'Well, that told me, didn't it?' the Proxy said to his droid.

Servicebot bleeped in agreement.

'Won't you do me a favour? Find Axel Lennart and bring him to me, please.'

Happy to help, Servicebot acquiesced with a single loud bleep and trundled off into the courtyard beyond. Axel and Blix were dancing an old formal group dance. Chuck was paired with Hellfrid Gis, the chubby red-haired daughter of a tavern owner, and Augustus Mork was with Agnete. They were laughing, red cheeked and happy, whilst the Proxy's Servicebot wound around people, trying to get to Axel, getting knocked and kicked by dancing couples as she did so.

Finally, the Servicebot reached Axel and Blix, just as they realised that the music had stopped but they were still holding hands. As Axel left, Blix noticed Berau, standing a little way off, watching her. She shuddered at his gaze, before turning away to talk to her sister.

*

'You sent for me, sir?' Axel said, entering the portico.

'What a pleasant evening it is, Lightbearer,' the Proxy said, smiling. 'But it is getting rather dark. Won't you see me safely to my ship?'

'Ah, so this is how it will be from now on?' Axel said, grinning back.

'Oh yes, every time I am in need of a light, I will call for you,' the Proxy said.

'See how the snake works his way in,' Mari whispered, placing her pale hand upon Berau's arm to draw his attention.

Berau's expression darkened as he caught sight of Axel and the Proxy walking together.

'It is of no significance, my love,' Berau said, smiling, running his fingers lightly over her cheek. 'Do not worry yourself.'

67

His eye moved back to Blix, who was talking with some friends on the other side of the courtyard.

'See something you like?' Mari said coldly.

'Oh, you have no need to be jealous. No need at all,' Berau said, looking at Mari, a cold smile tugging at his lips.

'Axel, Protector-9 will be watching you closely after today, I would not go out on the ice-wastes for some time if I were you,' the Proxy said.

They were walking in the ruins of what must have once been a pleasant formal garden, where the clouds drifted amongst them, like a thick mist.

'The wastes?' Axel said, as innocently as he could.

The Proxy gave him a penetrating stare. Axel's mouth twitched.

'How did you know?'

'Oh, I know everything,' the Proxy replied, with a small smile. 'Some old maps were taken from a crash site out there. You wouldn't happen to know anything about that, would you?'

'I might do,' Axel admitted, blanching.

After a moment, the Proxy asked, 'Are they still functioning?'

'Yeah – I found a pre-regime droid out there to read them.'

'Does anyone else know that you have them?'

'Balo Fuse, and all his friends. Why, is that bad?' Axel asked.

The Proxy shot Axel a horrified look.

'*That* gangster? Oh dear, this is worse than I thought.'

'What? Why?'

'The Regime want maps of Eleusis, and they know some were stolen from the wastes. If Balo discovers this, he'll inform on you for a reward.'

Axel grimaced. Of all the things he could have found out on the wastes, he'd found a broken sword, a tennis racket and something that would probably get him executed.

'So, I'm guessing that the Regime want maps to help them find object X-06?' Axel asked.

The Proxy's eyes widened. 'Oh, so you know about X-06 do you?'

'Kind of....So, what is it – this object?'

The Proxy said nothing for a long moment. 'Something I'm determined that the Regime should not find. X-06 is rumoured to be a powerful object of dark magic, buried somewhere on the wastes.'

'*Dark magic?*' Axel said, with raised eyebrows.

The Proxy surveyed him, an amused expression on his face. 'I take it you are not a believer in such things?'

Axel scratched his eyebrow, remembering the strangeness of the crash earlier, what had happened to him in the lift, the presence he could feel, even now. The truth was that he didn't know what he believed. His skin grew cool and pale as he thought on it.

'So, what's it meant do, anyway, this…object?'

The Proxy hesitated a moment before responding. 'It is called the *Lys Myrkr*, in the old language,' he said quietly.

'The Bright Darkness?' Axel translated.

His skin prickled. The name seemed oddly familiar.

'This object – it grants wishes,' the Proxy said, eyeing Axel curiously.

Axel grinned widely. He could not help it. But as he searched the Proxy's eyes for their usual sparkle of humour, he found none there. The Proxy was in earnest.

'Oh, come on, sir…You really believe in all of this stuff, don't you?'

The Proxy smiled a little. 'Perhaps, in time, you will come to believe in it too. Perhaps deep down, you are already starting to believe.'

Axel's thoughts flitted briefly back to the presence and the dull pounding in his head. A haunted look entered his eyes.

'It is a weapon, Axel…Of huge destructive force.'

69

'Hang on, when you say you're determined that the Regime shouldn't get their hands on this thing – you don't mean – you're not going to look for it yourself, are you?'

'I'm afraid I can't tell you anything more, Axel. I can't get you involved in this.'

'Now wait just a minute, here...I'm already involved! If the Regime get hold of those maps, well...that's *my* fault! I want to help,' Axel argued but the Proxy shook his head and waved a finger in Axel's direction.

'Axel, you must promise me you will forget about object X-06. And not another word on this – to anyone.'

Axel opened his mouth to speak, and the Proxy immediately shushed him.

Axel frowned discontentedly.

Scarto

6.

Axel woke suddenly, the air sticking in his throat as he gasped for more. It had been the pulse of the presence that had shaken him awake, and now a feeling of dread remained with him, heavy on his heart. Wiping the cold sweat from his brow, he got up and looked out of the window. Beyond it, the black, rocky ground slid down to the charcoal sea, waves choppy, reflecting the dim hues of the gradually lightening sky above.

Massaging his temples, he wondered if he was going mad. The throb of the presence had been bearing down on him for days. And it seemed to be getting stronger. He was trying to force himself to think of something else, when a low bleep heralded a visitor at his bedroom door. It slid open, revealing his tiny Chore Droid waiting meekly on the threshold.

'Morning, S-LO,' Axel said as the droid trundled in and squeaked something at him.

'A message from whom?' Axel asked, rubbing his eyes.

S-LO bleeped a response.

'Big eyes and great danger, huh? Yeah, I know who you mean,' Axel said, a frown clouding his face, as he thought for a moment. 'Did he say why I shouldn't go to Scarto?'

The droid bleeped to the negative.

Axel sighed.

'S-LO, when did he give you this message?'

Scrambling out of his hut, Axel held his scanner to his eyes and searched the Homestead for any sign of Bodo. But he found nothing

71

except for sleepy huts and the snow-filled wind, which howled against his ears. S-LO joined him outside.

'Well, looks like he's long gone. I wonder why he didn't come and talk to me himself.'

S-LO asked Axel what he was going to do.

'I'm going to go to Scarto,' Axel replied, matter of factly. 'And this time, you are definitely not coming with me.'

S-LO bleeped in horror.

*

'Did you hear? There was a prison break a few days ago - from Cyrene. A convict escaped,' Chuck said quietly, later that day, as they readied their crafts for a patrol of the triple moons.

He and Axel were in one of the vast hangars in the Black Mountain Spaceport, surrounded by a fleet of dormant Unity Regime star ships. Around them, mech droids bustled, as well as several other pilots.

'Uh-huh,' Axel said with a grin, his voice heavy with disbelief.

Cyrene was a desert world, a fiery wasteland, where no living thing could survive for long without shelter. Axel had never seen it with his own eyes, but desolate images of Cyrene had been shown several times in Regime propaganda films. The entire planet served as the Regime's prison district, where giant fortresses stood at regular intervals in the black sand. They entombed the convicts within, with the horrid certainty that there was no hope of escape, especially as they were executed once the Regime had no further use for them. So, Axel thought, Chuck's story was unlikely to be true.

'Who d'you hear that from?' Axel asked as Chuck passed him a hover-spanner.

'Hod – he's started to trade with some of the off-world Regime bases. So, sometimes, he hears things.' Hod was Chuck's idiot older brother.

'*Hod?* Chuck, you'd believe anything,' Axel said, with a smile.

'Hey - this is truth you're hearing here,' Chuck said, pretending to be offended.

'They tracked the ship he escaped in all the way to this sector. He's a Class-X criminal you know - highly dangerous.'

'Oh yeah? What did he do?' Axel asked, wiping his oily hands on a rag, whilst Chuck did the same on his bodysuit.

He shrugged.

'I don't know. Apparently, the Regime's desperate to find him.'

'You two talking about the convict?' their friend Mork chipped in, pausing to rest a moment as he carried a large part back to his Dronar.

'Shush!' Chuck cried, casting a weary look at the nearest Unity Guard.

Mork leant in. 'I heard they think he's come here looking for something – and whatever it is, well, I guess they don't want him to find it.'

'Oh, come on, guys, since when have you ever heard of anyone escaping Cyrene?'

'Since now,' Chuck replied stubbornly.

'Yeah, anything's possible,' Mork agreed, shrugging.

Axel shot Chuck and Mork a dubious look over the wing of his craft.

'Well, if it is true, that there's an escaped convict on the loose, then it would explain why they're acting a bit spooked,' he said, jerking his head towards the Unity Guards who were stationed near the entrance to the hangar, the visible parts of their faces as expressionless as usual.

'You can tell if they're spooked?' Mork asked. Axel smiled.

'Well, last time I went out on the wastes, almost every outpost on the border was manned by the time I got back. I was lucky to get back through. Usually it's too cold for them and they don't bother.'

'The wastes?!' Chuck said, trying to fix a propeller and only managing to break it further.

'Yeah, you know, beyond the borderlands,' Axel replied.

Chuck scowled.

'I know what you meant, idiot. You've been out there again?!'

'Yeah – for Balo – remember?'

'Oh yeah.'

'Aren't you afraid?' Mork asked.

'Afraid of what?'

'Well, besides the fact that Unity Guards will shoot you on sight if they catch you, *he* might be out there - you know, the convict,' Chuck said.

'Uh-huh,' Axel said in disbelief as he handed the spanner back, but then he frowned a little as he remembered Bodo's warning.

What if there was some truth to this convict story? What if he was the man Bodo had sought to warn Axel about, but he was not on the wastes, as the Regime expected, but out on Scarto instead? A Unity Guard nearby cleared his throat and Mork jumped, before reluctantly heading back to his Dronar, struggling under the weight of the part.

'See you later.'

'What's up?' Chuck asked. 'You still not sleeping properly?'

'Haven't had a good night's sleep since the Banren Run…Do you remember that strange fellow – Bodo, the one who tried to sabotage our ship? He sent me a message this morning – telling me not to go to Scarto.'

Chuck gulped.

'Well, don't you think that maybe you should listen to him?'

Axel scratched the back of his neck uncomfortably.

'I know this is going to sound crazy, but I feel like I need to go back there…I haven't felt…normal since the Run. And I think that *something* on that moon has the answer.'

'It does sound crazy. But, well…some weird things happened to us there. And especially to you.'

Axel tapped the wing of Chuck's plane with his palm.

'You need help with anything else? This one's probably almost ready to go if you'd stop breaking bits off it.'

'I'll manage,' Chuck said, grinning. 'You go on and get flying. I'll try and fix this and see you up there.'

'Sure. If I see the convict first, I'll say hi for you,' Axel said. Chuck scowled.

*

The snow was falling fast as Axel taxied out onto the runway. He was in a Dronar-60, a pure white, one-man fighter craft with long slim wings. Inside there was only room for him to lie in an almost horizontal position, separated from the world above by only a thin, domed glass hatch. He clicked the comm. system on.

'AL-28 to Control, requesting clearance for take-off, to do a patrol of Scarto.'

'AL-28, proceed to take-off position on Runway-10,' Control replied.

Axel maneuvered into position. 'AL-28 to Control, ready for take-off.'

'AL-28, weather conditions are poor. Check your Autobot is fully functioning.'

Axel reached behind him and flicked a switch on the squat flight droid that was in the Dronar with him.

'Autobot, respond.'

'Autobot on-line, sir,' the flight droid replied.

75

'Run diagnostics,' Axel ordered.

'Completed sir, all normal. Autobot fully functional, Tracking computer online, Dronar-60 fully functional and ready to fly, sir,' Autobot reeled off.

Axel nodded. 'AL-28 to Control, diagnostics completed, ready for take-off.'

'AL-28, do not proceed, repeat do *not* proceed,' Control responded. 'An order has just come through that all craft are to be grounded. Turn around and return to base immediately.'

Axel hesitated. Peering up through the clouds, he could glimpse Scarto hanging over him. The presence pulsed in his temples.

'What was that Control...? You broke up. Readying to take off.'

'N-negative AL-28 – do *not* take off.'

'Sir, I heard Control loud and clear – we must turn back!' the Autobot cried.

'Did you? I think you must be malfunctioning, Autobot.'

'But sir, I just said -'

Ignoring him, Axel pushed the throttle full forward and the Dronar stalled loudly. 'Sir – I think you have forgotten to -'

'I know – I *know!*' Axel said irritably.

As he gently pulled a lever back, the Dronar blasted upwards, rising through the air bumpily, buffeted by the harsh snow-filled winds.

'Eight thousand kilopars and rising, sir,' the Tracking computer stated.

'Ha-ha – see, I got us in the air, didn't I? Despite all this,' Axel said, motioning to the storm outside.

'Weather conditions adverse, advise landing, sir! The chances of a person of your *low skill* level landing safely are two-thousand and five to one! We had better turn back!'

Axel's eyebrows shot up.

'That *so*, huh? How interesting, please tell me more,' he said, reaching back to switch the droid off.

As he soared away, Axel looked down at Principality-5. The Black Mountains, where the spaceport was situated, were now behind him, and he could just about see the rocky coastline stretching out directly below. It snowed often on Eleusis, the winters harsh and the summer months short and rarely warm. The buildings were mostly simple huts painted grey. There were a few trading posts and towns, the largest of which was Vanmar, where merchants often stopped awhile and related stories about the goings on in the rest of the system.

There had been rumours of some trouble – some of the braver merchants mentioned it as they passed through – of a revolution rising against the Regime. Axel always wished to know more but such information was dangerous to come by and even more dangerous to ask for.

Suddenly Scarto loomed ahead of him, icy, stormy and ominous in the blackness of space. It seemed as though the whole moon was covered by a multitude of ice storms, the eyes of which swirled threateningly at him. Axel slowed a little and thought briefly about putting Autobot back on.

Breaking through Scarto's atmosphere, the Dronar was immediately hit by violent lashings of snow and hail. Getting through the worst of one storm, he flew through the howling winds of another, unsure of where he was even trying to get to. A multitude of flashing lights blinked at him from the control panel and alarms were sounding. Wearily, he flicked his flight-droid back on. 'Autobot, I've got a problem with the left-side stabiliser.'

'Of course, sir, I will look into it.'

'Dronebot approaching,' the tracking computer alerted. Axel caught sight of the Dronebot and groaned. They were flying droids programmed to fire on unauthorised craft entering the airspace of

Scarto. Diamond shaped, they hovered in the air, waiting for unwitting pilots to come into range. Their outer surface was of a dull grey metal, blackened and pockmarked through many years of being fired upon. Axel realised that he was unfortunately, unauthorised.

'Oh no…' Axel said, as the Dronebot opened fire, hitting and knocking out the left engine.

In response, Axel fired heavily on the Dronebot, but every bullet bounced back.

'Autobot? Locate the fuel-cell shaft on that Dronebot. It's a C-58 design. Armored.'

'Oh, yes sir, those are notoriously difficult to destroy,' Autobot replied.

'Yes, I *know*, Autobot,' Axel hissed. 'Have you located it yet?'

'Unable to locate, sir.'

With a groan, Axel took his best guess and fired. The Dronebot exploded.

'YES! Did you see that? I GOT IT!!' Axel yelled.

'Sir, my calculations show an unacceptable increase in danger should we continue flying in these weather conditions…'

'Autobot…Can't you be a bit more positive?'

'I will try. What a beautiful day it is here on Scarto. Where are we going, sir?'

Axel winced, unsure of the answer to that question.

'I'm not sure…I just thought, if we came here…well, I *don't* know…' he replied, the blood draining from his face.

A loud crackle told him that Control were still trying to reach him. The storm must be interfering with the Dronar's communication systems too.

'Ahh…maybe this was a stupid idea….Come on Autobot, let's go home. Ughh, I'm going to be in so much trouble when we get back.'

Axel tried to turn the craft around to go home. But something was wrong. A moment later the control wheel of the Dronar moved sharply to the right, seemingly of its own accord and then levelled out, steering them far into the ice-fields of Sector-7.

'Autobot – is this you?!' Axel cried.

'No sir...neither of us is flying this ship.'

Axel looked out of the window, freaked out. It was like the storm...or something had gotten a hold of the Dronar. As the craft slowed, it felt like the ship was in the field of a giant magnet that was pulling it down to the ground. The nose dipped in a frightening manner. Axel still had no control. The Dronar appeared to be stuck, suspended in mid-air, as though it was being drawn towards the ground, but was resisting it. Then, Axel thought he saw something dark move within the blizzard. He shivered, feeling the hairs rise on the back of his neck.

'What's going on, Autobot?'

'Sir, I believe the systems are being adversely affected by the snow-storm. We must land.'

'Can't you get us out of this, Autobot?'

'We can land, sir,' Autobot said. Axel sighed. 'Come on, what are the options, though?'

'Landing, sir,' Autobot said, stubbornly.

'That's *it*?'

'Yes, sir.'

'Fine. *Fine*. We'll land then! Bloody Autobot.'

'My pleasure, sir.'

After a rocky landing the Dronar dropped down to emergency settings. Axel flicked on his radio. 'AL-28 to Control...I've been forced to land on Scarto due to the storm...I'll have to wait it out until it clears. Do you copy?'

An incomprehensible crackle came back in response. 'Well…looks like the storm's interfering with our comms too, Autobot,' Axel said, dread filling his heart like lead.

'I would suggest you sleep until flight conditions are favourable again, sir. Perhaps then, your flight skills may improve to below-average.'

'*Would you*, Autobot? Well, thanks very much.'

'I will power down until the storm subsides, sir.'

'Excellent. That's the best news I've had all day,' Axel grumbled. 'Sleep well, sir.'

Axel drifted in and out of consciousness, the constant pelleting of snow against the glass was almost comforting until the bleeping of the tracking computer woke him up.

'Life-form located twenty kilopars from current location,' it said.

'Wh-what was that?' Axel said, wiping the sleep from his eyes.

The pulse in his head was stronger than it had been for days.

'Life-form located twenty kilopars from current location,' the tracking computer repeated.

'A life-form? What, like an animal or something?'

'Human life-form located nineteen kilopars from current location.'

'Human?'

Axel shifted slightly in his seat, his feet had gone numb. 'Autobot?' There was no response. Axel banged on Autobot's outer casing. 'Autobot! Wake up, you old rustbag.'

'Yes, sir?'

'There's someone out there in the storm – probably in need of assistance. Can we get the Dronar up yet to go and help them?'

'Running diagnostics…I am afraid that we are still unable to fly, sir.'

'Can we taxi?'

'These ice-fields are notoriously unstable, sir. We may hit a patch of ice-sand and sink.'

Axel closed his eyes for a moment. He knew that. 'Can you give me a visual on them?' he asked.

'Who, sir?' Autobot replied glitchily.

'What do you mean, who? The person I just told you was out there! Don't tell me you're malfunctioning too?'

'I'm afraid that our visuals are not functioning well, sir. I will do the best I can.'

A grainy, blizzard filled image projected onto the inside of the domed hatch. Axel could just about make out the distant mountains and a lot of snow.

'This is the sector the tracking computer located the life-form in.' Autobot said.

'Are you sure? There's no one there. Tracking computer, can you narrow down the location of the life-form?'

'The life-form is located nineteen kilopars from current location. Angle: 12 degrees east from current position.'

'There,' Axel said, pointing at a dark shadow on the screen. 'That looks like a man standing there!' The image pixelated and collapsed. 'Now what's happened?'

'My apologies, sir, something interfered with the signal. Our visual systems are now off-line.'

'Tracking computer, where is the life-form now?'

'There are no l-life-forms in the vic-vicinity,' the tracking computer stuttered.

'What?!'

'S-System mal-function. Restart required.'

Axel paled. 'Something must have happened to him. I'd better go and check,' he said, unstrapping himself from his seat.

'Sir, that is not advisable-'

'I'll put the external com system on.'

'Sir, it is against protocol to leave the cockpit -'

'Well, just don't tell anyone about it and we'll both be fine.'

'You have no weapons, sir!'

'Well, I'll just have to count on *you*, won't I, Autobot? Something I never thought I'd say,' Axel muttered to himself, unbolting the glass hatch door above his head.

'Sir, please wait!'

Ignoring Autobot's pleadings, Axel pulled himself out of the cockpit and onto a wing. The ice-fields stretched out in front of him. Vast, freezing, uncompromising...and the violent blizzard raged on.

'Keep an eye on me, yeah?' He said to Autobot as the cockpit hatch shut behind him with a quiet buzz.

He moved his legs, trying to get some feeling back into his toes before sliding off the wing into the soft snow. It crunched loudly under his boots.

'External com-on.'

'Hello, sir, reading you loud and clear.'

'Great. Autobot, give me the last known co-ordinates of our friend.'

'Sending them to your navwatch now, sir.

He walked for some time, moving slowly as he did not know whether the ground would give way under his weight. Eventually his navwatch bleeped.

'Sir?'

'Yes?'

'This is Autobot.'

'I know it's you, Autobot. What is it?'

'You are al-mo-st at tar-ge-t.' Autobot said, as his signal broke up into deep static.

Axel looked at the time on his navwatch. He had been walking for around forty minutes. 'Autobot, run a track scan,' Axel said, but there was no response. 'Autobot?'

Axel's breath caught in his throat. The sense of the presence felt just as it had been the last time he had been on Scarto. It had been getting stronger with every day, and now with every step. His head so pounded with it he thought it might split apart. His limbs felt heavy as lead, his eyes tired. The snow suddenly fell very fast around him, as if it had been speeded up somehow. The wind whipped and howled. *Weird weather*, he thought. And then, everything was back to normal. The pounding in his head receded to a bearable level.

'Sir, are you alright?' Autobot said through Axel's navwatch.

'I'm fine. Is the tracking computer reading anything?' he asked Autobot, whilst he looked through his scanner.

'Yes, sir.'

'It *is*?' Axel said. He could barely see anything through the snow. 'What's it saying?'

'It is saying that there is a human life-form present at your location, sir,' Autobot replied. Axel looked around and then slapped his hand to his forehead.

'Yes, Autobot. That would be *me*. Are there any other human life-forms around here, apart from me?'

'The tracking computer says no. It's just you, sir.'

'Divert all the power to the front sensors and scan again,' Axel said, rubbing his shoulders in an effort to get some heat going within them.

'Of course, sir,' Autobot complied.

'Nothing in the vicinity?' Axel prompted.

'Nothing. The tracking computer is saying that the earlier reading was probably just a system malfunction, sir.'

Axel exhaled. He looked down at the ground. His own footsteps had already disappeared in the relentlessly falling snow. Any other tracks would already be long covered by snow. If they'd ever existed at all. 'Yeah. Yeah, you're probably right. What was I thinking?' Axel said, rubbing his eyes wearily.

'On a positive note, conditions are improving, sir. According to my calculations, we should be ready to fly in one hour.'

'Ok,' Axel said heavily. 'I'm on my way back.'

Axel was as silent as the Dronar was as it glided through space, lost in his thoughts and wonderings as to whether there had been someone there, down in the ice fields of Scarto. Darkness had fallen by the time Axel landed back at the spaceport. All the lights were on at Control but the comm. was strangely silent as he taxied back down the runway towards the hangars.

'AL-28 to Control, everything alright back there?'

'Axel?' Chuck's voice said suddenly over the comm., his voice taut, anxious. 'Chuck?'

'I'm on the radio in my D-54 – they've jammed your navwatch! Listen, Axel – Protector-9 is waiting for you – they want to question you about your flight.'

'Protector-9?!'

'They're waiting for you -' He was cut off suddenly.

'Chuck? You ok? Chuck, come in.'

There was no answer. Axel slowed down. Bright light spilled out from the open hangar door, illuminating the soft, sparse snow that still fell from the night sky. As the Dronar glided to a stop, Axel could see that the hangar was unusually empty. 'Autobot?' Axel said, quietly.

'Yes, sir?'

'I'd like you to salvage everything you can from our mission today and clean it up for me.'

'My pleasure, sir, I will work all night to see that it is done.'

'Great. Once you complete your report, I want you to show it to *me* only. Do you understand?'

'For your eyes only, sir, I understand.'

Axel jumped down from the Dronar, looking all around him. There was not a soul one around, not even a single Unity Guard.

'Chuck?' he said.

No response. He took a step forward.

'Halt, Lennart!' A voice came through the hangar intercom.

Axel sighed. He recognised Protector-9's harsh tones and he did not sound happy. If the Security Chief of Eleusis wanted to see him, things didn't look too good. The hangar doors shut smoothly just as a small white door clicked open on the far side of the hangar. Five Unity Guards marched through it.

'Hands up in the air,' one of them said harshly.

Catching sight of the name XB-1 on his lapel, Axel grimaced. Very tall and broad shouldered, XB-1 was a Guard with a particularly vicious reputation.

'Hey look, I'm sure this is all just a misunderstanding. What's this all about?' Axel said, putting his hands up.

One of the Guards placed a small black case on the ground in front of Axel. With a series of metallic clicks the case opened revealing two black cylinders contained within. They automatically came free of the case, hovering in the air above it.

'Seize!' the Guard said, and the cylinders flew over to Axel and clamped themselves tightly onto his wrists. Axel grimaced.

'You're making a mistake!' he protested.

Like magnets, the cylinders suddenly came together, so that his arms were pulled straight up above his head. The cylinders painfully pulled him upwards, lifting his feet a little off the ground. Axel writhed uncomfortably in the cool air.

'Resist and you will be restrained further,' one of the other Guards said, looking up at him.

'Analyse the flight computers records,' the head Guard ordered one of his subordinates, who nodded and went over to the Dronar.

Axel heard him unscrewing the control panel on the underside of the craft.

'Move forward. Acceleration one hundredth of a kilopar.'

The cylinders slowly pulled Axel forward through the air, like a puppet on a string. The Unity Guards flanked him, one in front, two on either side and one behind. As they passed the other Dronars, Axel saw Chuck suspended in midair, his wrists also in cylinders, his head lolling unconsciously against his chest.

'Chuck?' Axel shouted, 'Chuck! What have you done to him?'

Axel tried his best to stop, but the cylinders were too strong. 'Chuck!' he shouted as the cylinders dragged him past.

Swinging his legs back, Axel tried to get them around the Guard behind him. There was the sound of another black case opening and a second pair of cylinders swiftly clanked into place on his ankles. They glided his squirming form through the door and up the stairs to Control, where Protector-9 patiently waited.

Control was an octagonal room shrouded in darkness save for some emergency lighting and the glow of several computer screens. With walls made entirely of glass and a floor of black reflective material, it seemed as though it was floating in mid-air, the stars bright above the jagged edges of the mountains outside. A continuous desk lined the walls, each containing a multitude of buttons that lit up randomly, so that the desks pulsated with light, snakelike in its movement from one part of the room to the next.

Protector-9 was standing near to one of the desks, his angular face submerged in darkness. Nine was the most feared of the Protectors. There was no warmth, no comradeship about him. He oversaw security in the realm, which meant that he controlled the Unity Guards, a power the Proxy used to have. The black visor that sat over his missing eye glinted as he turned slightly, the little coloured lights within them flashing as he did so. The gaze of his living eye moved across the room, coming to rest on Axel. His lips curved up into a slow smile.

Quality Time, With Protector-9

7.

'Halt,' the head Guard said. The cylinders stopped moving forward but kept Axel suspended in the air. His body twisted uncomfortably as it swung to a halt.

'What have you done to Chuck?' Axel asked, trying to get free of the cylinders and failing.

'Nothing that wasn't necessary,' Nine said, his voice deep and calm. It seemed like he was smiling to himself. 'The Guards are simply following protocol and so must restrain you both, for your own safety.'

'For *our* own safety?' Axel repeated incredulously.

'Yes,' Nine said.

'Against what?'

'Yourselves,' Nine replied. 'You might do something you would later regret, if you were free to act of your own accord.'

Axel shut his eyes for a moment, trying to ignore the burning pain in his arms and shoulders. 'What's all this about? All I did was a standard patrol. If you'd just check my flight computer -'

'How do you find flying, Lennart?' Nine asked.

'Find it, sir?'

'Do you enjoy it?'

Axel paused, trying to glean where Nine was going with this. 'It's okay,' he responded evenly.

Nine shifted his position slightly. He laughed a little. 'I'm not sure that's true, is it, Lennart? I heard that you need to fly, because you're desperate to leave this planet.'

There was silence for a moment.

'Why do you wish to leave? Is it so that you can join the revolution against the Regime?' Nine continued.

Despite the pain, Axel's face broke into a wide grin. 'I don't even *know* any insurgents, let alone want to *join* them!' he scoffed.

Nine's face remained stiff and taut, with no hint of amusement in his eye. 'Can you explain to me why you ignored a direct order from Control to return to base?' he asked.

Axel feigned surprise. 'Uh, I didn't get that order, Protector...must have been the weather conditions interfering with the signal.'

'That's very interesting, Lennart...None of the other pilots seem to have experienced any such difficulties.'

'Really? How strange.'

Nine placed his raw fingers to his curved lips for a moment, as if he were considering something amusing. 'What happened when you got to Scarto?' he probed.

'I destroyed a Dronebot and then I was forced to land due to the storm. So I shut down and waited for conditions to improve. Why don't you check my flight computer? You'll see all of this is true.'

'What happened whilst you were grounded?'

Axel hesitated before responding. A bead of sweat trickled from his forehead to his jaw as he thought about Autobot.

'Did you leave the Dronar?'

'No, I stayed in locked in the cockpit,' Axel lied, trying to keep his gaze casual.

'Did the sensors pick up any life sign readings?'

'No, sir,' Axel said, trying to hide the pain in his shoulders that the cylinders were causing him. He hoped Chuck was alright. 'Should they have?' Axel asked, curiously.

'You shouldn't lie to me, Lennart,' he said softly.

'I am not lying, sir.'

Nine's fingers tapped lightly on the control desk he was nearest to. 'You are an orphan, isn't that right?' Nine asked in an even manner.

Axel stared at him. 'Yes,' he murmured.

'Who were your parents?'

'I don't know...What's that got to do with anything?' Axel asked as the lights flickered suddenly.

Noticing this, Nine deepened his gaze. 'Nothing. Just a little suspicion of mine. I have another...' He came a little closer, his black eye sparkling in the dim light. 'Did you know that a number of pre-regime maps were stolen from the ice wastes recently?'

Axel did his best to shrug. 'No.'

'The thief matches your description closely.'

'Lots of people match my description, Protector. As per Regime rules, we all look the same.'

Nine narrowed his living eye, but before he could respond, a sudden bleeping emanated from his communicator.

'XB-1 to Protector-9, the flight computer contents have been analysed,' a Guard's voice crackled through.

'Bring me what you have found,' Nine said into the device. He looked at Axel, another horrid smile blooming on his face.

'Now we shall see whether you have been entirely honest with me, Lennart.'

A minute later, Guard XB1 entered Control. Axel groaned inwardly.

'Sir, the flight computer shows that the Dronar destroyed a Dronebot over Sector-7. The Dronar then landed in Sector-27 for four hours and forty-three minutes before returning to Base.'

'Were there any lines of communication opened whilst the craft was grounded?' Nine asked, without taking his eyes off Axel.

'Only an attempted communication with Control, sir,' XB-1 replied grudgingly.

Nine's brow furrowed slightly. 'No communication with anyone out on Scarto?'

'None, Protector.'

Axel looked up in surprise. So that's what all this was about. Nine thought Axel was meeting someone out there. Probably the escaped convict from Cyrene - if Chuck's story had been true. Axel almost laughed at how ridiculous it sounded.

'Did the pilot leave the Dronar at any time?' Nine continued.

Axel shut his eyes briefly. This was it. Autobot would surely have told them about the life form reading, and that Axel had left the craft to find it. And then Protector-9 would hypothesise that Axel was an insurgent spy who had met and aided the escaped prisoner. And he and Chuck would be shipped off to Cyrene themselves.

'No, sir, the pilot stayed with the craft at all times, as is protocol,' XB-1 said.

Axel opened his eyes in surprise. He looked at XB-1, trying to read him, before realising that Nine was watching closely. Axel stared back defiantly, trying to keep his face blank.

'Can an Autobot's memory be rewritten?' Nine asked, keeping his eyes on Axel.

'No, Protector,' XB-1 said. 'Any attempt to tamper with an Autobot's memory only builds more protection around it.'

Axel glanced out of the window that overlooked the interior of the hangar, hardly able to believe it. Autobot was down there, still being prodded and probed by a couple of Unity Guards.

90

'There, so you have your answer. Can I go now, *sir?*' Axel said, hardly believing his luck.

Nine said nothing but pursed his lips angrily. He seemed to be considering his options. '*Know this*, Lennart - if the Proxy was not still living I would have you sent to the Cylindric. And there would be no space for your lies there.'

At the mention of the Cylindric, Axel's eyes widened and his breath came faster and shallower in his chest.

'You are lucky....for now. Should we meet again like this, I will have no option but to subject you to further questioning at the *appropriate facility.*'

After a few long moments, he gave a curt nod to the Guards who opened up the black cases again.

'Return,' the head Guard commanded, and the cylinders flew back into their cases. Axel and Chuck fell sharply to the floor.

Groaning, Axel lay there for a few moments, crumpled and exhausted, whilst Nine angrily pulled on his gloves with short, sharp movements. Scrabbling over to Chuck, Axel satisfied himself that his friend was alright. 'Ensure that that Autobot is taken apart for analysis and break that Dronar up for scrap.' Nine said to the Guards, in a careless tone of voice.

'What? Why?' Axel asked, horrified.

Nine stopped in front of him. 'Axel Lennart, for rogue behaviour, you are expelled from the Proxy's Guard. And so...you have no need for that Dronar anymore...or any other craft for that matter.'

Axel slumped back in shock.

'But, Protector, I told you what happened -'

'Silence, Lennart!'

'Sir, I need this, I *need* to be able to fly.'

Nine surveyed Axel coldly.

'Lennart, I will personally ensure that you *never* leave this planet again.' And then, with a horrid smirk, Nine swept out of the room.

*

'I hate Protectors!' Chuck said, once they were free of the base. Breaking a huge icicle off an obliging rock face nearby, he held it gingerly to the angry looking bruise that had appeared over his left eye. 'Especially *that* one!'

'Hmm,' Axel agreed, his eyes on the ground.

'So…*did* you meet anyone out there?' Chuck said excitedly, as they rode their airbikes down the mountain, along the Airfield road that lead to the Homestead. 'You know – the convict?'

'I couldn't find anyone, even though the systems were saying someone was there...' Axel said. 'But everything was malfunctioning so much it was hard to know what was real out there.'

The black road tumbled down to the choppy sea below, and the triple moons shone mysteriously above it, their reflections rippling in the dark water below.

'I *bet* it was him,' Chuck exclaimed. 'Hod said that apparently the convict killed every Guard on his detention level on Cyrene, before escaping in one of their Unity Star Skiffs. And no one knows how he did it...'

*

In the darkness of his cave, Bodo reluctantly clicked his communicator on. A hologram of a hooded figure flickered into existence in front of him.

'Master? Has everything gone to plan?' Bodo asked.

'It is done…the protections are breaking.'

Bodo shuddered and his whole body slumped in resignation.

'Good, master...Very good.'

*

Back at the spaceport, footsteps echoed through the hangar as Nine slowly approached Axel's Autobot. Bending over so that his nose was almost touching the small droid, he ran his pale fingers over its metal casing. Nine scratched his long nails hard into the silver paint.

'*What are you hiding?*' he whispered.

Autobot shuddered. A Guard approached from the Control room, an urgent air about him.

'Sir, an encrypted transmission has been intercepted, between here and Scarto.'

Nine straightened up. 'Is Lennart's navwatch signal still being jammed?'

'No, sir, and the signal came from a cave situated on the Airfield road.'

'Send a squadron out immediately,' Nine said, his dark eye gleaming with the thrill of the hunt.

*

Bodo backed himself up against a wall, his dirty fingers scratching at the rock. He froze in breathless panic as a terrible bang shook his cave. 'They coming...they *coming*,' he breathed.

'The communication to Scarto came from further within the mountain,' Guard XB1 said, from the other side of Bodo's cave door. 'Blast the rock here, there must be a cavern within.'

Another bang vibrated around him, and the doors of the cave were blasted open with an almighty crash. Blinking at the Unity Guards storming in, Bodo whimpered in fear. With words whispered under his breath, there was a crackle of electricity from his hands and a sudden explosion, throwing the Guards back. They fell unconscious to the ground, but another troop was right behind them, emerging through the smoke. After a moment, Nine walked into the cave, flanked by more Guards. His eye swept the cave, until it came to rest on Bodo, who was cowering in a corner, exhausted by the use of his powers.

'A *Völvur*...? But a weak one. Stun him and take him to the Cylindric for interrogation,' Nine said coldly. 'You had better use the *white cylinders* for this one – we wouldn't want him to use those powers again.'

'No,' Bodo said, shaking his head and shuddering with fear, 'No...please...'

*

Saying a weary farewell to Chuck, Axel made his way through the Homestead to his own hut. It was set on top of the cliff overlooking the shadowy waters of the sea far below. From up here, the seemingly never-ending sea could be seen on one side and the endless wastes on the other.

The metal shield doors of the hut slid open, revealing a welcoming fire burning brightly in the central pit, casting a soft orange glow around a circular living room.

'Kolbjorn?' Axel said, stepping into the hut.

An excitable bleep sounded as S-LO rumbled into the living room to greet his master.

'Hello S-LO, how're you?' Axel said, patting his chore droid affectionately.

S-LO bleeped in response.

'Oh, cleaned the whole pantry did you? Well, that sounds like a day well spent.'

Wearily slumping against one of the cushions that lay scattered around the hearth, Axel let the glorious heat of the fire warm him. Sleep dragged at his eyelids.

A sound at the door caught his attention. He looked up, suddenly tense. Perhaps Protector-9 had changed his mind and had sent someone here to finish him off after all. As the doors opened, Kolbjorn appeared with a Unity Persuader in his hand, pointed straight at Axel.

S-LO bleeped in alarm and took cover behind Axel.

'I'm sorry, I promise I will clean my room tomorrow...' Axel asked, holding his hands up in surrender.

Kolbjorn exhaled and lowered the gun immediately.

'Axel...' he said, relief flooding his face as he came forward and pulled Axel into a rough hug.

'Alright, alright, what's all this about?' Axel said, patting Kolbjorn's shoulder, bemused.

'I heard you ran into some trouble with Protector-9. They wouldn't tell me anything – not even that you'd been released. I came back here to get some supplies...I was going back to get you out of there. Are you alright? What happened?!' Kolbjorn said.

'I'm fine, I'm fine...' Axel said, running a hand wearily over his eyes.

Kolbjorn lifted one of Axel's wrists up to the light of the fire, where the cylinder had left a long red mark.

'Fine, huh?' he said.

Axel shrugged it off. 'Protector-9 had some questions about my patrol.'

A shadow flitted across Kolbjorn's eyes. 'Did you see anything *odd* out there?'

Axel frowned a little, thrown off by Kolbjorn's intensity.

'No...Just a lot of snow.'

'And you didn't leave the Dronar - when you were grounded out there?'

'I-I might have.'

'Axel!'

'Look, I know alright? The computer picked up a life-form reading but when I got there...well, it must have been a malfunction. There was nothing and no one there.'

Kolbjorn stared at Axel a moment before nodding slightly.

'Nine expelled me from the Proxy's Guard. Now I'm never going to get off this cursed rock!' Axel said, the injustice of it bubbling under his skin.

Kolbjorn said nothing for a few moments.

'I'm sorry, son, but I think it's for the best that you can't leave Eleusis at the moment. You can be a Sheriff like me. No more flying around.'

Axel shook his head. 'That's what you always wanted, isn't it? For me to be stuck here forever.'

'Going to Chalkis is not going to give you the answers you seek about your parents.'

Kolbjorn looked out of the window that backed onto the wastes beyond the fence, and up to Scarto, which glowed brightly behind the clouds. 'It's not safe out there right now.'

Axel looked up. 'Why? What's out there?' he asked, thoughts flitting to the convict.

'Nothing that need concern you.'

'But it *does* concern me,' Axel said, eyeing the gun.

It had the markings of the Regime on it but looked longer and more angular than the ones the Guards used. An older model. PERSUADER-019 was printed on one side of it. Kolbjorn was one of the Sheriffs of Principality-5 - but only Unity Guards were allowed to keep weapons of any kind. For a Sheriff to do so was highly illegal.

'Where did you get that?' Axel asked, pointing at the Persuader.

Kolbjorn looked at him suddenly, a haunted look in his eyes.

'It doesn't matter. You must keep it with you from now on. For protection.'

'Protection against what?'

Kolbjorn offered Axel the Persuader. Axel shook his head. There was no way he was keeping that thing on him. He hated guns. With a sigh of exasperation, Kolbjorn put it on the table.

'Will you just tell me what is going on? Is this to do with the escaped prisoner - from Cyrene?' Axel asked.

Surprised, Kolbjorn reluctantly met Axel's eyes.

'How did you hear about that?'

'So, it *is* true?' Axel breathed.

Kolbjorn's ran a hand through his hair nervously.

'Yes,' he said, his voice quiet – almost a whisper. 'He's a very dangerous convict, known as 5257,' he added, after a pause.

'How did he escape?' Axel asked.

Kolbjorn swallowed uncomfortably and looked away. It was strange seeing him so rattled.

'I'm not sure...But it happened just before the Banren Run. Now, the Regime think he's been hiding around here, somewhere. Tell me again, are you sure you didn't see anything odd, out on Scarto?'

*

Axel slept fitfully, restlessly, even though he was exhausted. The wind howled at the windows and rain hit the panes with force. Bright moonlight flitted into his room, through the gaps in the fast-moving clouds, bringing with it a murmur, a whisper. In his dreams he could hear his name being called, over and over again, carried by the wind until it was very loud and close. He woke suddenly, his breathing fast and shallow.

He looked around his room. A small fire crackled in the grate, though the flames were low and close to dying. The door and windows were still shut. There was no evil spirit hovering around him, calling to him, wishing him ill. Axel climbed out of bed and moved over to the window. With the sudden feeling that he was being watched, Axel peered into the storm beyond the glass. But there was nothing there, except the glow of the moons through the clouds. His fingertips tingled strangely. Looking at them they seemed to almost be glowing as his skin reflected the light of the moons. Axel frowned, massaging his forehead wearily. Perhaps he really was going mad.

Before he could think more on it, a metallic tapping noise suddenly resonated through the hut.

What now? Axel wondered. Looking around for a weapon, his eyes came to rest on the old tennis racket he had found out on the wastes. Hearing the creak of Kolbjorn's chamber door open, Axel grabbed the racket and opened his door. Kolbjorn was in the corridor beyond. Putting a finger to his lips, he indicated to Axel that he should follow. They crept through the shadows of the living room to the front shield door, where the tapping sound was emanating from.

Kolbjorn placed his left palm over the door release, his right palm wrapped around the Persuader. He looked at Axel, who was holding the racket far back, behind his head. Kolbjorn raised his eyebrows.

'It was the only thing I could find,' Axel whispered, with a frown.

'You need a gun,' Kolbjorn hissed, before hitting the door release.

The Stolen Autobot

8.

The shield doors of the hut slid open, letting in the howling wind and the rain that had just started to pour. Kolbjorn pointed the gun at the intruder, but there was no one at eye level. Their eyes drifted down.

'Good morning, sir!'

'Autobot?' Axel said, surprised.

'Yes, sir, I am Autobot. Model 1162 dash 4 point 1.'

'You know this bot?' Kolbjorn said, lowering the gun.

'Unfortunately, yeah I do. He was the droid on my patrol today. Autobot, you'd better come in before anyone sees you,' Axel said.

'Thank you, sir. The rainwater has started to penetrate my inner systems.'

He rolled in and Kolbjorn shut the door. For a moment no one said anything.

'Autobot, not that I'm unhappy to see you again so soon, but what are you doing here?' Axel asked.

Autobot regarded Axel for a moment with his large, binocular-shaped eyes.

'Sir, you asked me to compile a report for you on our flight today. The report is now ready for your inspection.'

The report, Axel thought, looking at Kolbjorn suddenly. Kolbjorn's eyes narrowed and he cleared his throat. 'Anything you want to tell me, son?' he asked.

'No,' Axel answered. He looked at Autobot, who was dripping all over the floor. 'I think this bot's confused. Must have been all the excitement today. I'll…I'll clean him up and take him back in the morning.'

Kolbjorn looked unconvinced but shook some water off his striped pajamas and bolted the front door. 'Alright, Axel. Well, I'm going back to bed. Make sure that bot doesn't leave a watermark on my rug. And he'd better be gone by the time I wake up.'

Axel took Autobot to his room and rubbed him down with an old towel.

'How did you get here, Autobot? And how did you escape the Unity Guards?'

'I flew, sir,' Autobot replied.

'You flew the Dronar here?!' Axel asked incredulously.

'No, sir. It is a little-known fact that Autobots have self-flight capabilities, should their craft fail them.'

'You can fly?' Axel said, surprised, 'I didn't know that.'

'There are many things you do not know, sir,' Autobot said smugly.

'Hey, that's enough of that,' Axel said, putting the towel down and resting back on his haunches. 'Autobot, you do know that Protector-9 has ordered that you be taken apart and analysed?'

'Yes, sir. I am aware of Protector-9's wish to terminate me.'

'So, you flew away,' Axel said with a grin.

'I flew here to deliver my report to you, sir,' Autobot said, a little huffily.

'Of course you did,' Axel said, his smile widening. 'Autobot, I wanted to ask you – did you tell that Guard – XB-1 - that I didn't leave the craft whilst we were grounded?'

'Yes, sir, I did.'

Axel hesitated before asking the next question. 'So I never left the Dronar?'

'No, sir, of course you left the craft. For 3.5 hours, to be exact.'

The fire crackled a little in the grate, finally descending into ember and ash. Axel's forehead creased in confusion. He dried his hands with the towel thoughtfully. 'So…you lied?'

'Yes, sir.'

'But - that's *not* possible,' Axel asked, twisting the damp towel in his hands.

'Sir, Autobots are powerfully programmed to save the lives of their pilots – something Unity Guards seem to be unaware of. I calculated the probability of you being executed were I to tell the Guard, XB-1 that you may have been in contact with a stranger on Scarto, in the very quadrant of space where the Regime is hunting escaped convict-5257. It was ninety-nine point four per cent. So, I persuaded the flight computer to alter the flight record in your favour.'

'You…wow,' Axel said, astounded. 'Wait, you know about the convict?'

'That is all the information I have on him, sir. However…' Autobot projected an image on to the space in front of him. 'Here are the visuals the flight computer recorded from our journey today. A large proportion of the visual record was corrupted by the storm but I managed to salvage and clean up a great deal since landing,' he said scrolling through the footage fast.

'Did you see it, sir?' Autobot asked.

'See what?'

'I will slow it down, sir.'

Frame by frame, the figure of a man dressed in a dark cloak appeared on a distant snowy hillside.

'Stop it there, Autobot. Can't you zoom in at all?'

Autobot zoomed into the image, enlarging the section that contained the stranger. His bleeding, wounded face appeared blurrily. Pixelated though he was, his cold, dead eyes gave Axel a chill. Under his left eye, an empty black circle had been branded into his skin - the Regime mark of a criminal. Axel shrunk back as he stared at the image. The distorted, mangled face of the convict stared back at him.

'What happened next?'

'The next part of the visual record is corrupted, sir.'

Autobot played out the remaining footage, which quickly pixelated and then went black. For a few moments, they sat in the darkness, the pelting of the rain against the windows the only sound in the room.

'Thank you, Autobot, you know, for saving my life and everything.'

'My pleasure, sir.'

Their conversation was interrupted by a noise outside.

'Sir –'

Axel nodded, putting his finger to his lips to hush Autobot, before going to the window and looking out. There was nothing but rain and snow and darkness. Suddenly a figure loomed up against the glass. Axel fell backwards in fright.

'Axel?' the muffled voice of the figure said through the glass.

'Chuck, what are you doing? Are you *trying* to give me a heart attack?!' Axel said, hyperventilating as he opened the window.

'Did you see it?' Chuck said, eyes wide as he started to clamber in.

'I saw a rocket or something, flying in this direction.'

'It wasn't a rocket,' Axel said motioning towards the droid.

'What?!' Chuck said, catching sight of Autobot.

'Hello, sir,' Autobot said.

Chuck fell head first into the room. He scrambled onto his feet quickly, eyeing the Autobot suspiciously. 'Why have you got…how did an Autobot get into your hut?'

'He flew, that's what you saw – the rocket.'

'He flew?' Chuck said, raising his eyebrows.

'Yeah, I didn't know they could fly either, cool, huh?' Axel said, with a grin.

'Yeah, that is pretty cool,' Chuck admitted.

Running his hands through his hair, Axel frowned a little. 'Chuck, I think you'd better sit down.'

'Why?' Chuck said, not moving.

Axel looked at the droid. 'Autobot, replay the visual record from my patrol.'

'My pleasure, sir,' Autobot replied, spluttering out the projection into the air in front of them.

The convict appeared for a few seconds and then was gone. Chuck half sat, half stumbled onto the floor.

'Is that - was that - ?' he stuttered.

'Yeah, I think so,' Axel replied, joining Chuck on the floor.

'Spacenuts,' Chuck said as the last frame froze, so that the image of the convict hung in the air in above them. 'So it was true...'

They sat in silence for a few moments.

'But, hang on, if the convict's there in your record, how come the Guards didn't see it?'

'Autobot lied to save our lives, that's why,' Axel said, with a smile.

Chuck laughed. 'That's impossible, Axe.'

'Actually, it is partially correct, sir,' Autobot piped up suddenly. 'I actively chose to save Axel's life, but saving Mr. Bergo's was merely a happy consequence.'

'A happy consequence? A happy consequence!' Chuck repeated. 'Charming! *Thanks a bunch* Autobot!'

'My pleasure, sir,' Autobot replied, oblivious to Chuck's displeasure.

'Hey look - look at that,' Axel said, moving closer to the projection. 'Autobot, can you zoom in a bit, on his hands?'

Autobot complied.

'What's that?' Chuck asked, as a mark on the convict's left wrist became clearer.

'It's a prisoner number. 5257. He *is* the convict the Regime are searching for,' Axel murmured.

Chuck looked at Axel, all the blood seemingly drained from his face. Axel, however, was looking at nothing in particular, a nagging feeling in the back of his mind, that he could not quite place.

'Sir, I have managed to repair another section of the flight record,' Autobot announced suddenly. 'Playing now.'

The image flickered and changed. The convict was still present, but he had moved slightly. Axel froze as he looked at the image.

'B-but Axel, that's you,' Chuck stuttered. 'It looks like you're talking to him.'

It was true. The convict and Axel were facing each other, as though they were in conversation. Axel frowned and shook his head.

'That *can't* be. I didn't even see him, let alone talk to him!' Axel murmured, a cold shiver running through his bones. 'You do believe me, don't you, Chuck? I didn't see him, I swear.'

Chuck shifted uncomfortably. 'I believe you, Axe, but no one else would.'

Axel stared at the floor a few moments, lost in thought.

'Axel, do you know what Nine is going to do to us if he gets hold of that recording?!' Chuck asked.

The door to Axel's room suddenly opened and a panicked S-LO tumbled in, bleeping in panic. S-LO was dripping wet, he'd clearly been outside, somewhere, and had seen something.

'Who's coming? What are you saying?' Axel asked, struggling to understand the droid's garbled tones.

But then, a distant rumbling sounded, causing Axel and Chuck to freeze in horror. Rushing to the windows they looked out into the black night. A few little flickering lights had appeared in the distance, growing larger through the darkness with every passing moment.

Airbikes, grinding up the road that lead to the Homestead. Lots of them.

'It's Protector-Nine! He's coming for that droid!' Chuck cried.

Cold dread rose within Axel. 'Autobot, I'm sorry but you can't stay here!' Axel said.

'Do not worry, sir. I know just where to hide – Riin Dur. Protector-9 will not locate me there.'

Chuck and Axel exchanged glances, their eyebrows raised.

'Riin Dur? You mean the old mines?' Axel asked.

'Yes, sir.'

'Alright...Chuck, you'd better get out of here too,' he said pushing Chuck towards the door.

'They're coming for *me*. Go now, or they'll take you too.'

'I'm not going anywhere,' Chuck said stubbornly. 'Wherever they take you, I'm going too.'

The hum of the airbikes turned into a roar as they grew closer and came to a stop in front of Axel's hut, just as the Autobot trundled off into the dark, stormy night.

'What is going on here?' Kolbjorn cried, bursting out of his room, just as a troop of Regime Guards stormed the hut.

'Axel, you have a lot of explaining to do,' Kolbjorn said, as one of the Guards took the butt of his Snipe Rifle and hit Kolbjorn harshly over the head with it, knocking him out cold, whilst another picked up a struggling S-LO.

'Kolbjorn...Don't touch them. Leave them alone!' Axel shouted, as he and Chuck were dragged out into the freezing rain.

Their hands were bound and they were pushed down to their knees, in front of Protector-9.

'Didn't we just do this?' Axel said.

Protector-9 surveyed them both, his mask-like face hard and emotionless, his cold eyes glinting with suspicion. Nine inhaled sharply and stepped closer, the crunch of the snow and rock beneath his boots loud in the silence. He opened and closed his hands impatiently.

'Where is the Autobot, Lennart?'

'What are you talking about?' Axel replied, feigning ignorance.

Unfortunately, Nine was not so easily convinced. He produced a long white Correction Stick and hit Axel's arm with it, hard. Red bolts of electricity shot out of it like lightning, snaking round Axel's arm, burning him. Axel shuddered in agony, his cries shattering the peaceful quiet of the Homestead.

'How would you like to be Vanished, Lennart?' Nine hissed. 'Or better still, have your beloved *father* or *friends* disappear? The Proxy won't always be around to protect you.'

Axel felt his heartbeat quicken. He fought to kept his expression calm, composed.

'Vanish a Sheriff? Are you nuts? You'd have an uprising on your hands. Do you really want to be known as the Protector who lost control of the population?'

Nine stood up, losing patience, his metallic skin gleaming under the lights.

'Well perhaps just your friend, here? Or maybe that torchbearer, Blix Bo? Such a pretty little thing.'

Axel didn't trust himself to speak, as the blood pounded in his ears.

'I will find out what you are hiding, Lennart, whether you co-operate or not,' he said, the black hole that was his living eye gleaming with revulsion.

Axel stared back at him, equally repulsed.

'I am tired of being lenient to you, Lennart. That *Autobot*, the one I know *you* stole from the spaceport. *Where is it*?' Nine persevered.

'I don't…know…' Axel gasped, steeling himself as the stick came down again, this time on his back.

He shuddered, willing the pain to stop, or at least for the strength to stop himself crying out again. Out of the corner of his eye, he heard Chuck shouting for Nine to stop as the stick came down on Axel again. He slumped forward in the mushy snow, unable to think of anything but the pain.

A brief lull caused Axel to look up wearily, straight into Nine's amused face.

'Perhaps I am punishing the wrong person,' Nine's voice bubbled through the confused agony in Axel's head.

Nine turned to Chuck.

'Get away from him,' Axel spat. 'Whatever this is about, Chuck has nothing to do with it.'

Nine's lips curved up into his usual, ugly smile. And then he bought the Correction Stick down.

Chuck's screams cut deep into Axel's mind.

'Stop…Please, stop,' Axel wheezed.

He struggled up as Nine lifted the stick high, ready to hit Chuck again.

'Are you ready to confess, Lennart?' Nine said.

There was silence for a moment, the stillness interrupted only by falling rain. Axel knew that if he told Nine the truth, they would both be imprisoned and most likely sent to Cyrene. If he said nothing, there was a chance they would survive the Cylindric.

'No,' Axel said, desperation threatening to overwhelm him.

Nine's face twisted in rage as he grabbed Chuck and brought the stick down again. But something strange happened this time. Just before the stick hit Chuck's shoulder, something inside of it blew, and the electric shock that should have gone to Chuck spread through Nine instead. He yelled in agony as smoke emanated from

107

his wrist, as though his skin was on fire. He recovered quickly, getting the pain under control, with loud, yet restrained gasps.

Strangely, Nine laughed. Axel frowned at his reaction. He should have been angry, weary, yet the glance he shot at Axel was somehow triumphant. Axel shuddered under Nine's gaze, waves of agony still pulsing through him.

'Take them to the Cylindric…' Nine said quietly, a smile still stretched across his humourless face.

Everything around Axel merged into a blur as they were taken away. With a concerned look at Chuck, Axel felt himself drifting into exhausted unconsciousness, and he was unable to prevent the world around him disappearing into nothingness.

*

When Axel woke, hours later, it was to darkness, scorching heat and terrible fear. Freezing water dripped down onto him from above; his clothes and hair were soaked again. Shuddering, he found that he was lying on a small smooth platform that moved as he pushed himself upright, into a standing position.

'Axel?' a voice sounded from somewhere.

'Chuck, is that you?' Axel asked the darkness.

'Yeah, you ok?'

'I think so. Where are we?'

'Holding cells in the Cylindric. They're going to make us go into our Cylinders we're just, err, waiting our turn, I guess. Don't move, by the way, there's a sheer drop on every side.'

Axel blinked a few times. As his eyes adjusted to the darkness, he could see what Chuck meant. They were each standing on individual platforms that were suspended over what looked like an endless black hole. The air was hot and thick with smoke, filing Axel's nostrils with the acrid smell of burning.

'What a *lovely* place,' Axel said.

He ran his fingers over the chains that held his platform up, trying to see what they were connected to, but could only see darkness above. The screams of people already in their Cylinders drifted down from somewhere, echoing through the space.

'I'm really sorry, Chuck. About all of this.'

'Well...*can't* let you have *all* the fun,' Chuck murmured.

His voice was unusually subdued. Axel shut his eyes and leant his aching head against the ice-cold chains. After a moment Chuck piped up again, sounding a bit more like himself. 'I was thinking though, wasn't it weird how that Correction Stick exploded on itself?'

'Yeah,' Axel agreed, feeling strangely uncomfortable talking about it.

If he was being totally honest with himself, he could have sworn that *he* had made the stick explode, somehow. As though he'd willed it to happen.

'I guess the Regime's manufacturing standards aren't what they used to be,' Chuck mused.

In spite of the dark, grim setting of their surroundings, Axel could tell Chuck was grinning to himself.

The Cylindric had been used on Eleusis ever since Protector-9 was appointed Security Chief by order of Ragnar, the Grand High Leader of the Unity Regime. It was their interrogation facility, although they called this process a treatment, as though a stint in it could cure disease. Some never woke up from their treatments, staying trapped in their nightmares forever. The Regime called them Dreamers.

The sound of clanking metal and moving chains heralded an addition to the holding cell. As the new platform was lowered down, Axel could see a crumpled, shuddering figure lying on it, his large eyes wild and frightened, his hair a tangled mess.

'Leave him for a few minutes, then bring him back in for his next treatment,' a distant metallic voice said, from somewhere above them.

'Bodo?' Axel asked, uncertainly. 'Bodo, is that you?'

The man did not get up, but he looked around in an exhausted and confused manner, finally focusing at Axel. 'Ax…el…Len…nart?' Came the cracked and broken reply.

'Yeah, that's right - Axel, and this is Chuck.'

Through the silence there came a laugh, shrill and loud. Bodo was laughing. Axel found himself gripping the chains harder, more chilled by that laugh than any of the screams that surrounded them. His palms were sweaty from the heat, making them slip disconcertingly over the metal.

'It must be fate, to meet you here like this, so I can warn you once more, help you. I should have stop you! But now…Now, it done. It done!'

Axel tried to move closer, to catch Bodo's whispers, but the platform dipped disconcertingly and the water made it slippery. He moved back to the centre.

'How do you mean, *warn* me?'

Bodo's eyes were wide and over bright. '*He* has come back. *He* on Scarto. Soon, he will be here, on Eleusis.'

'Huh?' Chuck asked.

'*Ears everywhere.* Protections breaking. My fault. Soon he will be able to return, and *then…Terrible danger.* I should have told you more, stop you going to Scarto. I too afraid - *coward!* Now, no need be afraid no more,' Bodo whispered miserably through the gloom.

As the clanking sound resumed, Bodo's platform started to ascend into the gloom above them.

'It will begin with headaches and dreams. *Headaches and dreams.* Sabo can help…Sabo *will* help you.' came his last words.

'Wow,' Chuck said, once he had gone. 'That guy is a total nutjob.'

'Don't be too hard on him, that'll probably be us in a few hours,' Axel said, flippantly, but as his eyes drifted up to the point in the gloom where Bodo's platform had been winched up, Axel's brows knitted together in thought.

*

A few floors above, in a plain, white room, Protector-9 stood watching a holographic feed of Bodo's torture. Bodo stood trapped within the narrow glass cylinder, his eyes were wide and terrified as he saw his worst fears as though they were really unfolding, his wrists and ankles red raw from his attempts to escape from the restraints. As Nine watched, his face was indifferent. He tapped his communicator.

'Has Prisoner-5256 revealed anything of use, yet?'

'No sir,' the Guard overseeing Bodo's torture replied.

'Keep trying,' Nine said, his voice cold.

'Sir, if we go on any longer his mind will be destroyed,' the Guard countered.

'Then continue. He's no use to us if he won't talk,' Nine said. 'As is the case for Lennart and Bergo.'

*

Axel kicked at the chains in frustration and his platform swung violently. This was all his fault. Chuck should not be here and yet, Axel was ashamed to admit to himself that he was glad not to be in this place alone. A sudden clanking noise broke the temporary silence as the chains holding Chuck's platform started to yank it upwards.

'Chuck!' Axel cried.

'It's ok, buddy,' Chuck's voice drifted across the abyss. 'I'll see you after, ok?'

Axel stared at him, unable to speak as Chuck's platform disappeared into the smoky darkness above.

A while later his own chains were pulled upwards through the shadowy gloom, through a thick blanket of grey smoke. The platform stopped just above the cloud, through which the pit below could no longer be seen. He was now in the heart of the Cylindric.

The high walls curved around him, each glowing gently with white lights. With a quick movement, the platform moved sideways towards one of the curved edges of the room, almost throwing Axel off in the process. With a series of bleeps and clicks, the platform docked into a narrow ledge that ran around the abyss below. Chuck's platform stood empty to one side. Axel shivered and clasped his arms around himself to warm himself up. He stepped gingerly onto the ledge, wondering where all the Guards were.

A Correction Droid wheeled itself along one of the paths that radiated out from the central abyss. The droid moved closer and closer, a metal arm stretching out in front of him. Clamping a thick metal hand around Axel's neck, he pulled Axel forward, past cylinders full of people screaming in torment, some of whom he knew. The droid stopped at the first empty cylinder and pushed Axel into it.

With a push of a button, a curved glass door slid shut, encasing him tightly within the tube. This was it, Axel thought, steeling himself. As the Correction Droid pressed another button, the cylinder began to hum loudly with energy and pain pulsed through his muscles, getting stronger with every rhythmic hum of the machine. He felt sick. Black spots floated in front of his eyes and the cylinder was suddenly unbearably hot. Sweat rolled down from his temples.

It was then that he felt the floor beneath him give way, and there was no more Cylinder holding him. He was falling....falling into thick liquid-like darkness. The pain was still there. Still growing stronger with every hum. Screams ripped through the sudden silence.

'Axel...?' Kolbjorn's terrified voice cut through the darkness.

'Kolbjorn? Where are you' Axel said.

Kolbjorn's sobs were loud, amplified though the large, empty space. 'Axel...tell them...please tell them...'

'Tell them what?'

'What you *saw*...on Scarto.'

Axel's breaths grew shallow and fast. Time and space were spinning out of the realm of measurement.

'Please,' familiar voices cried.

'Axe, they're hurting us...They're going to kill us! Tell them what you saw...' Chuck's strained voice came through the background. More screams echoed through the endless black.

'I saw nothing,' Axel said through clenched teeth. More pain. Axel cried out, his hands pushing uselessly against the curved glass of the cylinder, his breath coming out in ragged gasps, catching in his dry, hot throat. The rhythmic humming was back and even louder, the pain more intense.

And then Axel realised he could hear something. An echo of a memory, or a dream perhaps. Something was being unlocked by the machine.

'*You....*' a whisper rattled through the air, carried on snowflakes blown through the blackness. '*You were the one saved from the fallen star ship, Ax-el Len-nart...*'

The sound of wings fluttering echoed around him.

'Who are you?' Axel asked, as he walked through the nothingness.

Pushing the lurching fear and pain deep down inside of himself, he started suddenly, catching sight of his reflection in many jagged mirrors. A stabbing pain in his head dropped him to his knees.

'How do you know my name?'

'*Ax-el Lenn-art*,' the voice continued in a low hiss. '*I have been waiting for you…*'

Axel's eyes snapped open. His reflection in the glass of his cylinder greeted him, eyes wide and terrified. With a crackle, a bolt of energy passed around the cylinder, blowing circuits as it went. Suddenly, there was a large boom and light filled Axel's eyes, and then the whole facility was plunged into darkness. Emergency lighting sprang up, along the floor and an alarm started to blare. Axel pushed against the heavy glass door, trying to calm his breathing down, his heart clicking irregularly against his ribs. Pushing the door hard, he slumped out of the Cylinder, and sprawled onto the cold floor beyond.

*

'Protector, we've lost all power to the Cylindric, there was a power surge…knocked all of our primary systems out,' XB-1 explained to Protector-9.

They were standing in a room close to the top of the facility, where Nine had been viewing a holographic video feed of Axel, Chuck and Bodo's hallucinations.

'I can see that,' Nine said, watching Axel's frozen feed with narrowed eyes. 'I want you to release the boy, his friend, and dispose of that creature – Bodo.'

'*Release* them, sir?'

'Yes. And have them watched. I am certain that Axel Lennart is connected in some way to convict-5257. He will lead us straight to him.'

Home Sweet Home

9.

Axel was still lying face down on the floor, shivering, body slick with a layer of perspiration, when a Correction droid rolled up to him.

'AL-28,' the Correction droid said. 'You are free to go.'

Axel shuddered with relief. But he could not believe it. He wondered if this was some kind of trick.

'W-What?'

A path suddenly lit up in front of his face, leading the way to the exit.

'Wait. What about my friend – C-Chuck Bergo?' Axel gasped.

'Proceed to the exit,' the droid replied curtly, and when Axel didn't move, it grabbed his wrists and dragged him forward.

After a long journey upwards through the bowels of the Cylindric, a pair of large shield doors opened, revealing a flat snowy landscape beyond. Glorious sunshine lit the snow, bathing it in golden light. To Axel's relief, Chuck stood out there waiting for him, looking like he hadn't slept for days.

The Correction droids finally released Axel, dropping him in the snow outside the last shield door. Chuck struggled over as quickly as he could, and helped Axel to his feet.

'Boy, am I glad to see you,' Chuck said.

'What happened in there do you think? Everything was malfunctioning when they dragged me out.' Axel shuddered. 'I – I saw...' he said, frowning, his voice drifting into nothing.

'Axe?' Chuck said, concern riding high in his eyes. 'Why d'you think they let us go?'

Axel shook his head. 'I don't know. Chuck – I - I saw the convict. It felt so real…'

'The convict?' Chuck said, blanching.

Axel nodded. 'What did you see, inside the machine?'

Chuck shook his head and looked away for a moment, to hide his face from Axel. 'Nothing as exciting as the convict, that's for sure.'

Axel put a hand on Chuck's shoulder. Casting a glance back at the Cylindric, Axel thought sadly of all the people who were still in there.

'There's nothing we can do for them, Axe,' Chuck said quietly. 'We were lucky to get out ourselves.'

They were interrupted by the sound of an alarm as the shield doors slid apart again. A Correction Droid emerged from the Cylindric, carrying an unmoving man over one shoulder. The droid slowly made its way over to them and dropped the figure heavily at their feet. Then, the droid turned and headed back into the Cylindric, the large shield doors shutting fast behind it. Exchanging glances with Chuck, Axel knelt in the snow next to the man and turned him over. He shot a glance at Chuck. It was Bodo.

And Bodo was now a Dreamer.

'Great,' Chuck moaned. 'Isn't this that creepy old nutjob?'

'Yeah - Bodo. The Regime must have thought he was as good as dead, or they wouldn't have dumped him out here.'

'Well, I don't think they're far wrong on that score,' Chuck said, lifting up one of Bodo's arms and letting it drop back down into the snow.

'Well, we can't leave him here,' Axel said, standing up stiffly.

Chuck groaned. 'I *knew* you were going to say that.'

*

In the gloom of twilight they reached the Homestead on foot. They had supported a snoring Bodo all the way, each taking a heavy arm looped around their necks. A light sleeting rain had started halfway home, so they were now soaked to the bone and exhausted. The sight of Axel's hut stopped them in their tracks, as the harsh blue light of Unity Regime floodlights spilled out of every window and the shield doors had been blasted wide open.

A loud, angry yell drew their attention down to Chuck's hut, where Chuck's mother, Binko, was being restrained outside of her home, unable to stop the Guards as they destroyed it. 'Get your hands off her!' Chuck cried, dropping Bodo as he hurried over to his mother. Axel stumbled towards them as he watched but he stopped suddenly, halted by his own guilt.

Kolbjorn's name hanging on his lips, Axel hurried into his own hut, his heart thumping in his chest. Unity Guards were swarming all over the hut, pulling the place apart, the air noisy with the sound of their scanners. Axel fully expected the Guards to re-arrest him, or at least drag him back out of the hut, but oddly, they did neither. 'What are you doing here?' Axel said, to one of the Guards. Getting no response, Axel pushed his way in.

'Kolbjorn....?' Axel called. The sound of something smashing rang out from somewhere and a thin layer of smoke hung in the air. Making his way through the rooms, he frantically searched for any sign of his father, or his Chore Droid. Reaching his bedroom, he saw Guards ripping a hole in his floor, where he usually hid things he didn't want anyone to find. He slumped back against the wall, relieved that for once, nothing incriminating was in there.

'KOLBJORN? S-LO?!' Axel cried.

Feeling stifled by the noise and the destruction, Axel pushed past the Guards and tumbled into the yard at the back of the hut. Kolbjorn was there, standing shackled to the border fence that ran around the back of the Homestead, separating it from the borderlands beyond.

'Ah, nice of you to turn up,' he said, as Axel rushed over.

'Kolbjorn…' Axel said in relief.

'You ok, kid?' Kolbjorn asked, the skin around his right eye blackened and a cut over his eyebrow was still wet with blood.

'Yeah. You don't look so good though. What did they do to you?' Axel asked as he fiddled with the wires to the cylinders around Kolbjorn's wrists.

'Nothing as bad as the Cylindric...' Kolbjorn said, shrugging off Axel's concern. 'Speaking of which, how did you get out? I was planning on coming to save you.'

Axel raised an eyebrow. '*You* save *me*?' he laughed.

Kolbjorn scowled. 'Yes. I've got a few tricks in me yet. Anyway, what happened? How did you get out?'

'There was a malfunction…a power outage, I think.'

'A power outage?' Kolbjorn mused.

'Yeah. And then…they just let us go.'

Kolbjorn's eyes narrowed slightly and drifted up to the clouds, where the pale glow of Scarto and the other moons could just about be seen.

'Ouch!' Kolbjorn said, as Axel short-circuited the cuffs and they fell off, smoking slightly in the snow. 'Thanks.'

'I'm sorry they're here,' Axel said, just as more bangs and smashes emanated from the hut. 'It's all my fault.'

'Yes, it is,' Kolbjorn agreed. 'Tell me the truth now - that Autobot - what's so special about him?'

Axel shifted uncomfortably on the spot. 'Nothing,' he said.

Kolbjorn eyed Axel curiously. 'You *did* see something, didn't you? Up there,' he said, motioning to the moons above.

Axel's gaze drifted up to Scarto. His breathing quickened.

'Did he speak to you?' Kolbjorn asked, drawing his cape closer around his body.

'Who?' Axel asked innocently.

Kolbjorn sighed and shifted uncomfortably on his feet. 'The man you saw on Scarto - the escaped convict.'

'How did you -?'

'Axel...' Kolbjorn pressed.

'No, I didn't see him...' Axel replied, perplexed. 'But the flight record shows me meeting him – or at least he was close enough that I should have seen him, but I didn't. I can't explain it.'

Kolbjorn pinched at his temples wearily, his gaze slipping from Axel's face to the ground. 'But you felt something, didn't you? In here,' he said, tapping Axel's chest.

Axel looked at Kolbjorn in surprise. 'Yes. I've felt it for days – a kind of *presence*. I can't explain it.'

Kolbjorn winced, and his gaze dropped to the ground. 'It's the convict's presence that you can feel.'

'How is that possible?'

Kolbjorn shook his head, he frowned, saying nothing for a moment. 'The convict is a Völvur, Axel.'

Axel's brow creased, until a grin broke through. '*Come on*...The Völvur aren't real, they're just an old fairy tale.'

'I wish that were true...' Kolbjorn murmured.

'The stories about the Völvur say that they practiced magic, that they had special abilities - *unnatural gifts*,' Axel said.

'Yes,' Kolbjorn murmured. 'Dark sorcery, the Regime called it, before they wiped the Völvur out.'

'*Dark sorcery*,' Axel repeated to himself, remembering some of the terrifying tales he'd heard of the Völvur as a child.

'Convict-5257 was a murderer. A nightmare...A *monster*,' Kolbjorn replied, a look of pain cutting deep across his face. Axel felt a chill that was nothing to do with the icy breeze that cut across him.

'You *knew* him?' Axel whispered, studying Kolbjorn's anxious face in the growing darkness. He seemed suddenly aged, his eyes tired, his skin wizened and weather beaten. Kolbjorn shook his head. 'I saw him once.'

Axel studied Kolbjorn's profile, trying to figure him out. 'Can you feel his presence too? Can everyone?'

Kolbjorn looked over, his gaze conflicted. 'No, I can't,' he murmured quietly.

'Then why can I?' Axel asked.

'I don't know,' Kolbjorn replied, his shoulders tensing.

'Come on, you've got to have some thoughts here.'

'I don't. But whatever the reason, it can't be good.'

Axel frowned. 'What is it you're not telling me...? Why do you think the convict is here?' Axel asked, his voice quiet.

Kolbjorn, who had been staring at the ground, opened his mouth as though he was going to reply, when he stopped himself. 'You shouldn't speak of this to anyone else, Axel. Not even Chuck. And don't think about leaving Eleusis. Not until he's recaptured.'

'But -'

'LET'S TALK NO MORE OF THIS!' Kolbjorn snapped.

The rain had ceased. Snow now fell around them in gentle, sparse drifts. Axel hit the fence with the palm of his hand.

'Stop trying to protect me. Don't you see it won't work? I'll find out whatever it is that you're keeping from me - one way or another.'

A haunted look entered Kolbjorn's eyes, and he turned away towards the wide and empty borderlands, his shoulder's slumping, his head dropping slightly in defeat.

*

120

Protector-9, who had recently arrived at the Homestead, was watching Axel and Kolbjorn from a distance, his expression curious. A Guard approached him, boots loud on the slushy snow.

'We have concluded the search, Protector,' he said.

'Has the missing droid been located?' Nine asked.

'No, sir.'

Nine was silent a moment. 'We must teach Lennart a lesson for his duplicity...*Burn every hut in this Homestead to the ground.*'

*

Kolbjorn took a few steps towards the hut, before he froze. The Unity Guards had formed a circle around every hut in the Homestead, each with a Flame Rifle in their arms.

'No...' Axel murmured. 'NO WAIT -' he cried, as the Guards shot incendiary bullets through the windows.

Flames blossomed within each hut. Kolbjorn caught Axel as he started to run forward, and held him back, the fire reflected in both of their eyes.

'There's nothing we can do, son. Protector-9 would never have left the Homestead standing,' he said, in a gentle voice.

'But S-LO could still be in there! And the other huts – he's burning them all!' Axel cried.

'Once Berau is Proxy I expect this will become the way of doing things. It was going to happen sooner or later,' Kolbjorn said. 'No...' Axel murmured, eyes wide as the flames engulfed the hut, gripping Kolbjorn's arm for support.

'S-LO...'

Headaches and Dreams

10.

'Access granted,' a computerised voice broke through the sound of the torrential rain.

Axel, Kolbjorn, Chuck and Chuck's mother, Binko, stared at the rusted shield door to the emergency quarters they had just rented, waiting for it to open. Nothing happened. Bodo, who was unconscious and draped over Kolbjorn's shoulder, let out a loud snore. Kolbjorn kicked the door hard.

'Acc-cce-sss Gr-aaa-ntte—ed,' the door stuttered as it shakily slid open.

They exchanged looks as they entered the cold, dark space. This was to be their new home. Axel looked out bleakly as he shut the shield door behind them. Vanmar - the very worst part of town, disappeared behind it.

'Well, this is cosy,' Chuck said, picking a dead Ratfink off the floor by its tail and swinging it gently in the air.

'At least it's dead,' Kolbjorn replied flatly.

Almost as though it were a challenge to Kolbjorn's statement, a loud squeak echoed through the space. There was a movement in the shadows and a very live Ratfink hurled itself at Chuck, all fangs and claws and dark matted fur. Chuck caught it just before it got to his neck, but struggled to keep it at bay, falling backwards to the dirty floor as it tried to get at him. Before Axel or Kolbjorn could react, Binko calmly got a Persuader out and shot the Ratfink dead. Everyone stared at her.

'Y-you c-could have killed me!' Chuck stuttered, still gripping the Ratfink tightly, it's green slimy blood dripping all over his face.

'You're welcome,' his mother replied huffily, cleaning a bit of Ratfink off her lined and freckled face and smoothing down her unruly hair.

For a few moments no one said anything, and the only sound was that of the drip, drip, drip of a leak in the roof, and Bodo's now rhythmic snoring. Then, the sudden, low hum of the door buzzer made them all jump. As the shield door slid open, Chuck's ancient looking Servicebot could be seen standing outside in the rain. He bleeped in greeting and rolled inside, immediately malfunctioning and blowing his top. Grey smoke filled the quarters. Chuck looked at Axel and sighed. 'Of all the things to survive,' he said, rubbing his face wearily.

Once they had repaired the bot, Axel and Kolbjorn coaxed a fire into existence in the central pit.

'I need to talk to you about what you said earlier -' Axel ventured but Kolbjorn shot him a severe look.

He glanced at Binko and Chuck before shaking his head at Axel. 'I told you to *leave* it!' he growled, turning away and busying himself.

Axel stared after him, frustrated.

As they settled down to sleep and the fire crackled down to nothing, Axel's gaze drifted around the grim surroundings and came to rest on Bodo, who was twitching slightly in his sleep. *If only he hadn't gone to Scarto, all of this could have been prevented,* he thought. He closed his eyes briefly and felt the gentle weight of a blanket being placed on him. Binko smiled at him reassuringly.

'Sleep now, Axel, and try not to worry,' she said quietly. 'All things pass, good or bad. Things *will* get better.'

*

That night, Axel slept restlessly, waking every couple of hours, thoughts of the Völvur and Nine's talk of Vanishings endlessly

123

running round his head. His dreams were indistinct, and somehow did not feel like dreams at all. They were more like fragments of memory, images collapsing and half forming, just beyond the grasp of his comprehension. The deep throb of the presence was also with him, constant, unrelenting, growing in power. Axel's head ached. It was as though someone was tapping loudly at a door to his mind, trying to find a way in. *The convict,* he thought, scarcely able to believe it, his eyes opening slightly at the thought. Through the grogginess of half-sleep, he noticed Kolbjorn was pulling on his cloak.

'You don't have to go tonight, do you?' Binko whispered to him. 'It's too dangerous. And Axel needs you. Now more than ever.'

'It's always dangerous, Binko, and Axel can look after himself. Don't worry, I hope to be back by sunrise.'

By the time Axel registered that this was not a dream, he heard the sound of an Airbike starting up in the street outside. Joining Binko at the open shield door, he watched as the lights of Kolbjorn's bike disappeared into the inky darkness beyond.

'Where's he going?' Axel asked.

'Oh…there's a dispute in the outer realm. Bunda tribes,' she said after a short silence. 'The other Sheriff's needed his help.'

*

The rain had eased a little by the next morning, but it still fell incessantly, running down the dark streets in fast rivulets. Axel watched it from the open doorway of the emergency quarters, a steaming cup of bright yellow Frick juice warming his hands. Kolbjorn had not yet returned from the outer realm.

'He'll be back soon,' Binko said, sensing Axel's concern.

As Chuck was still fast asleep, Axel decided to head back to the Homestead, to see if he could find S-LO, or what remained of him.

The huts were in a sorry state indeed, a mess of blackened stone and charred timbers, still smoking despite the rain.

'S-LO?' Axel called as he walked through the debris, checking every room as he went. 'Are you here?'

Outside, SL-O, who had been hiding in the snow all night, stirred. Reaching his bedroom, Axel stopped short. The walls had collapsed here, and most of the room had been destroyed, but something metallic gleamed within the debris on the floor. 'S-LO?' Axel called again, as he quickly cleared the debris off the floor, sure that it was his droid he could see buried there.

But as Axel uncovered the object, his shoulders drooped. It was just the old Tennis tool that he had discovered on the wastes. Somehow, it had escaped unscathed from the flames, and looked just like it had, the last time he'd seen it. Pulling it out from the rubble, Axel slumped back against a wall and let himself slide down to the floor. Outside, S-LO, who had gotten himself stuck, tried to flag Axel's attention for help.

'Oh S-LO...I'm so sorry old buddy. I didn't tell you... that, well, I know you were just a rustbag of bolts, with zero intelligence – I mean, literally *nothing*...but I – you were my friend, you know.'

Giving up on Axel, S-LO cast a cable out around a nearby rock to pull himself out.

The sound of tiny wheels carried from the broken doorway. Axel looked up from his depression. S-LO stood on the threshold, covered in a pyramid of hardened snow.

'S-LO?' Axel said, a grin spreading across his face as he rushed over to pick up his droid. 'S-LO! You ok, buddy? I'm so happy to see you!'

Smoking, slightly, S-LO vomited out a pile of snow, and then let out a severely unimpressed bleep.

*

'Reaching destination...' Axel's airbike announced, as they approached the abandoned mining colony of Riin Duur. S-LO was asleep in Axel's backpack, recharging his batteries and Axel felt the familiar drag of exhaustion under his own eyes. The sun was still low on the horizon and the sky was ablaze with orange and pink light. Glancing over his shoulder, Axel saw that his suspicions about being followed were correct. On a ridge he had passed not long before, he saw the glimmer of a transport – an Informer.

'Continue on without me,' Axel said to his airbike.

'Meet me back here in two hours, and make sure no one is on your tail.'

Axel's airbike bleeped in acquiescence. Steering behind a rocky outcrop, Axel jumped off, hitting the snowy ground hard and rolling painfully. As Axel's airbike zoomed off into the distance, the Informer followed at high speed, unwittingly trailing a bike with no rider.

'Haha, *what* an idiot!' Axel said, before losing his footing on some uneven ground and falling face first into an icy puddle.

He sighed into the water. 'Just once...just *once* it would be nice to have a little luck!'

Axel stayed hidden a little while longer, checking the horizon for the sign of any other spies. Satisfied he was truly alone, he got up and slouched bitterly into the derelict enclosure of the mines.

There were several man-made caves cut into the red rock which opened onto a large courtyard. Axel scanned the area for a sign of where the droid could be hiding. A fresh bout of snow and rain had washed away any tracks, if Autobot had chosen not to fly. There was nothing for it, he'd have to try every cave. By the fifth cave, Axel was starting to lose hope that the bot was even here. He switched his navwatch torch on and looked around.

'Autobot? Are you here?' he said, into the emptiness.

Nothing. Axel sighed and turned to leave, but stopped at the sound of a droid powering up. Autobot emerged from behind a large rock, looking rather dusty and a bit worse for wear.

'Sir!' he said, rolling excitedly over the rocky floor towards Axel.

'Autobot!' Axel exclaimed, relieved to have finally found the droid.

'Sir, I am so very glad to see you! It has been so long!'

'It's been less than a day, Autobot.'

Axel went back to the mouth of the cave. Holding his scanner to his eyes, he had a good look at the desert lands, leading up to the Black Mountains beyond.

'Do not worry, sir, no one would *ever* follow you in here.'

'Oh yeah? Why's that?' Axel asked.

'Because of the reactor leak, sir.'

Axel looked at Autobot in alarm. 'You bought me to a *radiation pit*?! I thought you were trying to save my life, not fry me alive.'

'It occurred some time ago, no need to trouble yourself, sir. But there is still some suspicion about the radiation levels in this sector.'

'Wonderful,' Axel said, not feeling very reassured.

He rubbed his upper arms to warm himself, and then he sat down, opposite the droid.

'Listen, Autobot, there is something I've been thinking about…'

'Yes, sir?'

'Well, it was what you said, about the amount of time I was out of the Dronar on Scarto. You said three and a half hours?'

'That is correct, sir.'

'But, I distinctly remember looking at my navwatch when I got to the target co-ordinates. I'd only been walking for around forty minutes. Can you confirm that, if you look through your records?'

Autobot was silent for a few moments, whilst he checked. 'That is correct sir, it took you forty-three minutes to reach the target destination and forty-seven minutes to return.'

Axel shook his head, puzzled. 'According to my records, you stayed at the target co-ordinates for some time.'

Axel shook his head. 'But, Autobot, do you remember when I told you I would head back? Well, I did, right then. I can't have spent longer than ten minutes there…'

'Sir, you stayed at those exact co-ordinates for approximately two hours, sir,' Autobot said plainly.

'*Two hours*? That *can't* be right…' Axel murmured.

'I am always right, sir. I analysed the daylight changes collated in my visual record and compared them to your departure from and arrival back to the Dronar. They are consistent with my timings.'

*

As Axel got back to the emergency quarters, he found a pale looking Chuck standing in the open doorway, his arms crossed tight around his chest. Chuck's mother looked equally frazzled, her brown hair a frizzy mess and dark circles under her eyes.

'Axel,' Chuck said, pointing at the inanimate Bodo. 'He *has* to go. And *where* have you been?'

'In any case, he'll die if you don't find a way to preserve his body, whilst his mind recovers from the trauma,' Binko said, eyeing Bodo with concern.

'Preserve his body?' Axel said. 'How're we meant to do that?'

*

'You met him *where*?' Blix asked, her eyebrows raised.

'Prison,' Chuck said, whilst chomping on some space beans.

'Well…the Cylindric. Hey, look I'm sure he's a stand-up guy. Axel knows him better,' Chuck added.

128

Axel grimaced. 'Hardly. Our friend here's the one that tried to stop us going to Scarto…But I think his intentions were good, maybe…Anyway, we heard that you might have a Hibernator here, that he could use?' he said.

They all looked at Bodo, who was propped up against a nearby wall, snoring lightly with his mouth wide open.

'Well…I do,' Blix relented. 'But, I'm not sure it still works. It hasn't been used since…' she trailed off, dropping her gaze to the floor. 'Well, for a while,' she added lamely.

They were in Blix's Uncle's maintenance hut, warming their bones by the fire in the central pit, whilst Blix hosed down her wayward Servicebot, who was battered and seamed with dirt. The task was hard going, as Blix's Servicebot, despite being built to clean, obviously disliked being cleaned itself, and kept trying to escape.

Outside, Blix's little sister, Agnete, was playing with S-LO, making a garland of brightly coloured flowers to adorn the droid. Blix watched them for a moment through the window, a small smile on her face.

The maintenance hut consisted of one large circular room under a low roof, filled with all kinds of mechanical bits and bobs, rusty tools and a couple of holographic star charts which flickered and changed as the planet rotated. Scarto was there, glimmering mysteriously, close to the two other moons. Axel recoiled from it without thinking, stumbling onto a small trapdoor hatch behind him. The door murmured something semi-threatening in response.

'Sorry about the door, it only says rude things for some reason,' Blix said. 'My Uncle tried to disable the talk function, but he couldn't work it out. Old circuitry, nightmare to fix.'

'I could take a look at it for you, if you want?' Axel said.

Blix froze. 'No thanks, that's okay. It's really not worth the trouble. Thanks though!'

129

'Where does it lead to?' Axel asked, curious. 'Oh - just an old storage basement,' she replied with a shrug.

Servicebot bleeped in annoyance as Chuck tried to rinse out his data tray. 'Ughh, how'd he get so dirty? I've seen mining droids that are cleaner than this,' he said, as Servicebot spurted oil all over Chuck's bodysuit.

'Well, he does love to clean,' Blix said, with a nervous laugh.

'*Does* he?' Chuck said, shooting a murderous glance at the droid.

'Yes, he's just not very good at it, stupid bot,' Blix said, 'I swear I spend more time cleaning *him* than he spends cleaning the hut.' In response to this, the bot emitted a tirade of angry bleeps, but Blix drowned him out with another blast of water. Servicebot bleeped so much that he short-circuited himself. Smoke issued from under his hood.

'I can fix that, I think,' Axel said, after a few moments of silence.

'Oh no don't worry,' Blix said casually. 'He does this all the time.' She hit Servicebot hard on his hood and he suddenly rebooted, lights flashing, bleeping all over the place.

'Hey – Rustbag, watch your language, okay? We have guests.'

Axel stared into the fire, his fingers wrapped around his cup of Smoke Gin, which had long since gone cold in his hands. Setting it down, he moved his knuckles over his chin and looked at Bodo, his eyes thoughtful.

'Bodo said that he wanted to warn me. That '*He*' had come back, whoever '*He*' is…' Axel said.

Blix seemed to pale a little at this. She shot a quick glance at Bodo and then busied herself quickly with cleaning. Bodo twitched suddenly, frightening them all, before he slumped to one side and started to snore. Setting his cup down, Axel moved closer to him, catching sight of something on Bodo's arm. Gently lifting the sleeve off his wrist, Axel dropped it again immediately. A prisoner number was burned onto Bodo's wrist. 5256.

'What is it?' Chuck said.

His eyes widened when he saw the number. 'Oh, this just gets better and better, doesn't it?'

'Wait - is he the one the Regime's looking for? The escaped convict?' Blix asked, coming over.

Axel shook his head, exchanging glances with Chuck, 'No, that's 525-7,' Axel said heavily. 'And anyway, he hasn't got a prisoner mark on his face, which means he must have been pardoned.'

'*Or* he escaped before they could mark him,' Blix said.

Chuck shuddered. Bodo grew agitated and murmured a stream of something incoherent under his breath. A moment later, his fingertips glowed with dim white light. They all took a step back.

'W-what was that?' Chuck gibbered. 'His fingers…why are his fingers lighting up?'

'He's a Völvur,' Blix murmured, her face white as a sheet.

Axel's breath quickened. He felt the skin on his forehead grow cool and clammy.

'*A Völvur…*' he repeated, so quietly the others could barely hear him.

'They're real?! I – I thought they were a myth,' Chuck said, moving away so that he was standing as far from Bodo as he could get without leaving the hut.

'They're real alright. Just very rare,' Blix said.

The convict, Axel thought to himself, *was that the man who Bodo had sought to warn him about?* Possibilities whirred through his head. It couldn't be a coincidence that their prisoner numbers were consecutive. He looked up at Blix, suddenly realising that her gaze was fixed on him.

'We have to find a way to wake him up,' Axel said.

'Huh?' Chuck replied.

'Look Blix. I'm in a bit of trouble…'

131

'There's footage of Axel meeting with the escaped convict – 5257,' Chuck chipped in.

'Thanks Chuck...'

'What do you mean?! Where?'

'Scarto…a couple of days ago.'

'You saw him? Talked with him?'

'Apparently. I don't think so! Look - all I know is something odd's going on here - I don't know exactly what. But whatever it is, well, *Bodo knows*. If we could only wake him up, he could tell us.'

'Axel…even if you're right – I mean, look at the state of him. His brains are fried! I don't think he'll be up for conversation anytime soon,' Chuck said.

'I know an old recipe for a draught which *might* revive him. I'll start to brew it immediately, but it may take some time for it to ferment before we can give it to him,' Blix said.

'Some time...? How long?' Axel asked.

Blix shrugged. 'A few weeks at least.'

'A few weeks!' Chuck exclaimed.

'It's the nature of the draught, I'm afraid. Give it to him too soon and it will likely kill him. But – well, when have *any* of us ever heard of a Dreamer waking up?' Blix said, a melancholy tinge to her words.

Her gaze fell to her hand, where she wore her father's old ring. Axel winced, feeling guilty that this situation was bringing up an old wound. Blix's father had never recovered from a stint in the Cylindric. Axel touched her shoulder lightly in comfort. A moment or two passed, with only silence within it.

'*Sa-bo...*' Bodo suddenly whispered, frightening them all.

'W-What did he say?' Chuck stuttered.

'Wait – that's what he said in the Cylindric – that I should see Sabo...That Sabo could help,' Axel replied.

'Are you sure?' Blix said, surprised.

'Yeah...I think so.'

'You know who that is?!' Chuck asked.

'Yeah. Well, my Uncle knows him, a little. He's a crook – a gangster.'

'Why does that not surprise me?' Chuck grumbled, pulling at his collar nervously.

'He's got a lair down in Kallestad,' Blix said. 'I could ask my Uncle if he can get us a meeting, but it might take a while – Sabo doesn't like new people.'

*

Blix's Hibernator sat just outside of the maintenance hut and had not been touched in years. Clearing the thick layer of snow off the surface revealed it to be a long, man-sized box. At the push of a button, a heavy glass lid slid smoothly to one side with a loud hiss, and the three of them shoved Bodo inside. A continuous white light at the base glowed gently when it was powered up, and a quiet whirring sound could be heard in between Bodo's increasingly loud snores.

'Well, he seems happy enough,' Chuck said, as the they surveyed Bodo through the glass. 'What happened to being 'trapped forever in a world of your nightmares'?'

'It comes later,' Blix said darkly.

Quality Time…With Oneself

11.

The next morning, Axel found himself up early again, unable to sleep. He was considering returning to bed when the roar of several airbikes filled the street, waking Chuck mid-snore. Squinting into the dim daylight, he stumbled over to join Axel at the open doorway, just as Berau and some of his cronies pulled up outside.

'So, it *is* true,' Berau said with a smile. 'The great *Lightbearers of Eleusis*, reduced to living in squalour.'

'What are you doing here, Berau?' Axel asked, trying to remain calm.

'Oh, I came to collect Chuck,' Berau replied.

'Collect me for what?' Chuck asked, wiping the sleep out of his eyes.

'Well, Bergo - you still have a Dronar, even if Lennart doesn't,' Berau said, a smug smile plastered on his face. 'We're leaving for a few days training at Danulix spaceport.'

'Training? For what?' Chuck asked.

Berau strained his neck to get a good look at the inside of the emergency quarters.

'You know, it's smaller than I thought it would be, even for a hovel. Just as dirty as I expected, though,' he said, his eyes lingering on Binko, who raised her eyebrows, unimpressed. The others laughed and Axel felt a pounding in his head that was nothing to do with any mysterious presence. Chuck's face grew red as beetroot and he clenched his fists.

'Alright, Berau...you've had your fun,' Axel said. 'Guess there can't be much going on at Glitnir Palace if you're here, visiting us mere peasants.'

Berau scraped idly at the icy ground with the tip of his boot. 'You know, I could speak to Protector-9. Get him to reinstate you,' he said.

Axel stared at him, trying to quell the wild hope that was blooming in his chest. 'And *why* would you do that?'

Berau smiled. 'I have one condition,' he said.

Oh, Axel thought, *here it comes.*

'Beg for it,' Berau said smoothly.

Axel laughed at his own naivety. 'I would rather eat that droid's cooking for the rest of my life, than beg *you* for anything,' he said, pointing at Chuck's Servicebot, who bleeped in appreciation.

Berau looked around and then nodded, as if deciding something. Then he smiled harshly. 'As you wish,' he said, with a cold smile. 'You coming, Bergo? Or are you going *nowhere,* like Lennart is?'

The others around him laughed again and the remnants of Axel's smile faded into an air of despondency. Chuck fixed Axel with an earnest look.

'I don't have to go,' he said.

Axel frowned. 'Huh? Don't be an idiot.'

Chuck sighed.

'It's okay, Chuck. Really,' Axel said, feeling anything but okay. 'I'll...I'll just find something else to do.'

The street started to vibrate again with a loud hum, as Berau and his friends started to power up their airbikes.

'Like what?' Chuck asked.

'Don't worry about me,' Axel said.

For a moment neither of them said anything.

'Chuck...' Axel groaned.

'Not without you,' Chuck insisted.

Axel scratched at his temple in agitation. 'Brother...we need the Kroner, I don't know about you, but I don't want to be going back to Balo for another loan.'

Chuck fidgeted a moment longer and then let out a sigh. 'Okay,' he said, reluctantly picking up his helmet. 'I'll talk to the Admiral...See if he can do anything.'

'Sure,' Axel said flatly, trying to look like he didn't care that he was being left behind. 'See you later.'

Binko put a steadying hand on Axel's shoulder as they watched Chuck and the others ride off, the roar of the airbikes slowly diminishing to a quiet hum as they quickly disappeared from the rain-sodden street. Axel's shoulders slumped. Binko's pitying looks were not helping.

'I'll...I'll be back in a bit,' he said, turning away.

Pulling his helmet on, he rode as fast as he could in the opposite direction to Chuck and the others, trying to ignore the pounding ache in his head. He finally stopped far into the desert lands, where no one could bother him, his only company the sheeting rain that froze him to the bone.

Hearing the sound of spacecraft above, he looked up at the sky, watching as the Dronars flew out in formation overhead. Before he knew it, they were out of sight and out of reach, gone without him. Powering down, he dismounted at the edge of Loom forest and sat dispiritedly on an uncomfortable rock.

'It's no good, Axel,' Axel's Airbike said.

'What isn't?'

'Wallowing,' the bike replied.

Leaving his Airbike hovering at the tree line, Axel walked into the darkness of the forest. Groaning in frustration, he kicked a rock and then grimaced in pain. *What a terrible day.* The trees around him creaked in the wind, their trunks stiff with ice. They were arranged in straight lines and geometric shapes, an indicator that this place was anything but natural. *It was a Unity Regime creation,* Axel thought, as he started to feel the effects of the past few days hitting him. He had been walking for some time now, and his feet felt like lead. Sitting himself down on a felled tree, he intended to rest only for a few moments, but soon felt his eyes start to shut. Drawing his cloak tighter around him to fend off the chill wind, he lay back, onto the tree. The frozen branches around him rattled in the breeze, scattering snow through the dark air.

Struggling to keep his eyes open, the world around him drifted away as he fell fast into a deep slumber. Suddenly, he was flying...on a patrol, but his craft was on fire. He was crashing into the wastes, crawling out of the burning wreckage, from the fire onto the fast melting ice of a frozen black lake. And then, '*Ax-el...*' came the call, the broken whisper that was somehow loud enough to be heard over great distance, because it was in his own head.

'Ax-el Len-nart...'

The whispering call belonged to the black silhouette of a man standing on the middle of the lake. The flames of the crash lit his face - a face that was full of wounds and burns, each one angry and deep and red. Axel recognised the face. It was the convict. Dressed in finery; a cloak of black shiny feathers was draped over his curved back. On his face he wore a black beak, its dark surface glimmering in the light from the fire. His hands were clawed with long, black fingernails, pointed and sharp. His eyes were lidless and glowed red.

Axel got up shakily, blood running from a cut on his forehead. A fluttering could be heard, unnatural in the still, windless air. Black birds - a flock of ravens suddenly appeared. Swarming around him, they seemed to be saying his name, over and over again.

'Who are you?' Axel shouted to the convict, as the birds dived past, their beaks and claws nipping and scratching his skin, herding him forward.

'Come to me…' the convict said, somehow talking without moving his lips.

Axel wanted to escape, to run away, in the opposite direction, but instead he felt compelled to go to the convict. Axel tried to resist but his bare feet were uncontrollably sliding over the center of the frozen lake, where the convict waited for him.

'I am the *Raven*,' the convict whispered, his voice deep and thick, the words echoing around them through the blackness.

The convict reached out his hand, offering it to Axel. With stilted breaths, Axel realised that the Raven's fingertips were glowing slightly. The convict smiled. The ice started to tremble and crack around them.

'What's happening? What do you want from me?!' Axel shouted, but the Raven only smiled, his teeth glinting in the flames of the crash.

Axel looked around in panic as the ice beneath him suddenly gave way, plunging both him and the Raven into the water below. The Raven was still smiling, even as the dark water pulled them down into the depths of the lake.

'Axel Lennart,' the Raven's voice vibrated through the blackness. 'You cannot escape me…We are *one*, you and I.'

Axel kicked hard, pushing his body upwards through the dark, icy water. As he broke through the surface of the lake, he awoke, gasping for air, cold sweat drenching his bodysuit. He sat up properly, trying to calm his breathing down, his heart pounding irregularly against his ribs. With growing horror, his eyes drifted down to his hands. His own fingertips were glowing, with a bright, white light. Gasping, he struggled backwards, and promptly fell off the log.

'W-what is this?' he murmured, staring at his hands.

The glowing resided and his fingers suddenly looked normal again. Kneeling in the snow, he stared at his hands, his breaths ragged and fast as he tried to make sense of it. *Was he losing his mind?* Axel thought, with genuine fear. He looked at his hands again and they looked perfectly normal. It must have been part of the dream. Just a dream, he comforted himself.

The cracking of a twig in the forest around him snapped him out of his thoughts. He pushed himself to his feet, and looked around for any sign that he might not be alone - that someone might have seen him. A long moment of silence passed. Seeing no one, Axel massaged his forehead wearily.

He had no idea how long he had been asleep, but the shadows were rapidly deepening within the trees. Without further ado, he stood shakily and headed back to his bike. Shuddering, Bodo's words came back to him: *it will begin with headaches and dreams.*

*

Clasping a metal cup of Banbo juice tight in his hands, Axel shakily lifted it to his lips and drank the whole thing in one go. He was standing at the bar at Banchan Tavern, a smelly hole of ill-repute that was full of crooks, merchants and droids, where a fight was more certain than the possibility of a decent cup of ice-ale. It was Axel and Chuck's favourite drinking establishment by far.

A flat layer of light grey smoke hung densely over the place, which was large and dark, with a large counter around which its patrons clustered, like flies to a light. There were a few dimly lit booths towards the back, which most folks avoided unless they wanted in on a dark deal or two - or were desperate for a loan to keep themselves afloat. He looked at his hands for the tenth time since he'd been here. Still normal.

Wanting another cup of Banbo, Axel looked around for Hellfrid Gis, the rotund daughter of the tavern owner. He found her fast asleep on the other side of the bar, her head buried deep in her arms, her snores vibrating the drinks atop the bar with every snore.

'Hellfrid?' Axel said, gingerly prodding her arm.

She woke immediately, a look of wild rage on her chubby face. 'TOUCH ME AGAIN AND YOU WILL DIE, FUNKFACE!' she shouted, the colour of her skin matching that of her mess of flaming red hair.

She paused for a moment, lifting her hands to her temples to steady herself as she focused her eyes on Axel.

'Oh, hi Axel, how're you?' she said, recognising him.

'Still alive I guess….' Axel replied morosely. 'How're you?'

'Oh, I had a bet with a Ddudkkie that I could drink more cups of Lo Fo Punch than him. Take my advice - never bet a Ddudkkie anything!' she said, swaying slightly.

'You lost?' Axel asked, with a frown.

Hellfrid leant across the bar and grabbed Axel by the collar, pulling him towards her so that their noses were almost touching.

'You should know by now, Axel, I take my drinking very seriously,' she said emphatically. 'That's him, over there,' she whispered, nodding over to a dark corner.

Axel could just about see the triple legs of an unconscious Ddudkkie sprawled out on the floor.

'Is he…okay?' Axel asked, aghast.

'Oh, he'll be fine,' Hellfrid said nonchalantly, releasing Axel and pouring him another cup of Banbo juice with jerky, uncoordinated movements.

'So where's Chuck?' Hellfrid asked, pouring herself a cup.

Lifting it to her lips, she smelt the thick, orange liquid gingerly.

'Oh, he's out at Danulix Port for a while – training.' Axel said, nursing his drink in a brooding manner.

Hellfrid winced a little. 'Oh yeah. Sorry, Axe, I heard about what happened. Protector-9, huh? That's too bad.'

'Yeah,' Axel nodded bleakly and took a sip of his drink.

A moment later, someone wiped Axel's elbow off the bar, causing him to spill his drink down his front. He looked up in slow rage, ready to punch whoever it was in the face, when he cracked a smile. His friend, Augustus Mork was propping up the bar next to him, grinning like a Cheshire cat.

'Thought I'd find you here, Axe.'

'Mork?! What are you doing here? How come you're not training with the others?'

Mork squirmed slightly and winced. 'I ugh – I tried to quit, so they suspended me for a while. Chuck persuaded me to stay on. I leave for Danulix tomorrow.'

'You wanted to quit? Why?'

Mork shook his head and tapped the bar for a drink. Hellfrid obliged. 'Ahh...it's just not for me anymore.'

'Hmm, well I don't blame you, I guess. Chuck just said they're going to increase his Patrols.'

'Well,' Helfrid said, leaning in. 'I'm not surprised they're doing more patrols, what with that convict on the loose. Hod told me there's some kind of big blockade up there now. You have to have a military movement order to be able to leave.'

'Hod's back in town?' Axel asked, surprised.

It was typical of Chuck's idiot brother to visit Banchan Tavern before his own family. He was such a tool.

Hellfrid nodded, and then moved a little closer as she spoke in a conspiratorial tone.

'I heard that the convict has *powers*. And during the wars, he could bring whole star ships crashing down, just with the flick of his wrist.'

'Uh-huh...' Axel said, massaging his temples - he'd come here to forget about the convict.

Hellfrid moved even closer. 'They say that he has a death sentence on him, but nothing works. That's why he's still alive. He *cannot* be killed…'

Axel looked at Hellfrid for a moment and then burst out laughing.

'Hellfrid, I think you'd better stay off the Lo Fo for a while.'

'You know, Axe…Well, have you heard what people say, about the convict? That he's a Völvur…a dark sorcerer? I have to say, I'm starting to believe it all myself,' Mork said.

Hellfrid slapped the bar and poked Axel in the chest. 'See? laugh all you want, birdbrain, but I hear a lot of things at this bar, mostly rubbish, but this, *this* I believe.'

'The Regime think he's on Scarto but what he *really* wants is to come to Eleusis,' Mork added.

Axel looked up, interested. 'Why d'they think that?'

'They found his apprentice here,' Hellfrid said, yawning widely.

'Apprentice?'

'Yeah, apparently he bit it in the Cylindric. His mind couldn't take the torture.'

A chill raised the hairs on Axel's arms. His brow furrowed as he made a connection in his mind. It *couldn't be*, he thought.

'Hellfrid, do you know the name of the apprentice?' Axel said, the familiar sense of dread rising in his stomach.

'Yeah – Bono or…or something,' Hellfrid mumbled.

'Bodo? Hellfrid, was it Bodo?' Axel asked, but Hellfrid was past responding.

She slumped down into her palm and a small snore escaped her lips. Axel sat back a little processing all this. *Was it possible? Could Bodo be the convict's apprentice?* he wondered, staring at his fingers with a frown.

'You ok, Axel?' Mork asked, bemused.

A guttural laugh drew Axel's attention to one of the booths at the back of the Tavern. He knew that laugh. Moving closer to the booth, a familiar cloying scent filled his nostrils, and Axel caught sight of Balo Fuse lounging languidly in the booth, surrounded by a collection of his fellow crooks, his fish-like face wreathed in pink smoke, a half-spent Smoke Dart hanging limply from his lips.

'Balo,' Axel said, with an unenthusiastic smile. 'My favourite money lender. I've been trying to get hold of you.'

Balo smiled. 'I heard. Money problems perhaps, now that your hut has been reduced to nothing?' Balo laughed meanly.

He puffed on his smoke dart with a semi-continuous rhythm, every so often reaching forward and tipping the dart's pink ash off the side of the table.

'Maybe you would like a loan? Or another wager?'

'No loan, or wager…But, I do want something.'

'Oh? And what is that?' Balo smiled.

Eyeing Balo's friends, Axel hesitated, scratching at his neck thoughtfully. It was a risk, telling Balo and his friends anything. 'I need to get hold of some Gilead Water – you know, that Unity healing tonic.'

Balo stretched his long slimy lips into another wide grin. Mork came over, even more bemused than before. 'Ah, so you have an ill friend?' Balo asked.

'A Dreamer that I need to wake up.'

'A *Dreamer*?' Balo said incredulously. 'Who is this Dreamer?'

'That's none of your concern. Do you know where I could get some Gilead Water?'

Tilting his head to one side, Balo surveyed Axel, a smile tugging at his long lips. '*Perhaps*. For the right price.'

'And what would that be?'

'Ten thousand Kronar.'

'*Ten thousand*?! You must be out of your mind.'

'Gilead water is hard to come by…And *you* could never afford it. You're washed up, Lennart. Done for. Just like your *Dreamer* friend,' Balo said with another low, guttural laugh.

'Yeah, well, we'll see about that,' Axel said, with a deep frown.

Balo smiled greasily. 'You don't even know the worst of it. Your *father*, Kolbjorn. You don't know where he is, do you?'

'Are you saying you do?'

'You have no idea what he's involved in.'

'What do you mean? Involved in what?'

Balo started to laugh. Axel had just about had enough. He reached forward and grabbed Balo by the collar. 'Come on, *friend,* I can tell you're just *itching* to tell me.'

The sound of several blasters powering up made Axel rethink his grip on Balo's neck. As the noses of the guns nudged at Axel's face, he backed off slowly, a forced grin on his face. But seeing Balo's smug smile, Axel stepped forward again, fists balled. Mork pulled Axel back before he could go any further, stumbling in the process. 'Okay, alright – come on now, we're all friends here, aren't we? No need to overreact.'

*

'Kolbjorn, are you there? Can you hear me?' Axel said into his navwatch. Nothing but static returned. Standing in the doorway of the emergency quarters, Axel realised that a velvety darkness had fallen, whilst he'd been lost in his own thoughts. The rain had finally ceased, only to be replaced by a solemn, howling wind. Balo's words haunted him.

'What is it?' Mork asked.

After being thrown out of Banchan they'd ended up back at the emergency quarters for a bowl of Servicebot's good slop.

'It's probably nothing.' Axel said, with a wince. 'Just Balo yanking my chain. But I can't shake the feeling that something's wrong – like Kolbjorn's in trouble.'

'Where did he say he was going?'

'The Outer Realm, with the Bunda tribes.'

'He probably can't get much of a good signal out there. If we were closer to him, you might be able to speak.' Axel brightened and nodded, wagging his finger at Mork in excitement. 'You're right.'

Jumping on their airbikes, they rode out across the desolate ice plains, all the way to the outer realm. It was here that the Bunda tribes lived, in small clusters of huts, sparsely spread through the icy wastes.

Taking his scanner out, Axel took a look around. He saw nothing but a flat expanse of snow, leading up to the tall cliffs of ice that marked the border to Principality-6. To his right, the wastes stretched out past the border fence.

'Did you see that?' Mork said, pointing behind them.

A faint glimmer of a light flashed in the distance. But as soon as he focused his scanner on it, the glimmer disappeared. Frowning, he shook his head.

'I think Protector-9 is having me watched.' Axel said.

Putting his scanner away, they continued on, looking for any sign of Kolbjorn or the Bunda.

After riding for hours, they finally stumbled upon a Bunda settlement. Jumping off his airbike, Axel padded through the snow towards the desolate life pods the tribespeople inhabited, his body tense. The Bunda were not known for their friendliness, but Axel hoped that they would tell him if they had seen Kolbjorn.

'Something's wrong here...' Mork said, shivering.

There was not a soul around. Silence hung heavy here and thick snow draughts were piled up against the pods. This place seemed to have been deserted for some time.

Riding further along the outskirts of the outer realm, they found another abandoned settlement and a few kilopars along yet another. Pulling his cloak tight around his nose, Axel approached a row of dead Batfnats, strung up ready to be cooked, now rotting in the wind. It seemed that the Bunda had left this place in a hurry.

'Where would they have gone without their life pods?' Mork asked.

Cold dread pushed in on Axel's chest. *What had happened here? And where was Kolbjorn?* He tapped his navwatch again and it bleeped negatively. No signal.

'I'm getting nothing at all here. You?' he said, turning to Mork, who shook his head.

'Axel, Battery Low. Recharge required,' Axel's airbike piped up, once he'd gotten back to it.

'Oh no,' he sighed. 'Do we have enough power to get back?'

'Yes…if we return now.'

His navwatch suddenly trilled with a short message from Kolbjorn. It simply read, '*Need to stay in outer realm for few days. Resolve dispute, Bunda tribes. Do not leave Eleusis.*'

'Hmmm,' Mork said, reading the message.

He looked at Axel, unconvinced. Axel frowned. Kolbjorn was lying to him, but Axel could hardly ask about it over a navwatch signal, which anyone could intercept.

'Come on, Axe, I agree it's strange, but there's nothing more we can do out here tonight.'

'Uh-huh,' Axel agreed heavily, turning his bike around.

Taking one last forlorn look around him, Axel reluctantly started back on the long journey home, the glimmer of light appearing again in the distance behind them.

Far away, in the bowls of the Cylindric, Protector-9 peered at a holographic feed of Axel and Mork riding through the wastes. The

Protector's fingers tapped on a nearby table top as he watched, his human eye glinting darkly in the gloom.

*

When Axel arrived back at the emergency quarters, he found Sheriffs Eidor Voll and Ferry Wolswinkle waiting for him in the freshly falling snow. Voll was a tall, pale man with a pinched, mousey looking face. Wolswinkle had a beard the colour of straw and the build of a serious Ice Ale drinker.

'Sherriffs…' Axel said, dismounting his airbike and opening up the quarters. Servicebot bleeped cheerily in greeting and S-LO eagerly stoked up the firepit, excited by the prospect of company. 'What can I do for you?'

'We were looking for Kolbjorn. Do you know where he is?'

'He's in the Outer Realm, resolving a border dispute,' Axel said as convincingly as he could.

Voll looked at Axel curiously. 'The Outer Realm? How interesting. And when will he be back?'

'At a guess…probably when the border dispute is over. Why?'

'There's been another attack on the supply transits…' Wolswinkle said.

'Yes…and there have been some disturbing rumours that some Sheriffs might be aiding these attacks,' Voll added.

Axel's eyebrow's shot up. 'Uh-huh. And what's that got to do with Kolbjorn, exactly?'

'I'd very much like to speak with him about it. Would you tell him that, when he returns?' Voll said, his watery blue eyes glinting just like Nine's did, when he suspected something.

'There's nothing I'd rather do, Sheriff Voll,' Axel said shepherding them towards the door, and motioning to Servicebot, who was cooking again.

147

'Now if you don't mind, gentlemen, I've got some inedible stew to eat.'

Axel watched as his visitors reluctantly mounted their airbikes and rode off.

'*Kolbjorn*...what have you got yourself into?' he murmured under his breath, resting his forehead against the icy metal of the door frame.

Then, he closed the shield doors against the freezing night.

The Raven

12.

'What can I do for you, Axel?' the Proxy asked, the next day. He and Axel were standing by the fire in the Proxy's study, in his Palace, Glitnir. The study was a large room, with white walls that stretched up to a glass ceiling, which afforded an early view of the first stars.

The back wall was also constructed largely of glass, revealing the stormy sea beyond, as the villa stood on the very edge of a rocky shore, just beyond the grasp of the dark, frothy water. Outside, the light had already begun to fade as evening approached, the threatening darkness drawing closer with every passing moment.

'Well...I didn't want to bother you, sir - but it's – well, I think Kolbjorn is in some kind of trouble.'

'Trouble?'

'He told me he was in the outer realm resolving a dispute with the Bunda, but yesterday Sheriff Voll came to the quarters looking for him.'

The Proxy's eyebrows shot up. 'Did he now?'

'Wolswinkle was with him too. Something to do with supply transits being raided - they suspect Kolbjorn.'

'Indeed?' the Proxy said, his expression thoughtful. He said nothing for a moment, and then smiled.

'Not to worry, Axel. I'm sure there is some explanation, which will become clear once he returns.'

'But, sir...what if it - I mean...what if he *is* involved, somehow...? I didn't buy that he was with the Bunda so I rode out to the outer realm myself. Every settlement I found was empty - deserted. I'm telling you – *something's off.*'

The Proxy smiled a little and then shook his head. 'Axel, trust me... Kolbjorn can look after himself.'

Axel frowned, frustrated.

'Do you trust me, Axel?'

'Yes.'

'Then do not worry. I will send Kolbjorn an encrypted message warning him of the situation. No one will be able to read it but him.'

Axel blinked a couple of times, and then nodded slowly. 'Thank you, sir.'

'I heard about your stint in the Cylindric...and that Nine burnt down your Homestead. I am sorry I could not stop him. It seems that he only listens to the Proxy-in-waiting now...he has no use for the ramblings of an old man.'

Axel raised his eyebrows. 'Berau and Nine are working together? Wonderful.'

Axel stared into the ever-growing darkness beyond the glass, lost to his thoughts for a moment. Then he turned to the Proxy, who was watching curiously.

'Something else on your mind?'

'I was wondering...Sir – what do you know of the escaped convict? 5257?'

The Proxy raised his eyebrows, but did not seem surprised by the question. 'Ah yes...Protector-Nine told me of his suspicions, that you had some communication with the convict on Scarto.'

'Mmmm,' Axel said, non-committally.

Tilting his head to one side, the Proxy surveyed Axel thoughtfully. 'What do you know of him?'

'Only that he's a murderer, and…a Völvur.'

'Does this mean that you are starting to believe in such things, Axel?' the Proxy said, with a small smile.

Axel pinched at his temples, trying to ease the throbbing in his head. 'Let's just say I'm more open to the possibilities.'

The Proxy looked out through the glass wall, into the churning sea beyond. 'It is true, Convict-5257 was once a Völvur - a powerful sorcerer. No one knows where he came from - it was as if, one day, he was simply born of the darkness itself. He became the monster everyone feared the Völvur to be. He slaughtered all who crossed him. He sought power at all costs, and swore vengeance against the Regime for the slaughter of his people. And then, one day, something caused him to lose his powers, and with the help of his apprentice, 5257 was captured by the Regime.'

'Was his apprentice called 'Bodo'?'

'Yes – I believe that was his name. Convict-5256. I pardoned him in return for his assistance in the matter. Unfortunately, the convict's abilities are slowly returning to him, just as I feared they would. That is how he escaped from Cyrene.'

Running his knuckles over his chin, Axel considered this. 'This convict – 5257 – what is his name?'

'He has no name,' the Proxy replied. 'But here on Eleusis – his home - he was known by many by his Völvur name - *The Raven*.'

Axel felt the room around him swim.

'The *Raven*?' he breathed, the feeling nausea rising in his dry, hot throat.

'Are you alright, Axel?' the Proxy asked, concerned.

For a few long moments, Axel said nothing. 'Yeah,' he finally said, blinking swiftly, trying to regain his composure.

The Proxy frowned a little in thought, his eyes sparkling with curiosity. 'Are you sure?'

'I'm fine,' Axel said. 'Why do you think he is here? What does he want?'

'Do you remember Object X-06 – the Lys Myrkr?'

'Of course – *The Bright Darkness* - the wish granter.'

The Proxy nodded. 'The Lys Myrkr is hidden somewhere on Eleusis.'

Axel was silent a moment as he made the connection. 'And the convict – he wants it?'

The Proxy nodded. 'Convict-5257 seeks it and that is why the Regime are in such a hurry to find it.'

'But how do you know this convict – the *Raven* - hasn't got it already – the Lys Myrkr?' Axel asked.

'Believe me, if he had it, we would know. Protector-9 thinks the Raven has not left Scarto.'

'That doesn't make any sense. If he knows where the Lys Myrkr is hidden here on Eleusis, why wouldn't he just come and get it? It's not like he seems to have any trouble avoiding Unity Guards.' Axel said.

The Proxy shrugged. 'There are many things we do not understand. But there is one thing I know for sure. He *must* not retrieve it, Axel, and *neither* must the Regime. The Lys Myrkr is a treacherous object. It works by trade – it will grant a wish only in return for the number of lives it thinks fit, for the wish in question.'

'Lives? It *kills*?'

'Oh yes, it longs to kill. But it cannot do so without the wish-maker's life energy. His or her soul, if you like.'

The Proxy moved a little closer. 'There's an old friend of mine, who's an expert on these sorts of objects, his name is Einaar Laan. He went into hiding as soon as he heard the Regime started looking for the Lys Myrkr. I am sure that *he knows* where it is hidden. Now, I have a couple of trusted bounty hunters trying to find Laan, but it is no easy task.'

Axel's brow furrowed. 'Trusted Bounty hunters?' he said, incredulously.

The Proxy nodded slowly, lifting his gaze to meet Axel's.

'Axel, I mean to find the Lys Myrkr myself. And destroy it before it can do more harm. I have the maps, Axel – the ones you found on the wastes, I acquired them from Balo Fuse myself!' the Proxy said, looking very pleased with himself, and motioning to a pendant that hung from a long chain around his neck.

Axel paced the floor for a few moments, his anxiety levels reaching fever pitch.

'Sir...what you're talking about is treason...If Protector-9 finds out - not to mention the wastes are crawling with Regime patrols looking for this thing! I don't mean to be rude but what chance have you got of finding the Lys Myrkr before them?'

The Proxy nodded in reluctant agreement.

'You are right. Unless Laan can be found, and persuaded to give up the co-ordinates, there is no hope of finding the Lys Myrkr, before either the Regime or the Raven does. Last time the Lys Myrkr was used it bought the ice to Eleusis, ending all life on the surface in an instant. I dread to think what further harm it could do, Axel. It *must* be destroyed!'

*

With Chuck away, Binko working all hours and Kolbjorn still gone, Axel found himself in the Emergency Quarters with nothing to do and S-LO and a senile Servicebot as his only company. The unfortunate consequence of all of this was that Servicebot had taken charge of dinner, and as a result, something truly terrifying bubbled away in a cauldron over the smoky fire.

After a spoonful of the broth, which had both the flavour and consistency of mud, Axel grimaced and then jumped, startled, finding Servicebot standing uncomfortably close by, eager for feedback.

'Oh, it's lovely, Servicebot,' Axel said, trying to feign enthusiasm as he subtly dropped the ladle back in the cauldron. 'Tastes great! Truly...'

Servicebot bleeped happily, ladling a large amount of the broth into a bowl and handing it to Axel.

Axel sat down next to the dim, flickering fire, which was providing the only heat and light in the room. Moving his spoon distractedly around the bowl for a while, Axel lost himself in his thoughts, trying to ignore the dull thudding presence that now constantly bore down on his mind. He examined his shaking hands, for the glow in his fingertips he had seen earlier. They looked perfectly normal now.

'Thanks,' he murmured distractedly as S-LO dropped a folded blanket onto his lap. 'Servicebot...' Axel said, an idea occurring to him. The droid rumbled over and bleeped uncertainly.

'Would you be able to access the General Record?'

Servicebot bleeped to the affirmative.

'Can you bring up all records on a Völvur known as '*The Raven*'?'

Servicebot was silent for a few moments and then bleeped negatively.

'No records?' Axel said, frowning to himself. 'Ok....bring up anything to do with the Völvur.'

A minute later, Servicebot splurged out a glitchy hologram of found records. Axel peered at them, his heart beating strangely in his chest as he read.

'*Völvur murder of ten people, Völvur murder of thirteen people, Völvur torture of children, Disappearances of children....*' Axel murmured to himself, as he scrolled through the records.

He paused at a record which was titled '*Völvur massacre of entire village.*' Tapping on the record, it opened and holographic text appeared in the air in front of him:

'*The Völvur known as the 'Red Lady' was the sole survivor of a starship-wreck when she was but eight-years old. She was saved from the sea by Lord Mildren himself, who took her in and raised her as his own. Eight years later, Lord Mildren announced he would marry a Lady from the neighbouring*

Homestead. The Red Lady, who was sixteen by this time, and in love with Mildren, fled to Stoffe Forest, where she was taken in by a Völvur coven. Stricken with grief, Mildren searched for the girl, to no avail. For two years, nothing was heard of her, until one day, she returned to the manor. She drove Mildren's lady from the house and bewitched Mildren. They married, however the villagers knew of her powers and rose up against her. As the villagers arrived at the manor, the Red Lady used her powers to drown each and every one of them, without the presence of water. When Mildren saw what she had done, it broke his heart, and he took his own life. The Red Lady fled to Stoffe Forest with her new born son and was never seen again.'

S-LO shuddered at the story. Axel shivered and raised his eyebrows at his droid. 'Creepy, huh?'

The black smoke of the fire thinned momentarily, revealing a sliver of the triple moons through the open shield doors. His eyes reluctantly drifted up to Scarto. Pulling the blanket around his shoulders, he forced a few spoonfuls of hot broth down his throat.

It was no use, Axel thought, slamming his bowl down. He needed to find out what happened on Scarto, and what this *'Raven'* wanted with him. But Axel found that he could do no more today, a sudden exhaustion took hold of him and he could no longer keep the thread of his own thoughts. He drifted hazily into a deep and troubled sleep.

Escape from Riin Duur

13.

A loud bleeping sound woke Axel the next morning, and to his chagrin, he found that he had fallen asleep face first into his bowl of broth. Groggily searching for the source of the bleeping, he realised it was an incoming message to his navwatch.

'Chuck?' Axel said, wiping the sleep from his eyes to focus on the hologram that had fluttered into the air in front of him. 'W-What's up?'

'Axe...I can't talk for long. How are you? Listen - I heard the Regime are stepping up their search for – well whatever they're looking for - out in the wastes. Interesting, huh? I heard they're even forming a new base...at Riin Duur.'

Axel's heart thumped loud and fast in his chest. 'That *is* interesting,' he said. 'Well, nice of you to call. I'd better go – you know – chores.'

'Yeah sure, call me when you've taken care of those chores.'

'Will do!'

Throwing the blanket off his shoulders, he slammed on the door release button and rushed outside to his airbike. As S-LO emitted a reproachful bleep, Axel stomped back in, grabbed his Chore Droid and ran back out to his bike. Servicebot stared after them in mute surprise.

*

Reaching Riin Duur, Axel climbed to the top of the rocky ridge that rose above the mining caves. Peering over the edge, he immediately sunk down again, horror struck. S-LO shuddered in fear. The basin below them was crawling with the largest number of Unity Guards Axel had ever seen in one place, as well as a terrifyingly healthy number of Air Tractors.

Holding his scanner to his eyes he saw the Air Tractors blasting the ground, just as he had seen them do so before, but this was on a much bigger scale. As Axel watched, a vast expanse of ruins started to emerge from the melting ice, and frozen artefacts were being pulled out of them at an amazing speed. *Protector-9 sure wanted the Lys Myrkr*, Axel thought with a groan.

'Take the finds to the old mine. They'll be analysed there,' a nearby Guard said, just as a fast-moving cloud of snow and dust indicated that a couple of Air Tractors were heading straight towards him.

'Great,' Axel hissed, scrambling back down the hill as fast and invisibly as he could.

'Err, Autobot, we've got a problem,' Axel said, running into the cave and flicking Autobot on. A growing rumbling sound and a sudden shaking of the cave disturbed their conversation.

'W-what is h-happening, sir?' Autobot asked, falling over.

'Well, we have to leave, *now*.'

'Leave, sir?'

'Yeah, unless you want to make friends with around three hundred Unity Guards.'

'But sir - that cannot be!' Autobot said, as Axel helped him off the ground and started pushing him towards the opening of the cave.

'We're *going*, Autobot.'

'But sir, where will we go?'

'*Anywhere else* – just *hurry up!*' Axel groaned, as the rumbling around them grew louder and the earth shook again.

They hurried into the central courtyard of the mine, just as the Unity Air Tractors turned into it, blowing a cloud of snow up around them. Axel pulled Autobot into the nearest cave, where they hid behind a large rock column. After what sounded like hundreds of Unity Guards jumping off the Air Tractors, Axel heard a familiar voice. His heart sunk. *Of all the luck*...he thought to himself as he chanced a glance into the courtyard. Protector-9 was standing, surveying his operation. He turned his head quickly, almost spotting Axel, who quickly shifted back behind the column.

'Set up analysis pods in each of the caves. Every Völvur object that comes out of the ruins must be catalogued before it is sent to the Cylindric,' Nine said.

Axel grimaced. Unfortunately, it looked like Nine would be sticking around for a while. As his eyes adjusted to the darkness, it became apparent that he and Autobot were standing on the edge of a giant circular abyss - the old mine shaft. Oddly, despite whatever crisis had befallen this place, power still served it; dim lights pulsed at intervals down the shaft. A strange sound also filled the space - like breathing - like many breaths at the same time. The increased shudders of S-LO signaled that he had noticed it too. With rising dread, Axel slowly looked up. Hundreds of bloodshot eyes looked down at him from the ceiling, each pair belonging to a hungry looking Batfnat.

Excellent, Axel thought. He hated Batfnats, especially as it was rumoured that they liked to feast on eyeballs. They were large and extremely ugly creatures, with mottled, purple skin that hung in greasy folds around their long, wrinkled necks. Large bat-like wings sprouted out of their hunched backs. Their razor clawed feet clung to the ceiling as each one shuffled in excitement, preparing to attack.

Axel tensed. Footsteps were approaching the entrance.

'And this is the place where the Völvur Calle Los met his end?' Nine said, stopping somewhere close to the column Axel was hidden behind.

'Yes, sir. He fell here, and was never seen again,' the Head Guard replied.

Nine stepped closer, lingering for a few moments as he looked into the abyss. 'And his body was never recovered?'

'No, Protector, the radiation from the reactor leak made it impossible.'

Nine said nothing for a moment, thoughts flickering rapidly behind his dark eye.

With a jolt, Axel noticed that a particularly large Batfnat was slowly crawling down the column towards him, yellow gloop dripping out of its beak in hungry anticipation. Axel did not know what to worry about more. Another step and Nine would discover him, another moment and the Batfnat would be upon him.

Nine turned to leave. 'Send a party down to retrieve the remains,' he ordered.

The Batfnat suddenly swooped down on Axel. He caught it by the neck as it did so, struggling to keep it at bay as it tried to peck out his eyes.

'But sir, the radiation levels down there have not been checked,' the Guard said, but Nine put a hand up to silence him, before turning back towards the column, listening.

After a moment, he turned back to the Guard.

'Radiation does not interest me. It is rumoured that Los hid object X06 himself,' Nine argued. 'Therefore, there may be some clue on his body, some hint as to where the object is hidden. You will head the party personally.'

'Yes, sir,' the Guard said, his voice strained. 'I'll arrange it at once.'

'Sir!' A Unity General said, as he approached Nine. 'A transmission has come in from a bounty hunter called Raku. He claims that the Proxy hired him to find an old friend of the Proxy's, an expert in Völvur objects, who went into hiding two years ago. Goes by the name of Einaar Laan.'

'I knew the Proxy was up to something. I wonder if he hopes this old friend of his can help him find object X-06.'

'You think he means to find X-06 himself?'

'If he does, then the capture of this friend of his will provide the evidence to have him arrested and executed for treason.'

Axel's breath stopped for a moment. This did not sound good.

'Tell the bounty hunter that if he lets *us* know when he finds this Laan, instead of the Proxy, I will triple whatever the Proxy has offered him.'

'Yes, sir,' the Guard said, his footsteps retreating back into the general hubbub.

The Batfnat was almost free of Axel's grasp, a viciously hungry look in its bulging eyes, when it accidentally knocked itself out by lunging at Axel, hitting its head against the rock column instead. Wearily, Axel dropped it on the floor, wondering how much time he had before the Unity Guards started heading down the mine. The courtyard was still very busy - there was no way out through there. Hesitantly, Axel peered into the mineshaft, wondering how deep it was. There was no light at the bottom. Above him, the Batfnats were shuffling excitedly again, and several more were climbing down the wall towards him. Things did not look promising.

'Autobot,' Axel hissed. 'Any ideas on how we can get out of this?'

'No, sir,' Autobot replied.

Multiple footsteps approached the entrance. A Guard caught sight of Axel.

'Oh no...' Axel muttered.

'YOU – YOU THERE! HALT! IDENTIFY YOURSELF IMMEDIATELY!' the Guard shouted, rushing forward.

Grabbing the unconscious Batfnat by the neck, Axel swung it up to the ceiling. The limp, rubbery body hit the other Batfnats, causing them to panic and swarm down towards him. As the entrance filled up with sharp beaks and large flapping wings, Axel grabbed Autobot and jumped into the mineshaft.

'Autobot!' Axel gasped as they fell. 'Use your thrusters!'

Autobot tried to start up his flight engine, but it would not start.

'Oh no,' Axel said, noticing that his flight fuel gauge was almost empty. Autobot tried again, but still had no joy.

'Come on, Autobot, one more try,' Axel begged, eyeing the bottom of the shaft, as it rapidly rose up to meet them.

Scrunching his eyes to brace for impact, he realised with a jolt that they had come to a stop mid-air, not far from the base of the shaft. Axel sighed with relief.

'Thank frick for your thrusters, Autobot, I *knew* you could do it!' he gasped.

'My blasters are not on, sir,' Autobot replied.

'Huh?' Axel asked, frowning.

'I cannot explain why we have not hit the ground, sir.'

Carefully shifting his gaze down to Autobot's unlit blasters, Axel could see that this was true. They were inexplicably floating, neither moving up or down, but simply hovering in space. With a feeling of cold dread, Axel peeled one of his hands off of Autobot and looked at them. The tips of his fingers appeared to be glowing, with a bright, white light.

'Do you see that, Autobot? You do see that, don't you?' he gasped, just before they fell the remaining distance to the hard, rocky floor.

Axel lay there for a moment, trying to process what had just happened. His fingers were no longer glowing, but he felt a wave of tiredness crash over him, as though he'd just run a few kilopars uphill. S-LO tumbled out of the backpack and squirted water in Axel's face. 'For frick's sake, I'm awake, S-LO!' Axel groaned, squinting into the darkness. 'Autobot, you okay?'

'Cook on high heat for t-twenty minutes,' Autobot said, pushing himself back into an upright position.

'I guess not, then,' Axel said. He stared at his fingers again in mild horror. A dead Batfnat dropped down the shaft, hitting him in the face. Gunfire rained around them as the Unity Guards shot down at them from above.

'Come on, Autobot,' Axel said, grabbing S-LO. 'We've got to find a way out of here!'

Several passages radiated out from the main shaft, each one dark and foreboding. Up above them, the Guards had stopped shooting, and the sounds of their descent started to drift down the shaft.

'Great...they're coming,' Axel said, pushing Autobot up against one wall as he tried to decide on which passage to take. From what he knew of this mine, some of them would surely be dead ends. They had to choose carefully, or else he and Autobot could end up trapped underground with a whole load of Unity Guards for company. Unfortunately, each tunnel looked identical.

'Come on, *come on*,' Axel said, slapping his navwatch, which was malfunctioning.

'I have calculated a route out, sir,' Autobot said, suddenly regaining his faculties and heading down one of the tunnels.

S-LO bleeped uncertainly.

'Yeah, I know...' Axel agreed.

He stared at the Autobot for a moment, until blue gunfire rained down again from above. S-LO shrieked in terror as the gunfire narrowly missed him, hitting the ground hard and making it sizzle.

'Are you sure you know where you're going?' Axel said, stumbling over the rough, uneven ground as he hurried after the droid.

'Yes, sir,' Autobot replied.

Sweat dripped off Axel's brow as they stumbled through the darkness; the heat down here was incredible. His mind drifted to the Guard's comments about radiation in the mines. He hoped that there was nothing to worry about on that score. Voices sounded in the tunnel behind them.

'Halt, stop right there!' a Guard shouted, catching sight of them.

'Hurry, Autobot!' Axel said, as they speed down the path.

'Almost there, sir,' Autobot replied chirpily.

'Almost *where*? Oh, you'd better not be malfunctioning,' Axel muttered.

They reached a junction of several, identical looking tunnels. Resting his hand on the tunnel wall for support, he found it wet to the touch. Water ran over it fast, collecting into a small stream that ran down into a tunnel that forked off to their right.

'Which way do we go?'

'This way,' Autobot said, rolling into the wet, steeply sloping tunnel.

The tunnel narrowed and a sudden gush of water caused Autobot to slip, and Axel with him, and soon they were sliding down the tunnel at breakneck speed whilst blue gunfire flashed past them. The Guards were catching up.

Tumbling around a corner, they came to a sudden, painful stop against a smooth rock wall. Axel winced in pain. The stream they had been following did not lead to a way out, as Axel had hoped it might. Instead, it led only to a small drain beneath his feet. A horrid realisation dawned on him. This was a dead end and the Guards would soon find them here.

'Sir -' Autobot piped up.

'Autobot, I only have one nerve left and you're getting on it,' Axel said tersely. 'It's over. We're trapped!'

S-LO bleeped in angry agreement.

'No sir, we are not,' Autobot replied, fiddling with something in the rock wall they had come up against. With a low hum, a secret door in the rock wall slid open and Axel rolled backwards through it. Autobot followed quickly, shutting the door behind them.

The Guard who was following them slid down the tunnel and hit the rock wall hard. Getting up, he stared at the dead end bemusedly.

'Have you got them, TQ-1?' Nine's voice echoed through the Guard's communicator.

'No, sir…they've just…disappeared.'

*

Axel laughed in shock and S-LO ran circles around them in relief.

'Autobot, that was amazing! I could kiss you!'

'That won't be necessary, sir,' Autobot replied.

Pushing himself up off the floor, Axel surveyed the large, dimly lit cavern that they were now standing in. It was filled with numerous mechanical objects in various stages of completion, with several oddball droids working busily on them. The air was thick with smoke and smelt strongly of machine oil. Axel looked around, trying to work out what functions the machines being built could serve, but they were unusual in the extreme.

'Where are we?' Axel spluttered. 'I do not know, sir – it is a secret exit, not marked on the maps. I can tell you that we are somewhere beneath the ice fields.'

'But…why would a mine have a secret exit?' Axel asked.

'Because it doubled as a secret base during the wars, sir,' Autobot replied, matter-of-factly.

'Huh?! Hang on, why do you know about secret exits in secret bases?' Axel asked, suddenly realising how strange it was that an ordinary flight droid should have such information stored in its memory banks.

'I was not always an Autobot, sir,' Autobot replied mysteriously.

The droids working around them seemed to have been built from salvaged parts. They certainly looked recycled and terrifying. Engrossed in their tasks, they did not seem to notice Axel, S-LO and Autobot as they moved quietly through the cavern, until another tiny Chore droid crossed their path and screeched in wild alarm. The hum of the drills and machines suddenly ceased as all the droids stopped what they were doing and turned to look at their visitors. Axel raised his hands in surrender.

'Hi there. How are you? Nice…er…nice place you got here. Look, we don't mean you any harm,' he said, as he started to back away from the approaching droids. 'We're just passing through. Tell them, Autobot, you're a droid. They'll listen to you.'

The strange droids advanced on them, spanners and wrenches held high. Autobot shuddered nervously. Axel looked around the cavern for another way out. Spotting a hatch in the ceiling he climbed a short ladder up to it.

'Sir!' Autobot shrieked.

The other droids were closing in on him in a menacing manner. Axel tried to open the hatch, but it would not give. Instead it simply mumbled something he could not quite make out, in a deep menacing tone.

'It *can't* be!' he said to himself, his face breaking into a wide grin. Looking down he said, 'Hey, Autobot, I think I know where we are!'

*

165

'Axel....' Blix said, eyeing Autobot wearily. 'Don't you think I know that Protector-9 is looking for that bot? He's *the one*, isn't he – with the footage of you talking to the convict? And how did you find that secret door? And why are you both so wet?'

The surprise of finding Axel, S-LO and Autobot dripping water all over her secret basement was still bright in Blix's eyes. At her command, her wayward droids had ceased their attack. They were now back at work, busily building their strange machines.

'So many questions...' Axel groaned, rubbing a hand exhaustedly over his face.

Blix shot Axel an expectant look. Axel sighed.

'Ok, well, I hid Autobot in the abandoned mines, but we ran into a couple of Unity Guards. The tunnels were our only way out,' Axel said, pulling his boots off and emptying them of water.

'There are Unity Guards in the tunnels?' Blix said, blanching.

'Uh-huh. Luckily Autobot knew about the door – he's got an old map of the mines somewhere inside that rusty head of his.'

Blix looked at Autobot, her eyebrows raised. 'Does he? That's interesting,' she said, bending down to examine him.

'Blix, er, what exactly are you're building in here?' Axel asked, looking around.

Blix paled. 'In here? I – nothing!'

'Nothing huh?'

Shooting her a puzzled look, Axel moved past her to look at her work. Blix followed him hurriedly. Axel picked up something that looked like a tuning fork, and Blix with a panicked look immediately took it out of his hands and laid it extremely gently back down on the table.

'Axel, you can't tell anyone about this place. Do you promise?'

An alarm sounded and Blix hurried over to where a grizzled looking droid was welding circuits onto a small silver cylinder. Blue smoke was billowing out of one end.

166

'Oh dear,' she said, grabbing a small extinguisher and spraying the cylinder and droid with a healthy coat of foam for good measure. 'Do I have your word?' she prompted.

'Sure, if you tell me what this place is,' Axel replied.

She shifted uncomfortably on the spot.

'So, this is how you knew how to fix the P-600,' he said, noticing an ancient looking droid behind Blix.

An old infobook labelled, '*Advanced Spacecraft Flight Performance, Vol.13*' was jammed into its reader slot. The words of the book were projected above it, glowing a dim green as they hung expectantly in the air, waiting to be read. As he moved closer, however, he noticed that most of the words and diagrams were not about spacecraft at all. In fact, the page she was on was titled '*Sabotage Code Machines.*'

'Yeah, my Uncle Rune gave me all his old infobooks. Would you like to see some?' Blix asked, quickly moving between Axel and the droid and shutting it down.

Just before she did so, however, Axel noticed a much shabbier, dirtier infobook spine sticking out of a second reader slot further down the machine. It read '*Disrupter Mechanics, The Art of Sabotage.*' He reached down behind Blix and grabbed the infobook out of the droid, who powered back up just to emit a low bleep in irritation.

'Sure. What's this one about?' Axel said, waving the infobook at her.

She stared at him wide eyed and then grabbed it back. 'Nothing, that's - it's pretty dull actually...I just found it in Fosse junkyard.'

'Uh-huh,' Axel said, as an awkward silence stretched out between them. 'Come on Blix, just tell me what's going on? What's all this for?'

Her hands faltered on the machine. 'Nothing! Nothing's going on. I mean, well, everyone needs a hobby, right?' Blix continued, her smile floundering.

'Sure…' Axel said, unconvinced, looking at the variety of strange machines that surrounded them.

He took the infobook from her hands and set it down on a nearby desk.

'Blix, you know you can trust me, don't you?'

They were very close together now, their faces inches from each other. Blix's eyes roamed over Axel's face. Then she looked away from him, trying to hide the sudden colour in her cheeks. He could feel her anxiety, her fear.

'Axel, that's not it -' Blix said quietly, the shadow in her eyes deepening. Axel frowned. *Why did she look so guilty? Well, she wasn't the only one with secrets,* Axel thought, his gaze slipping down to his fingers.

'It's ok, Blix, I won't tell anyone about this place,' Axel said, stepping back slightly.

She looked up at him and smiled, relief flooding her face.

'Listen, I guess I can keep your droid here. But he'll need a disguise.'

They both looked at Autobot. 'A disguise? Oh no, sir, I'd much rather come with you,' Autobot said.

'Now's not the time for vanity, Autobot,' Axel replied evenly, enjoying this.

He moved over to a pile of scrap parts in the corner of the room.

'Hey, would you look at this! Here are some old Slop Droid casings. These should fit pretty well.' Axel said with a wry grin.

Autobot said nothing.

On his way out, Axel approached the Hibernator that stood outside Blix's hut, the light on its base glowing brightly in the gathering darkness. Wiping a fresh layer of snow off the glass hood, he saw that Bodo still slept a troubled and tortured sleep. As Axel watched, Bodo's face contorted in agony.

'No,' he murmured. 'Please don't hurt them…not them, *not them.*'

'He's been getting worse,' Blix said, joining Axel at the Hibernator. 'I doubt he'll last much longer.'

S-LO bleeped in concern.

'Would you keep S-LO here for a little while too?' Axel asked. 'There's something I have to do...And he'll be safer here, with you.'

*

Borrowing an airbike, Axel rode fast across the ice fields. He had to warn the Proxy.

Jura

14.

'What you tell me is very concerning,' the Proxy said, once Axel had relayed everything he had heard.

'Yeah, well I guess some of your trusted Bounty Hunters weren't so trustworthy,' Axel said.

They were standing in the Observation Chamber of the Proxy's villa, which was a large room with a domed ceiling made entirely from glass. Through it, the dying light of the day could be seen disappearing from the deep blue sky, which was slowly brightening with the light of the stars. The Proxy sighed.

'I've put Laan in danger. The Regime will soon find him. They will torture him, Axel. And then, when they have the information they need, when they have found the Lys Myrkr, they will *kill* him. And *through* the Lys Myrkr, many more will die.'

'Protector-9 mentioned someone called *Calle Los*...said he hid the object – do you know who that is?'

The Proxy looked up at the name, and a shadow crossed his face. 'No...I'm afraid not.'

He sat down heavily. 'I am a fool. I shouldn't have got involved.'

Axel shook his head and moved closer to him. 'So did this bounty hunter at least have the courtesy to give you Laan's location as well?'

The Proxy nodded. 'The message just came through. Jura.'

'Jura?!' Axel said.

He'd heard tales of that vast, dusty planet, and they weren't pleasant. He swallowed, contemplating the options. 'Do the bounty hunters know exactly where Laan is, on the planet?'

170

'No – they only know that he left Elara on a transport bound for Jura.'

'Okay, so what if I were to go to Jura? If you know where he might be hiding out, I might be able to get to him first. Save him. And you can deny the charges. Without Laan they've got nothing!'

The Proxy shook his head. 'No, Axel. It's too late. And it's bad enough that Laan is in danger because of me. I couldn't risk your life too.'

Axel twisted his hands together in an agitated manner. 'Come on, sir, I'm trying to help you here.'

'And I'm telling you, it's too late!'

Axel grabbed the Proxy's arm as he turned to walk away. 'Sir, I can do this – you *know* I can. Jura's a big place, right? It's going to take them a while to find him. You know Laan. Where's he likely to be hiding?'

The Proxy's shoulders slumped a little. He opened his mouth to say something when the doors to the Observation Chamber suddenly opened and a troop of Unity Guards marched in, their red robes bright in the gathering gloom.

'Proxy Cephalus Feovold. You are charged with Treason against the Regime,' the Head Guard said.

Axel looked at the Proxy in alarm.

'On whose authority?' Axel asked, trying to buy some time.

'Protector-9 has received a special order from Ragnar himself.'

'No...' Axel said, noticing a familiar looking black case being placed on the floor.

'It's okay, Axel,' the Proxy said, in a placating tone.

'You *know* I have some part to play in this, sir,' Axel said quietly. 'I-I think I'm like *him*...The Raven. But I think you knew that already.'

The Proxy frowned slightly at this, and a deep sadness entered his eyes and he nodded slightly. He pulled the pendant from his neck and placed it in Axel's hands.

'*Don't* let them get these.'

With a series of mechanical clicks, the Guards' case opened and a pair of black cylinders flew out.

'Wait - you can't do this!' Axel said.

One of the Guards hit Axel hard with a correction stick. The red electricity burned through him and he dropped to his knees, shaking.

Axel pushed himself to his feet and readied himself to fight, hideously outnumbered and weapon-less though he was.

'Axel, don't!' the Proxy said, offering his arms up for the cylinders. 'This is *not* a fight you can win.'

The cylinders clamped shut over his wrists with a horrid finality.

Axel watched helplessly as cylinders glided the Proxy towards to the door. Axel suddenly ran forward, trying to get past the Guards as they jostled forward.

'Cephalus, *please*. Don't be an idiot! It's not too late,' Axel pleaded.

The Proxy thought for a moment and then looked back at Axel.

'Have faith, Axel.'

'*Faith?*' Axel replied incredulously.

'Yes. Through *faith*, many things that are lost can be found.'

*

Running amongst the merchant freight ships that were landed in the Mugu Spaceport – the trader's port - Axel wound his way over to one tiny, dilapidated, murky green supply ship called the Unicorn.

Strange off-world music blared out through the open shield door as Axel approached. *Good,* he thought to himself, this meant that Hod was in.

'No, Axel. No, no, no, no, no,' Hod Bergo said, his mouth arranged in a thin line of negativity.

He rearranged the black bandana that ran tight over his tangle of sandy hair and shook his finger at Axel. '*No!*' he added emphatically.

Hod was Chuck's older brother and was similar in looks to him, with the same freckly skin and blue eyes, but his shoulders were broader and his arms much more muscled. Hod liked to work out, a lot. Axel had found Hod at the helm of his small ship, swearing to himself, his head buried deep inside a control panel as he attempted to repair the ancient wiring within.

'Come on Hod, I *need* your help,' Axel said.

Hod shook his head. 'There is a *blockade* out there that is checking everything going out and everything coming back in for irregularity, see, all because of that damn convict. Now, you, being a stowaway on my ship with no authorisation to fly...well, I'm *no* expert, but I'm pretty sure that counts as an irregularity.'

Ignoring Hod, Axel frowned in concentration.

'Faith...*Through faith that which is lost can be found...*' Axel muttered to himself as he went over to Hod's flight computer and tapped in a search for Jura.

The Proxy wasn't religious, Axel thought. *It had to be a clue of some kind.* Hod watched him as though he was crazy.

'Hey, Funknuts, what are you doing? Are you even listening to me?' Hod asked, pulling the plug on his flight computer. It gurgled something rude at him as it shut off.

'*Through faith, that which is lost can be found...*' Axel said, undeterred. 'What do you know about Jura...is there a big temple or something on there?'

'No,' Hod said, frowning. 'No temples, at all. It's kind of – a dead place.'

Axel slumped back, dispiritedly. Hod paused, remembering something. He looked at Axel and sighed.

173

'There is a monastery though…not many people know about it. Tuis…something…Tuis Bake…Tuis Baku,' he said reluctantly.

Axel's face lit up. 'Okay, well, that's a good place to start,' he said, plugging the flight computer back in and typing away on it.

Hod shifted uncomfortably. 'Well I don't know what you're so happy about, noid. I'm still not taking you *anywhere*,' he said simply.

'Come on, Hod. If we don't do this, the Proxy, he'll die,' Axel said, trying to appeal to Hod's better nature.

Hod sighed heavily. 'Axel, you know I don't get involved in politics. It doesn't bother *me*, and *I* certainly do not bother with it.'

Axel sighed, wondering what he could promise that would be of interest to this idiot. He remembered Chuck saying Hod had a weakness for machines.

'My airbike - you can have it,' he said, trying not to worry about the fact that he had no idea where Sandra was, or even whether she was still in one piece. She had still not returned from Riin Duur.

Hod paused a moment. 'You mean *Sandra*? The one with all the crazy modifications? Self-drive, and she talks to you?'

'Yeah,' Axel winced, it would be a wrench parting from his airbike.

Hod scratched his nose thoughtfully. 'And you just want to go to Jura, get this weirdo and come back?'

'Uh-huh,' Axel said, hopefully.

Hod surveyed him with narrowed eyes. 'Bet you could fix my ship too?' he asked.

'Sure,' Axel agreed.

He looked around, suddenly doubting the accuracy of this promise. There were wrecks rusting in Fosse junkyard that were in better shape.

Hod seemed to be considering the offer. 'Okay,' he said, slowly. 'But we only spend one day in Jura.'

'One day?! But that's not enough time -' Axel cried.

Hod nodded. 'It'll *have* to be, noid. Bad things happen on that planet. It's cursed.'

*

Breaking out of the upper atmosphere into the darkness beyond, they stared wide-eyed at the vast blockade of Unity ships ahead.

'Quite a sight, huh?' Hod murmured.

'Yeah,' Axel agreed, not taking his eyes off the blockade.

He had never seen so many Unity ships in one place. Scarto loomed just beyond them, and Axel could feel the dull throb of the presence growing louder in his head.

'Ah,' Axel groaned, raising a hand to his head.

'What's up? Headache?' Hod asked.

Axel nodded. 'Uh-huh.'

Something bleeped ominously. Hod flicked some switches quickly, tapping the glass of a monitor in the control panel to check it was still working.

'Well, it looks like the scrambler is working fine,' he said with a tense smile. 'They should only detect my life sign. We'll be okay as long as they don't decide to board us.'

The Unicorn glided forwards smoothly, moving ever closer to the silent Unity ships that faced them.

'Shouldn't they have made contact by now?' Axel asked.

'Yeah. They are being remarkably quiet,' Hod said, tugging uncomfortably at his collar.

Axel thought fleetingly of the spy who had been trailing him. If they had seen him boarding Hod's ship, the Regime would know that he was here.

'Maybe they just don't find us that interesting,' Axel said optimistically.

'Well, let's hope so,' Hod sighed, adjusting his bandana nervously. 'Man, I can't believe you talked me into this...' he muttered, shifting uncomfortably in his seat. 'Risking both our necks on a *fool's* errand.'

'It is *not* a fool's errand!' Axel replied heatedly, although he didn't know who he was trying to convince more...Hod or himself.

'I don't like this,' Hod said, spooked. 'I'm turning us around.'

He started to move the steering wheel but Axel stopped him.

'No! If you do that, they'll know something's wrong. *Come on,* Hod. I know it's a long shot, but this is important. If we don't pull this off, things are going to get bad. And not just for the Proxy. For *all* of us,' Axel said earnestly.

Hod grimaced. 'Ugh. You're such a little sap.'

'Control ship to merchant vessel, identify yourself and state your business,' the nasal voice of a Guard suddenly burst through the ship's communicator.

Hod raised his eyebrows at Axel and slowed to a stop. The Control ship hung almost above them to their right, noticeable due to its sheer size and its strange hexagonal shape.

'Unicorn to Control ship. Hod Bergo here. I'm transporting some supplies to Kagbeni...to the Deoria outpost.'

'What is your cargo?' the Guard asked, his tone sharp, his voice clipped.

'Uhh - Mechanical parts for the Unity base out there - a few converters and object shockers. I have a movement order, ah...number 4077 dash 2.' They drifted slowly in silence whilst they waited for the response, exchanging anxious glances.

'You are cleared to proceed, Unicorn,' the voice finally announced.

Hod and Axel looked at each other and laughed, slumping back in their chairs with relief.

'Okay, noid, we got through the first hurdle,' Hod said, flicking some switches.

Axel grinned. Once they were past the blockade, they hurtled through the stars at breakneck speed, past great gas giants and distant nebulas full of colour and light.

'You'd better get some sleep,' Hod said after a while. 'It's not far to Jura but trust me, you'll need your wits about you when we get there.'

Axel didn't want to take Hod's advice, but as he drew the rough blanket up around his neck he felt his eyes droop. Sleep nagged at his tired mind.

*

Pain cut through Axel's body… Stretching out his hands in front of him, he saw that they were burnt, cut and scarred. He was lying flat on his back in a kind of glass coffin - a Hibernator. Above him stretched the silhouetted leaves and branches of a gloomy forest.

The Hibernator was moving forwards, gliding silently above the ground as it weaved its way between the trees. To his right, a strange black box also hovered close by, matching the speed of the Hibernator. The black surface of the box was mirrored, reflecting the dim light off it as it moved. Pushing the pain of his wounds deep inside him, Axel focused on the box. It seemed to be whispering something to him - words of another language that he could not understand…and did not want to. The whispers grew louder and louder, making Axel thrash about within the Hibernator, holding his burnt hands to his ears as the whispers became a roar.

Axel woke with a start, gasping for air. Stretching his hands out in front of his face, he stared at them for a moment. Relief flooded through him. Turning his head slightly, he noticed Hod was watching him curiously.

'Bad dreams?' Hod said, with raised eyebrows.

Axel settled back down again, trying to calm his swiftly beating heart. 'Yeah,' he murmured uncertainly.

Hod veered violently to the left. 'Hey, what are you doing?!' Axel exclaimed groggily, struggling to stay on his chair.

Wisps of pink and red gas rushed past the side of the cockpit window. Hod's upper lip twitched slightly. 'That's the Mara Beni Nebula. No need to go in there,' he said, looking pale with fear as he continued to swerve away from it.

Staring blearily into the dense pink clouds, Axel frowned, feeling his usual pull, out to a spot that lay far beyond the edge of the nebula.

'Hod. Have you ever tried to go into deep space? Say to Chalkis?'

'Chalkis?! Are you kidding? Do you know how far away that is?'

'Yeah, I know…'

'Why are you interested in Chalkis anyway? From what I heard, it's a total dump.'

'Oh…it's just, that's where Kolbjorn found me - in the wreckage of a star ship. I've always wanted to go there. Try and find out what ship I was on. I don't know, it's stupid, I guess.'

Hod raised his eyebrows, looking eerily similar to Chuck for a moment. 'What, you think you could find out who your parents were?'

A bleeping issued from the control panel.

'We're coming up on Jura,' Hod added, pressing some buttons to stop the noise.

Axel pushed himself up and gazed through the glass window of the cockpit. Growing larger in the dark expanse of space before them was a vast purple planet.

'You know what people say about this planet, don't you?' Hod said grimly. 'That people who come here never leave…'

The further they got from Eleusis, the less the dull thud of the presence seemed to bother Axel. With every kilopar he found that

178

he felt a little lighter, less burdened. But as Axel stared at the fast approaching purple planet, a shadow clouded his features.

'Hey look – aren't those a couple of Unity Air Tractors around the monastery?' Hod said, squinting at an enhanced view of Jura's surface.

Axel felt his stomach drop. 'Go faster,' he said to Hod, who looked at him as though he was insane. 'We need to speed up!'

'Alright, alright noid! Keep your pants on!' Hod replied.

Hod set the Unicorn down inside a small crater in an isolated stretch of desert.

'Look, Axel, *I mean it*, we can't stay here for long,' Hod said, powering the ship down. 'It won't take those Air Tractors long to spot us...I mean...are you sure about all this? How do you know this guy is even still alive?'

'I don't,' Axel shrugged. 'But I have to try.'

Purple dust swirled through the air in violent gusts as they jumped onto the dark purple ground. A sandstorm.

'What is this stuff? It's worse than snow!' Axel said, pulling his cloak up around his face to protect himself against the sand.

Squinting into the dull glow of sunlight, they found the air hot and the hazy sky dark, despite the fact that a distant sun hung high above the horizon. The sound of gunfire broke through the still air. Axel and Hod exchanged glances. Climbing up the crater walls, Axel and Hod peered over the edge.

From what they could see through the sand, a flat desert landscape stretched on for kilopars, leading up to a range of angular pinkish mountains in the east, from which black smoke billowed ominously. Hod looked through his scanner. 'That's Tuis Baku over there...Looks like it's under attack,' he said, passing the scanner to Axel.

'I've got to get there,' Axel said, readying himself to leave.

'What? *Don't* you understand? That's exactly where the Unity Guards are!' Hod said incredulously, pointing at the smoke. 'Chances are that the Regime's already got your friend. All you're going to do is get yourself killed!'

'Maybe,' Axel said, pulling himself over the edge of the crater and onto the flat plain above.

Hod rolled his eyes and grabbed Axel's arm. 'Look, moron, whatever crazy mission the Proxy sent you on, it's not worth losing your head over.'

'More than the Proxy's life depends on this. I have to do this,' Axel replied.

Hod shook his head and dropped his hold on Axel's arm, allowing him to stand up. 'Hey, listen. I meant what I said. If you're not back by nightfall, I'm getting the hell out of here, okay?'

Axel nodded. 'Thanks for everything, Hod...' he said, with a small smile. 'If I don't make it back, tell Kolbjorn that I...just tell him I...*never mind.*'

*

Leaving Hod open-mouthed at the side of the crater, Axel moved as quickly as he could through the hot, dusty desert towards the billowing smoke of Tuis Baku. When he arrived at the monastery, he was surprised to find that there were no Guards of any kind standing around the periphery. In fact, he was able to walk straight in, gaining a little respite from the sand filled air.

Inside, he found nothing but a smouldering ruin, recently burnt and recently dowsed with water. The floor was soft and damp beneath his feet, giving way a little under his weight. Blackened walls crumbled around him, their surfaces pitted with gunshot holes, their X-shaped mark familiar.

Stepping into another room he found the floor strewn with the bodies of slain monks, their skin still warm, their eyes glassy and full of terror. The bodies of a few Unity Guards also lay scattered around the room. The monks seemed to have given a good fight, but no side had won this particular battle. Axel shivered, his heart thumping in his chest, his breath shallow. As he moved carefully past them, a small cry stopped him in his tracks.

A wizened old monk lay shuddering on the floor, his white hair bright in the smoky haze. '*You*,' the monk whispered, a look of recognition flitting over his face.

'I knew *you* would come.'

Frowning in confusion, Axel examined the Snipe Rifle wound in the monk's chest. It was clear that the man had only moments left.

'I'm sorry...the wound is mortal. There's nothing I can do,' Axel said, his voice quiet.

'Good,' the old monk breathed. 'Let me die...'

Axel frowned, trying to make the monk more comfortable.

'Please - I'm looking for someone called Einar Laan. Has the Regime taken him?'

A strange look flitted across the monk's face.

'You are so...young.'

'Please, sir - I need to find Laan. The Proxy of Eleusis sent me. Do you know where I could find him?'

There was a flash of recognition at the Proxy's name, but the light in the monk's eyes was growing dim. The rumble of a transport outside made Axel pause for a moment. Air Tractors. Several of them. Approaching fast. The monk heard them too, and with surprising strength, he grabbed Axel's wrist.

'*I* am Laan,' the monk uttered, in a broken whisper.

Axel stared at him in shock.

'Help me. I...have been...*selfish. Kill...me...*It is the only way... Do it now...before...they...take me.'

181

'What?!' Axel asked.

'Do it…' Laan said, tightening his grip on Axel's wrist with surprising strength. 'Or else *all* will be lost…They will find *it* through *me.*'

Axel shook his head, as the rumble of the Air Tractors became a roar.

'I *can't*…I'm here to save you – take you back home.'

The sound of footsteps approaching the door forced him into a hiding place behind the charred wreck of an old table as a troop of Unity Guards entered the room, the thud of their boots heavy against the still smoking floor.

'I told them not to kill the monks until we had Laan,' a General with a simpering face said, the red of his cloak sweeping over the still faces of the dead monks as he walked amongst them. '*This* is the one we want. Barely alive. Bring him back to base and have the Medibots patch him up. The Eleusian Protector wants him back alive and fit for interrogation.'

The General, whose name was Cylix, pushed his boot into the wound on Laan's chest, causing him to cry out in agony.

'What a shame he is *necessary*. I would have taken great pleasure in ending his pitiful existence. Fool thought he was safe from the Regime, hiding here amongst the dead.'

Axel watched helplessly as a hover stretcher was brought in and Laan was pulled onto it. The room quickly emptied until only two lower Guards were left. One of the Guards knelt by one of the dead monks and pulled a pendant from his neck, pocketing it smugly.

'A memento of our time here,' he said to the other, stockier Guard, who laughed harshly.

'We'd better get going,' the other Guard replied. 'The air tractors won't stay here for long.'

'You go, I want to see if these monks have any other treasures for me.'

The sound of footsteps clomping past Axel's hiding place told him that one of the Guards had left. The other still remained, however, and he was getting closer and closer to the table behind which Axel was situated.

Axel looked around for a weapon, anything at all that he might use to defend himself. Grudgingly he thought Kolbjorn's Persuader would have come in very handy right now. The only thing around was some kind of ceremonial tray that was lying on the floor next to him. The Guard, who was now on the other side of the table, suddenly froze, as he noticed Axel's boot. Axel lay very still, his hand loosely grasped around the edge of the tray.

Drawing his Persuader, the Guard pointed it at Axel, but was suddenly distracted by the sound of gunfire and explosions outside. Re-holstering his weapon, he knelt quickly to pick Axel's pockets, but as he did so, Axel whipped the tray up and hit the Guard over the head with it, knocking him out cold.

'Well, you wanted a memento of your time here,' Axel said, to the unconscious Guard.

Moments later, Axel was dressed in the Guard's clothes, reluctantly holstering the Guard's Persuader. With haste, Axel pulled all of the stolen items out of the Guard's pocket and put them back into one of the monk's open hands. Running outside, he saw that the Air Tractor had a giant hole in its side, and black smoke was billowing out of it. Unity Guards were everywhere, firing at some unseen enemy who had fired from further up the mountain. Axel took cover and scanned the area for Laan. Under heavy fire, he was being loaded into the damaged Air Tractor, and into a recovery chamber, where his injuries would be treated.

Axel took his chances and bolted through the crossfire, trying to catch up with the Air Tractor, which had started to move off and was now gaining speed. As a shot glanced off his arm, he realised his navwatch had been hit. *No more contacting Hod...*Axel thought to himself, his heart sinking. The door hatch was closing. Giving it all he had, Axel jumped forward and managed to grab on to the air tractor, pulling himself inside just before the door shut. He stood shakily, finding himself with the two Guards who had bought Laan in, who were looking at him bemusedly.

'I…er…Hail Ragnar!' Axel said, saluting them.

'Hail Ragnar,' the two Guards replied, scowling as they saluted back.

As the Air Tractor trundled through the vast purple desert, Axel looked out of the window for landmarks, hoping he would remember his way back to the Unicorn. They had been travelling for some time now and the sun was already starting to fall past the midday mark. He shot a glance at Laan, who was unconscious but still breathing. Axel could see that Laan still needed special treatment that could only be administered back at the Unity base. If Axel broke Laan out of the Air Tractor now, he would surely die. And although that was what Laan wanted, Axel was hopeful that there was another way. Laan's eyes opened briefly, fixing confusedly on Axel.

The Air Tractor slowed to a stop. They had reached the outer fence of an extremely large and foreboding Unity Base. The main building within the fence rose vast and tall out of the purple sand, black walls reaching up to the sky, windowless and monolithic. Axel felt his heart thumping. It would be a miracle if *he* got out of this alive, let alone with Laan. As the Air Tractor came to a final halt, Axel stepped outside, hoping he could stay close to the prisoner.

'Hey you - FQ-1' a harsh voice shouted across the yard.

It took a while for Axel to realise that the voice was addressing him, as a short, stout man approached, his large face as red as his uniform.

'FQ-1, what are you doing out here? You should be in the Control Room, cleaning the base units.'

'I…sorry, sir, right away…' he said, saluting.

Out of the corner of his eye he saw Laan's hover stretcher being taken off somewhere to his right. He turned to follow it.

'Where are you going?!' the Guard addressing him shouted. 'I see I will have to escort you to the Control Room myself!'

Axel's heart sunk. The short Guard took him deep inside the warren like complex, so far within that he felt he would never find his way out again. However, just as a troop of Guards approached from the other direction and filled the corridor, Axel took his chance and made a break for it, running down a narrow side passage as fast as he could, turning corner after corner until he was sure his new friend couldn't find him. Then, he noticed a console in the wall that was still active. Accessing it, he bought up a schematic of the base, and located where the medi-bay was - that was where Laan was being taken. *Five floors up from his current location*, he realised, memorizing the route.

Axel found his way to the medical hub as quickly as he could, catching sight of the Medibots working on Laan, just as they injected him with a silvery liquid. Axel quietly entered the room, racking his brain for an excuse to give to explain his presence, should they ask him for one. The Medibots stopped their work and looked up at him.

'The lot is ready for collection, and transport to the furnace…' one of the bots told him, pointing towards a stack of white body bags in the corner of the room. 'You can take them now.'

Axel raised his eyebrows. 'Right.'

He moved over to the body bags, a chill running through his veins as he drew closer to them. Dead prisoners lay within them. There was a chute close to the middle of the room. He opened it and reluctantly pushed one of the body bags down it. It slid down a long way, finally stopping with a thump somewhere far away.

'General Cylix to Medibot-5, what is the status of prisoner-9054?' a voice came through the speakers in the room.

'Stable…' Medibot-5 replied. 'We have completed our work on his heart.'

'Good. He will be collected for interrogation immediately.'

Axel felt his pulse rise, the blood thumping through his veins at speed. *He had to do something now…or Laan would be lost forever.*

Einar Laan

15.

Berau's breaths came in short, shallow gasps as he let his fingertips run over the raised pattern on the Proxy's circlet. But his eagerness to touch it caused the circlet to jump away from his grasping hands. With a loud clatter, it fell to the floor and rolled away from him, under the gaze of the blue-cloaked Heimdall, the Proxy's personal Guard. They stood at intervals along the two longest walls of the Gallery in the Proxy's villa, silent and still. Berau glared at the Guard closest to him.

'What are you smirking at?' he snapped quietly.

The Guard, who had no hint of a smile on his face, said nothing. Berau picked the circlet up and moved closer to the Guard.

'I said, what are you smirking at?' Berau asked louder.

The Guard shook his head slightly. 'Nothing, sir.'

The doors of the study opened suddenly, admitting the Proxy's silver Servicebot with a visitor in tow.

'Protector,' Berau said, in greeting. 'To what do I owe this pleasure?'

Protector-9 smiled a little, his dark cloak sweeping over the shiny surface of the floor. 'I came to offer my congratulations, to the new Proxy of Eleusis.'

With an insincere gentleness, Nine took hold of the circlet and examined it. Forcing a smile, he placed the circlet on Berau's cherubic head. Berau smiled, flattered.

'I'm not quite Proxy yet,' he corrected. 'But I am getting much closer, thanks to you. It is a matter of days, is it not, until my father's execution?' Berau said, eagerly.

Nine tapped his fingers against the Proxy's desk, thoughtfully. 'It is a serious thing - to accuse a Proxy. As soon as I have proof of his treason, then Ragnar himself shall authorise us to proceed.'

Berau let out an exasperated sigh. 'Well, while we are waiting, we can have a little fun, can't we? I want all these tiresome blue Guards executed. I have no need of them, and they irk me.'

Nine smiled accommodatingly. 'I will be happy to arrange it, Proxy,' he said with a bow.

The Proxy's Servicebot shuddered in fear.

'Oh, one more thing,' Nine said, just before he reached the door. 'When you ascend, Ragnar will expect you to take a wife.'

'I will do my duty,' Berau said, a blank expression on his face.

'The Lady Mari Slette would be an admirable choice,' Nine suggested, but Berau shook his head slightly.

'No,' Berau said simply. 'My sights are set elsewhere.'

Nine struggled to hide his frustration. 'May I ask where?'

'No,' Berau said haughtily. 'You may not.'

*

Checking to see if anyone was watching through the glass windows that led out into the corridor beyond, Axel considered whether to use the Persuader on the two Medi-bots that were still bustling around the room. Deciding it would cause too much noise, he instead approached them quietly and engaged them in a passionate but mostly silent fistfight, which he finally won. Shoving the smoking Medibots in a cupboard, he noticed that it was full of vials of Gilead Water.

'No way…' he said, grabbing a handful and stuffing them into his pocket.

Then, as quickly as he could, he opened one of the body bags and heaved out the poor soul that was inside.

'I'm sorry, friend…' he whispered, pulling the man onto the hover-stretcher next to Laan.

Breathlessly, he dragged Laan into the empty body bag and zipped it up, just as two Guards came in to take him up to the interrogation room.

'He doesn't look too good…' one of the Guards said, looking at the body Axel had substituted for Laan. 'Are you sure he's been cleared to leave?'

'The Medibot signed the order,' Axel said, pointing to a hologram that was floating in the air above the hover-stretcher, that read 'CLEARED.' His eyes moved anxiously to the cupboard he had put the Medibots in, as smoke was now curling out of the doors. One of the Medibots' batteries must have caught fire.

The Guards didn't move, sensing something amiss.

'Where are the Medibots?' one of the Guards said.

Axel shrugged. 'I don't know! Look, I'd hurry if I were you. There'll be hell to pay if he croaks it before the interrogation.'

The Guards exchanged anxious glances and started moving. Axel watched incredulously as they guided the hover-stretcher out of the room, their faces taut with tension. Once they were gone, Axel wasted no time in pushing the rest of the body bags down the shoot, Laan's bag last.

Finally, he gulped one last breath of cold, sanitised air and went down the chute himself, just as the cupboard holding the Medibots exploded with a loud bang. The dark, dank tunnel seemed to go on forever, Axel's alarm and dread rising with every twist and turn. He hoped that this did not lead directly to the furnace.

Finally, the tunnel came to an end and spat him out at speed. He flew horizontally for a few seconds, landing hard onto a pile of body bags. A small groan escaped from the bag underneath him. Laan must be waking up.

'Quiet in there!' Axel said, pushing himself off Laan's bag.

Standing dizzily, he tried to gauge where they were and how they were going to get out. Around him was a vast, dark, rectangular room, with a ceiling so high it disappeared into the darkness above him. Pipes of all sizes lined the walls, the biggest of which being the chute he had just come down. A low hum constantly reverberated through the walls, making it sound like some mechanical process was occurring close by. Anxiously running his hand through his hair, Axel looked for a way out.

*

Several stories above Axel, the Guards carrying the substitute prisoner reached the interrogation room and loaded him into a Cylindric. Slowly, the curved glass of the lid shut with the sound of suction and the horizontal cylinder tilted upwards smoothly, until it stood vertically, the prisoner trapped inside it. His head lolled downwards, to his chest. General Cylix watched from behind a glass wall, in the control room next door.

'Start the interrogation,' Cylix said.

A Guard at one of the control stations tapped a few buttons, frowning slightly.

'General,' he said. 'There's a problem. I'm reading no vitals, of any kind. The subject is dead, sir.'

The smug smile on Cylix's face slowly waned.

'This is not Laan. You've bought the *wrong* prisoner!'

*

Axel watched anxiously as a shield door opened revealing a dusty courtyard beyond, the distant fence of the base just visible through the hazy air. Just outside the door, a slight Guard with MN-9 stamped into his uniform stood waiting next to a very dirty looking rectangular transport. It hovered a little way above the ground, its back door wide open. MN-9 walked into the room, a dissatisfied look on his face.

'Who are you?' he asked, stopping as he noticed Axel walking out from amongst the body bags.

'I...er...I was told to take these er- off-site.'

MN-9 raised his eyebrows, his eyes shifting down to the number stamped onto Axel's uniform. Axel tensed, hoping this guy didn't know the real FQ-1. 'New?'

Axel felt his breathing slow down as relief washed through him. He nodded. MN-9 scowled. 'Shift them onto the transport.'

Laan chose that moment to groan loudly. MN-9 looked at Axel curiously, who nodded awkwardly.

'Of course, sir. Right away...' Axel said quickly.

'I'll be speaking to your supervisor about this...insubordination,' MN-9 said, his eyes narrowed.

Axel nodded again. He almost felt sorry for the real FQ-1.

Whilst MN-9 watched, Axel moved the bags as quickly as he could, taking care to put Laan's on the top of the others.

'Get in,' MN-9 ordered. 'I'll need you to unload again at the furnace.'

Axel nodded, finally feeling a little hopeful as MN-9 started up the transport and they started rumbling towards the boundary fence. Perhaps somehow, Axel thought, by some strange and wonderful miracle, he would pull this off and they would get out of this alive. But just then, a loud yell emanated from the stack of body bags.

'What was that?' MN-9 asked, slowing the transport down.

Axel winced. They were so close to the exit.

'What? I didn't hear anything...' Axel bluffed, but MN-9 wasn't buying it.

He powered down the transport just as Laan yelled again.

'There's someone alive back there...' MN-9 said, looking at Axel.

191

'How can that be?!' Axel said, feigning ignorance.

Both of them jumped out of the driver's cabin and over to the back of the vehicle. Opening the door, MN-9 jumped in, followed closely by Axel. Laan was now both yelling and flailing around, but he was still trapped within the body bag.

Suddenly, an alarm sounded at the base behind them. Axel's heart sunk. A message crackled over their communicators.

'A prisoner has escaped from sick bay…he must be recaptured immediately.'

MN-9's eyes narrowed in suspicion. He tapped his communicator to respond.

'This is MN-9. I think we have the prisoner. Send backup to Transport 54 in the outer courtyard.'

He looked at Axel.

'How did this happen?' MN-9 asked testily.

Axel shook his head. 'I don't know…' he said, leaning back on the button controlling the back doors, causing them to slide shut quickly.

'What are you doing?!' MN-9 asked reaching for his Persuader.

Luckily, Axel was faster and managed to knock MN-9 out cold before he could fire. As quickly as he could, he unzipped Laan's body bag.

'Will you shut up? I'm trying to rescue you here.'

Laan sat up, looking dazed. 'Oh…it's you…' he said, recognising Axel.

'Hurry up and get out of those clothes…' Axel said, quickly stripping MN-9 of his bodysuit.

'What are you doing?' Laan said, aghast.

'Quick,' Axel said, throwing MN-9's bodysuit over to Laan.

'Put that on. Now. And give me that hospital gown.'

There was banging on the door too soon, before they were ready.

'Open up…' an authoritarian voice said on the other side. 'What's going on in there?'

'We…er…had some trouble with the prisoner…' Axel replied. 'Just getting him subdued, now…' he continued. MN-9 started to stir and Axel knocked him out again.

'Wait…' Laan said, just before Axel opened the door. He had a wound on his arm where something had been inserted into the skin. Ignoring the pain, he dug his fingers into the wound, pulling out a tiny metal disk. He put it into MN-9's mouth and Axel watched in disgust as MN-9 swallowed it.

Axel opened the door.

'Here's the escaped prisoner,' Axel said, pushing the unconscious MN-9 out of the door towards the troop of Guards that were waiting outside. He landed flat on his face, on the dusty ground.

'Tried to escape in a body bag…violent one, that one.'

'Yes, knocked the Persuader right out of my hand!' Laan said.

The other Guards looked at each other, unimpressed.

The sand now swirled thickly in the air around them, the storm was picking up.

'Wait, how do we know this one's the real Laan? The visuals on my communicator aren't working…' one of the Guards said, turning MN-9 over with his foot.

'Mine neither…it's the storm. Check his tracker,' Laan suggested. The Guards took his advice and scanned MN-9. The metal disk he had swallowed still appeared to be working.

'It's him. Get him straight into the Cylinder…General Cylix wants him interrogated immediately.'

Axel and Laan watched breathlessly as the Guards moved back towards the base and the alarm sound shut off. They looked at each other.

'Now what?' Laan asked.

Back in the transport, they moved towards the boundary fence.

'Clearance code?' the Guard at the gates said through the communicator.

'Err…8743,' Axel said, making something up.

'That is an incorrect code…Who is this?'

'This is FQ-1…just delivering some bodies to the Furnace.'

After a silence, the voice said, 'FQ-1, The Furnace is within the boundary fence. Please power down and wait to be boarded.'

Back at the base, the explosion in the medi-bay had inadvertently set off a chain reaction. Axel and Laan watched as small blasts occurred at intervals along the entire base. The blares of the alarms grew louder. Laan looked at Axel, open-mouthed in shock. 'What did you do?!'

'That's…unfortunate,' Axel said, revving the power up as Laan hurriedly put his seatbelt on. 'Hang on to something!' Axel cried, as he accelerated madly and the little transport blasted through the boundary gates, breaking them apart in one go.

*

'Now what?!' Laan said, once they were trundling out into the purple desert, being buffeted by shots and blasts from the army of Unity Guards who were now chasing them.

'Is that the *only* thing you say?' Axel yelled, firing back, as the transport shuddered violently and threatened to keel over.

'W-Warning…warning…el-lectrical s-sandstorm imminent,' the transport's computer said. 'T-Turn around…Turn around.'

Axel looked at the bleeping warning on the console in front of him. Turning the steering wheel hard to the left, he headed straight for the storm.

'What are you doing?!' Laan asked, horrified. 'If we go into the sandstorm, the transport will seize up and…well, if by some miracle we are not recaptured, well…*do you know what lives in the desert…?*'

Axel gulped and shook his head. 'I think I liked it better when you just said, *'now what?'* he said, accelerating into the storm.

As visibility deteriorated, the number of shots hitting the transport also lessened. The Air Tractors above were forced to fall back. It seemed that for now, Axel's plan was working.

'We can't stay out here much longer...' Laan said, squinting through the glass window into the wall of purple sand beyond it. 'The transport won't take much more of this...'

Axel nodded in agreement, wracking his brain for any possible solutions.

Setting the transport onto autopilot, he placed a hand on Laan's shoulder.

'Laan, we have to get off this thing, and soon,' Axel said.

Laan stared at him open mouthed. 'What? Are you crazy? We'll die in minutes out in that storm. The sand - it'll get into our lungs. Choke us.'

Axel looked outside. He didn't particularly want to go out there either. Several things on the console were now bleeping and flashing. They didn't have much time before the transport stopped dead.

'I have a plan. It might not work, but it's our only option. The Guards will follow this transport, but we have an opportunity to escape, whilst we have the storm to cover us. We just need to get into the back.'

Axel moved to the back of the driver's cabin, to the partition that separated the cabin from the back section of the transport, where the body bags were. Getting out the Persuader, Axel shot at the partition, trying to blast it away. The shot bounced off the walls, until it finally hit one of the consoles, causing it to explode and the transport to lurch violently to one side. Laan stared at Axel in horror.

'See, *this* is why I hate guns - absolutely useless!' Axel said, holstering the Persuader with disgust.

Axel looked around for something else they could use and found a laser cutter in the glove compartment. 'Wait!' Laan said, pressing a button on the control panel.

To Axel's relief, the partition slid open.

A bleeping emanated from the console.

'A-Attention! Mal-malfunction in j-joints in the motivator…Urgent main-maintenance r-requested…T-Turn back…T-Turn back!'

Laan looked at Axel in wild panic.

'Don't say it!' Axel said, incensed.

As fast as they could, Axel unzipped two body bags and threw one to Laan.

'GET INSIDE!' Axel shouted, over the now deafening roar of the failing engine. 'GOOD LUCK,' he added, zipping Laan's body bag right up.

Then Axel got into a bag himself and zipped it up to his waist. Bracing himself, he hit the door release button.

A howling wind ripped through the transport, bringing with it sharp shards of sand that cut sharply into Axel's face and hands. Holding his breath, he rolled Laan out of the transport as gently as he could.

A sudden blast knocked him backwards, knocking his Persuader out of his holster, and almost as though it was spiting Axel for his earlier outburst about guns, it bounced a few times and fell out of the back of the transport, immediately lost to the sand below. Axel had no time to think about it. He was running out of air. Going red, he sealed himself into the bag and jumped, landing in the sand with a thump and rolling along for a while until he came to a sudden stop, face down on the soft, warm sand.

As the hum of the transport faded into the roar of the wind, he heard several more of them as they hovered past in pursuit. An almighty bang heralded that the transport must have exploded, and then there was no sound except the howling wind. The soft pressure of sand collecting over him filled him with horror as he remembered how Laan had said they could be buried alive. He tried to shake the sand off, but it was no use, it was piling up too quickly. He thought regretfully of Laan. Had Axel rescued him only to give him a more horrible death?

What seemed like hours passed and the storm finally subsided.

Axel kept trying to move, but there was so much sand on him it seemed impossible. He tried again.

'LAAN?' Axel shouted, into the heavy silence that now surrounded him.

There was the slightest possibility that Laan was not as buried as him. That he had cut himself out and was now looking for Axel.

'LAAN?'

No response. Axel tried to control his breathing, as air now seemed to be in very short supply.

He frowned, refusing to be beaten by this. There had to be a way out, he thought, there just had to be. And then, on the wind, he could have sworn he heard his name as though a hundred voices were whispering it at the same time.

'Ax-el Len-nart...'

Axel shuddered. He must be imagining it.

Amongst the whispers of the desert, Axel found his thoughts ran to Blix.

*

And far away, back on Eleusis, Blix was thinking of Axel too. She looked up to the stars, pulling her cloak around her shoulders for warmth. S-LO was at her feet.

'Did you have any luck?' Blix said to Autobot, who had just rolled out of the maintenance hut, looking for her.

'I have been unable to locate Axel, my lady. His navwatch appears to be out of range.'

'Out of range?' Blix repeated, twisting her hands together.

S-LO bleeped anxiously.

'Do you think Berau's...*done* something to him?'

Autobot considered this. 'No, my lady. If he had, I do not think he would keep it a secret.'

Blix sighed, relieved and then smiled a little. 'You're right, Autobot. Thank you.'

'What strange company you keep...' a drawling voice behind Blix made her jump.

'Conversing with a Slop Droid *and* a Chore Droid?'

'Berau...' Blix said in surprise, tensing up as she turned to face him.

Her eyes flitted over to the Hibernator, hoping Bodo wouldn't give himself away by shouting something in his sleep.

'I didn't hear your airbike,' she said, as she looked for it.

'Oh, I left it at the Cylindric...I felt like a walk.'

Frowning a little in confusion, Blix wondered how long he had been watching her. 'What are you doing here, Berau?'

'I came to see you...' Berau said.

He smiled a little and then moved towards Blix until he was standing right in front of her, his face close to hers.

'How's Mari, these days?' Blix asked, stepping back slightly, her throat suddenly dry. 'I haven't seen her since the Banren Run...'

Berau smiled, running a hand through Blix's hair. 'I don't know. I confess I have not been thinking of Mari much lately...'

'No...?' Blix said, a heavy dread creeping in beneath her skin.

Berau shook his head. 'It's *you* I have been thinking of, Blix…And *now* that I am soon to be Proxy…It is *you*, that I have chosen to be my companion.'

Blix stumbled back, away from him. 'I am…honoured, Berau…but I – I can't…' she stuttered.

'Let me guess…it's because of *him*, isn't it? It's *always* him,' Berau said bitterly. 'You care for Axel…Well, where *is* he…?'

Blix turned away, trying to hide the shine in her eyes. 'So, *you* don't know where he is?' she asked quietly.

Berau laughed. 'No…I haven't done away with him, if that's what you're asking. But he is missing. Probably fled the system because now I am Proxy in all but name…'

Pausing, Berau edged a little closer, keeping his eyes fixed on Blix. '*He's* not here, Blix…But I am. I can take care of you…protect you…*and your sister.*'

At the mention of Agnete, Blix froze.

'Why did you kill all those Guards – The Heimdall?' she breathed.

Berau laughed a little. 'Because fear is stronger than love…' he said, drawing close behind her, his breath hot on her neck.

As he moved forward to touch her, Blix closed her eyes, her body tense. The lights around the hut flickered a little. Then, Autobot turned suddenly and punched Berau in the groin.

'Arghh! Stupid Slop Droid! What's wrong with you?' he cried out, doubled over in pain.

'Oh, I'm so sorry, sir, I do not know what came over me!' Autobot said. S-LO bleeped in approval.

Blix suppressed a smile. 'I'm sorry, Berau – my droid is obviously in need of some urgent maintenance. I must repair him straight away. Good evening.'

*

199

A faint snuffling sound broke Axel out of his thoughts, and a mixture of dread and hope ran through him. As the snuffling grew louder and the weight of the sand started to reduce, Axel realised that someone, or something was digging him out. As the weight on him lessened enough for him to move his limbs, he dug around the bag for the Persuader. Then, with mild terror, he remembered that he'd lost it. Without the gun, there was no way Axel could get himself out of the bag, and his Navwatch was not working.

As the last of the sand came off him, Axel tried to push himself up, but felt something sharp, like a long stick, hit him across the back.

'Ouch! Laan, that you?' A voice in a strange language sounded from somewhere near to Axel's feet.

A moment later, another voice replied, prodding him with a broad stick.

'Hey – who is that?! Who's out there?' Axel couldn't understand their words, but he had a feeling that he wouldn't like what they were saying…whoever they were.

As the stick prodded him again, there was a cracking sound of glass breaking and Axel felt a cool liquid start to spread quickly out of his pocket. That was the Gilead Water gone, he thought to himself with a groan.

'LAAN?' Axel yelled, giving it one last try. 'CAN YOU HEAR ME?'

Footsteps grew nearer to Axel's head, and a moment later the stick came down on him hard, knocking him out.

Attack of the Knoda

16.

When Axel regained consciousness, he was still in the bag, being dragged slowly along the desert floor. His head was taking the brunt of the dragging, hitting pebbles and rocks as he moved, whilst his legs were tied together at the ankles and raised a little off the ground. Judging by the heaviness of the footsteps ahead of him and the strange musty smell that carried on the wind, a large animal of some kind appeared to be doing the dragging. A bright orange glow seeped through the material of the bag...the sun must be setting. It now seemed horrendously impossible that Axel would get back to the Unicorn before nightfall. He didn't even know where he was, and with his navwatch broken, he had no way of contacting Hod.

They came to a sudden stop and Axel's feet were dropped to the ground. Then, as the hum of strange voices surrounded him, many small hands picked him up and carried him somewhere dark and cool. Axel lay very still for a moment, trying not to panic. *At least he wasn't back at the Unity base,* he thought to himself. *Yes. That would be worse.* He tried to open the bag for the hundredth time. It was impossible, and even though the stones must have worn the fabric during his long drag here, he could see no sign of even the tiniest hole. These bags were ridiculously strong. The Regime couldn't be faulted on quality at least. He yelled in frustration.

'Lennart...?' a voice said suddenly. 'Is that you?'

Axel froze, stunned. 'Laan?'

In response, there was a strange humming noise and a few moments later, both Axel and Laan were out of their body bags, and armed with one laser cutter between them.

'Boy, am I glad to see you,' Axel said, standing shakily, banging his head on the low rock ceiling above. It appeared that they were in a small, darkish cave stacked full of supplies, presumably all stolen from Unity transports. Ripping open cartons of frick juice, they drank thirstily, faces shining with sweat.

'Oh, look, my favourite!' Laan said, grabbing a small tin of Unity Regime Roasted Crunters and stuffing them into his pocket.

Making their way to the mouth of the cave they saw a collection of tents arranged around a low fire.

'Knoda - deadly, treacherous little fiends,' Laan surmised, not taking his eyes off the tents.

Axel had heard of Knodas, they lived on Eleusis too, but they were secretive creatures. In fact, Axel had never seen one, he'd only heard tales of them stealing machinery and weapons at night.

'But they're just nomads...What do they want with us?' Axel asked.

'To eat us, I suppose,' Laan said, seemingly nonplussed. 'There's not much in the way of fresh food out here.'

Axel winced and looked back towards the horizon. The sun had set and the sky was now intensely dark purple, generously smattered with white stars.

'Do you know how to get back to Tuis Baku from here?' Axel asked.

Laan looked at him, his eyebrows raised. 'Of course, but that's exactly where the Unity Guards will be expecting us to go.'

'I know but...I have a ship waiting for us, just outside of the monastery,' Axel said, hoping this was still true.

Would Hod really be heartless enough to leave them stranded here? *Probably,* Axel thought. Still, it was the only hope he and Laan had left.

'If we can just get to it, we can go home.'

'Home?' Laan said, his voice breaking on the word. 'To Eleusis?'

Axel paused before replying. 'Yeah,' he said softly, roughly patting the shoulder of his new friend. 'I did not realise that Eleusis was home to you.'

'Yes....it was once...I never thought I would see it again. It will...be nice.'

After a moment, Laan grinned at Axel, unashamed of the obvious shine in his eyes. He tensed suddenly, his gaze moving to the distant horizon.

'You see something?' Axel asked.

Laan shook his head slightly. 'Listen...' and on the wind, there was a whisper made of a hundred whispers.

'Wait - you can hear that too? I thought I was going nuts.'

Laan shook his head. 'Believe me, that would be preferential.'

'*Ax-el Len-nart...*' the whisper drifted on the hot, faint breeze.

Axel grew pale and stepped back from the mouth of the cave.

'Who's Axel Lennart?' Laan asked.

'T-That's me!'

Laan looked at Axel. 'It *is*? How is it they know your name?' he said.

Axel stared at Laan wide eyed. 'Well, *I* don't know! What are they?'

'Wraiths of the desert. They were Dreamers once. When faced with death, they gave themselves up to the dark magic, and now they are cursed to exist in a kind of half-life, neither living, nor dead. This is why the Regime takes Dreamers away. Just in case they rise again. Should one touch you, you will become like them. Soulless. Heartless. Empty.'

Axel stared into the horizon too, the sweat on his forehead cold. 'Why are they saying my name?'

Laan's gaze slipped down to the dusty ground. He did not reply straight away. 'They are drawn to darkness.'

Axel frowned. 'What do you mean?' he whispered, suddenly feeling very sick.

Laan looked at him, his eyes kind. 'It isn't *you*, Axel. It's something I sensed…from the moment we met. It's something you are connected to. I believe it is *that* to which the wraiths are attracted.'

Axel opened his mouth to ask more, when, suddenly, something very small, black and furry with a long, snuffling snout approached the cave and stopped short, his large grey eyes wide in alarm as he noticed that the prisoners were lose. He gave a high screech followed by a few short loud whoops.

'That's a Knoda?' Axel said, pointing incredulously at the creature.

Laan nodded, his expression serious. ''Deadly and treacherous?' But, he's so -'

'Don't say it!' Laan interrupted, shaking his head. '*Don't* say they're cute. Come on!'

And with that, Laan suddenly bolted off, surprisingly fast for a man of his advanced age, making a beeline to a large, dopey looking creature that was tied up on the edge of the camp. Axel stared after him open-mouthed, before realising that the large, angry mob of Knoda were headed straight for him. He sprinted after Laan, just as several spears whooshed past his chest.

'Hurry up! You're young. You're meant to be fast! I almost died and I'm faster than you!' Laan shouted.

Axel scowled, he *hated* running. Raising his eyebrows in curiosity, he surveyed the large, purple beast whose back Laan was scrambling on to. 'What *is* that?'

'It's a Knorlat. Get on, Get on!'

Axel didn't argue, but he wondered how fast this thing could really go. It looked like it was in danger of falling asleep at any moment. Regardless, he struggled on whilst Laan tried to persuade the Knorlat to get going. It seemed reluctant.

The Knoda were approaching fast behind them.

'Come on, come on!' Laan pleaded.

'What's, err. What's going on?' Axel asked nervously.

'Not much,' Laan replied.

The Knoda were almost upon them and they were still in the same place. A spear flew through the air, narrowly missing Axel's head. Another spear flew towards them, hitting the Knorlat in the rump. It yelped in agony and started to gallop at high speed, away from the Knoda. Laan started to laugh, only stopping when another spear just missed his ear.

*

'So, where's your ship?' Laan asked, as they reached the crater where the Unicorn had landed, breathless and thirsty. They had got here with relatively few troubles, as Laan knew where the flesh-eating quick swamps were and knew how to fight off the Dopnot snakes...*and* how to defeat the Blue Sandworms. All in all, it had been an eventful night. But night it definitely was, and the Unicorn was nowhere to be seen. The Knorlat was slumped against the crater wall, snoring slightly.

'I *really* thought he'd wait...' Axel said desolately. 'I didn't think he'd really go and leave us here! Bloody Hod.'

He sat down heavily on the crater floor, throwing a pebble into the darkness.

Laan said nothing for a moment. Then he clambered up the wall of the crater and peered over the edge, back towards Tuis Baku. The blue lights of several Unity Air Tractors were trained onto it. Several other Air Tractors were out searching the desert for signs of life, illuminating spots of land all around them with their bright floodlights.

'We can't stay here,' Laan whispered, as Axel joined him. 'Besides those Tractors, they'll send Guards out on sweeps, looking for us.'

Axel stared at the dark, dusty ground and sighed. Laan looked at Axel.

'Why didn't you just kill me when you had the chance?' he whispered irritably.

Axel stared at him in surprise. 'If you'd just killed me when I asked you, we wouldn't be in this position!'

'Oh, I'm sorry,' Axel whispered back, annoyed. 'I've never killed someone before. I don't just go around, *killing* people, you know.'

Laan stared at him in horror. 'Oh no. Don't tell me I'm being rescued by a pacifist? Let me guess, you're a vegan too?'

Axel narrowed his eyes. 'No. I just don't eat anything with a face.'

'This thing was doomed from the start!' Laan groaned.

'Well, look - we haven't been captured yet,' Axel said, trying to look on the bright side.

'Hands up!' A sharp voice suddenly said behind them.

Axel shot a glance at Laan and dropped his head back in exasperation. They slowly turned to find two Unity Guards standing in the crater behind them, armed with Snipe Rifles. Reluctantly, Axel and Laan put up their hands.

'You were saying?' Laan said.

One of the Unity Guards tapped his communicator, to tell his commander that they had found the missing prisoner, when there was the sound of a Persuader firing twice and the two Guards suddenly fell forward, collapsing onto Axel and Laan. They squinted into the blackness where the shots had come from but could see no one there.

206

'Come on,' Axel said, shrugging the Guard off his shoulder. 'Someone would have heard those shots.'

They scrambled out of the crater and ran towards the direction the shots were fired from, finding themselves suddenly amongst a small rocky outcrop. Suddenly, a pair of large hands clamped over both their mouths and dragged them backwards, further into the rocks, just as a troop of Unity Guards ran past, heading towards the crater.

Struggling to free himself, Axel pulled something off the head of his captor. Staring at the item with puzzlement, he realised it was remarkably familiar. There was only one person he knew who wore a black bandana. The hands finally loosened their grip.

'Hod!' Axel exclaimed, grinning like a maniac.

Hod reluctantly grinned back. 'Well, I couldn't just leave you in this armpit of a planet, could I? Especially with your newly liberated weirdo...who *everyone* seems to be looking for by the way,' Hod replied, motioning to Laan. 'Had to move the Unicorn. When I realized you'd dropped out of contact, I figured I'd wait for you here a few extra hours, see if you were, by some miracle, still alive.'

*

They ran as fast as they could after Hod, unfortunately attracting the attention of a nearby troop of Unity Guards, who started firing at them.

'Tell me you have a plan,' Axel groaned wearily.

'Just shut up and run, noid!' Hod said, as an Air Tractor fired at them, momentarily knocking them to the ground.

'RUN FASTER!' Hod urged.

'Run...faster...' Axel repeated breathlessly.

No one seemed to understand how much he truly hated running. A shot hit Laan and red liquid gushed out. Axel stared at him in concern.

'Oh! The crunters!' Laan said, sorrowfully, stopping and pulling the broken tin of food out of his pocket. 'I was looking forward to those...'

Hod rolled his eyes in exasperation and ran back to pull Laan on. 'Now is *not* the time, old man!'

And then, on the wind, came the whisper again. 'Ax-el Lennart...'

Laan looked at Axel in alarm. 'Wraiths!' he shouted.

'What?' Hod asked.

'Remember, don't let them touch you!'

Hod's frown of confusion melted into horror as they saw thin hooded figures emerging from the darkness behind them, illuminated by the blue lights from the Air Tractors.

Turning around, they ran as fast as their legs would carry them, sometimes stumbling on the uneven ground, as both the Unity Guards and wraiths drew ever closer. Suddenly they stopped, having reached the end of a sharp cliff, beyond which was a very deep dark ravine.

'Oh no,' Hod said. 'We must have taken a wrong turn! This isn't the way I came.'

The Air Tractors and Guards suddenly stopped firing. With slight relief, Axel remembered that they wanted Laan alive. They wouldn't shoot him off a cliff. Turning away from the edge, they watched as the faceless wraiths moved closer and closer to them, all whispering Axel's name.

'Axel,' Hod said, freaked out. 'You *know* these guys or something?'

One of the Wraiths extended an arm out, skin red and raw, his spindly fingers moving closer and closer to Axel's face.

'What's going on?' Hod breathed, but Axel had frozen, somehow mesmerized by the Wraith, whose hand was very close now, almost touching his skin.

'Hey, get back - stay away from him!' Hod said, moving to swipe the Wraith's hand from Axel's face.

'*Don't* touch them,' Laan said, stopping Hod's hand just in time.

The other Wraiths moved closer towards them. Hod exhaled. 'Jump,' he said quietly.

'What?' Laan said, but before he could object further, Hod pushed both Laan and Axel off the cliff, before jumping himself.

They hit the bubbling water of a river hard and dropped far into it, breaking Axel out of the trance. Struggling to the surface again, the lights from the Air Tractors blinded them from above.

'WHAT NOW?' Laan yelled, over the roar of a nearby waterfall.

'FOLLOW ME,' Hod shouted back, leading them back under the surface and further down river to the Unicorn, which was waiting for them on the riverbed.

*

'What the hell were those things? And why did they know your name?' Hod asked, once they were safely locked inside the Unicorn.

'Err…' Axel replied, still in shock.

'Actually, forget it, I'm going to have enough trouble sleeping tonight as it is. Let's just get out of here. We'll go along this river for a while, get away from all those Tractors and then, it's goodbye to this dump.'

He squelched his way over to the console, looking traumatised. Axel looked over at Laan, who was sitting in one of the passenger seats, twisting his hands in his lap in an agitated manner.

'We're going to make it,' Axel said comfortingly. 'We'll be back home before you know it.'

Laan looked at Axel, a sad smile on his face. 'Yes. Home. Thank you, Axel, for everything.'

Axel looked at Laan, puzzled. There was something strange in his tone.

'What's up?' Axel asked.

Laan's hands were white as he gripped the armrests of his chair. His face was just as pale.

'It will be safe now. No one will find the Lys Myrkr...that terrible black box.'

Axel blanched. 'The Lys Myrkr is a black box?' he said.

Laan looked up at him suddenly. 'Yes...why?'

'Oh...' Axel said. 'It's nothing. I just...I dreamt of a black box...just before we got here,' Laan stared at him, fear clouding in his eyes.

'What is it?' Axel asked, freaked out.

'You saw the box in your dreams?' Laan asked.

'I dreamt of *a* box,' Axel corrected.

'What else have you dreamt of? Anything that feels strange? Unusual?' Laan asked quietly.

Axel hesitated before replying. 'A lake. And...I dreamt of the escaped convict...5257. The Raven.'

'He has escaped?' Laan breathed.

'Yes...he's on Scarto, the Regime think he's looking for the Lys Myrkr too. You didn't know?'

Laan stared at Axel open mouthed, and then shook his head. 'And his powers - they have returned?'

Axel paused before responding. 'It is believed so, yes,' he said.

Laan grew even paler. 'When did these dreams start?'

'A few days ago. After I went to Scarto. The convict was there...but I didn't know it at the time...'

Laan's gaze dropped to the floor, thoughts rushing through his mind at lightning speed, unuttered questions hanging on his lips. Axel watched him, curiosity burning within him.

'What did you mean, back in Tuis Baku, when you said you knew *I* would come?' he asked, tensely.

Laan looked at Axel, his face very white. 'I knew that *you* would be the one I saw last...I knew that *you* would come seeking the Lys Myrkr...just like *him*....'

'What do you mean?'

The tail of something large thrashed against the Unicorn, and a mouthful of giant teeth emerged from the darkness of the river around them. They snapped outside the window of the helm, narrowly missing them.

'Right. That's it!' Hod said. 'Time to leave.'

'No – wait, there's something I must say!' Laan said, but Hod didn't listen.

'Whatever it is, you can say it in space, old man!' he said, pulling the steering lever as far down as it could go.

The Unicorn lurched violently from side to side as it burst through the surface of the river and rose up through the atmosphere at terrifying speed. But, the further they got from the surface of Jura, the more unwell Laan started to look. Suddenly, he slid down his chair and started convulsing.

'Laan...LAAN!' Axel shouted, unbuckling himself and rushing over.

'Oh. We've got fighters coming in,' Hod said, priming the ship's meagre guns. The Unicorn shuddered as shots hit it from all sides.

'Axel, I could *really* use your help here!'

Axel unbuckled Laan and lay him flat on the floor. The convulsions lessened and his eyes opened a little.

'There is nothing you can do,' Laan whispered, his body shuddering in pain. 'The Medibots...injected me with a...poison. It only becomes active if the prisoner leaves the planet,' Axel stared at Laan, his mind racing.

'What? Why didn't you tell me?'

Another loud shot shook the ship.

'You wanted to die. Didn't you?' Axel said, angrily. 'This was your plan all along, wasn't it? But it's not going to happen! What's the antidote?'

Laan smiled weakly. 'Only the Regime have it.'

Axel shook his head. 'Hod, we have to go back. He's dying. Laan's been poisoned!'

'Are you crazy?!' Hod replied. 'We can't go back. We're *all* going to snuff it as it is, if we don't get out of here now!'

'He's right,' Laan gasped, putting his hand on Axel's shoulder. 'We can't go back.'

'There must be something we can do,' Axel said miserably. Laan shook his head slightly, as another shot hit the Unicorn. 'No,' Laan said. 'This is for the best. This is how it was meant to be,' Laan looked at Axel sorrowfully. 'Listen to me, carefully now Axel. Do not let it corrupt your heart, as it has so many…others. *Promise me.*' Axel shook his head, confused. 'I don't understand…'

Laan blinked slowly, as though he was very tired.

'Find the Lys Myrkr, Axel…and destroy it…Promise me you will…' he shut his eyes briefly, and then forced them open again, shuddering with the last of his strength.

Axel frowned and then nodded. 'How will I find it?'

'The Lys Myrkr is treacherous…Your *father*…gave his life…to hide it…He wanted me to tell you where it was when you were ready….But I-I was so afraid…of what it might do if it was found. You *must* destroy it…Stop him from using it. Only *you* have the power to do this…You must not fail…' Laan gasped.

'My *father*?' Axel breathed, his heart thumping fast in his chest. 'Laan…W-was my father Calle Los?'

'You look *so* like him...' Laan's eyes were glassing over, but they flitted to Hod briefly. 'Be careful who you trust...*Tell my daughter that she may have my cloak...ice stones...and staff...*' he whispered, his voice so quiet Axel could barely hear it over the hum of the engines.

And, with a final breath, Laan was gone.

Secrets of the Dead

17.

Another loud blast hit the Unicorn and everything shuddered. Axel looked upon Laan's empty eyes a moment longer, before closing them and gently covering his body with a blanket. Axel stood slowly. Running the rough surface of his palm over his face, he joined Hod at the helm, fighting back tears as he took control of one of the blasters.

'WHAT HAPPENED?' Hod shouted, over the noise of gunfire.

Axel shook his head in response. 'LAAN'S GONE.'

Hod was silent for a moment. 'I'M SORRY AXEL, BUT THERE'S NOTHING MORE WE COULD HAVE DONE...'

The ship shuddered under the force of another hit.

'THERE'S TOO MANY OF THEM! WE'LL NEVER OUTRUN THEM,' Hod said, aiming his gun on a fighter and blasting it out of their way. 'AND YOU CAN BET THOSE TRACTORS ARE ON THEIR WAY TOO, WHEN THEY GET HERE, WE'RE REALLY DONE FOR!'

Axel shook his head and scrolled through the flight computer to see what was around. 'HEY LOOK,' he yelled, tapping the screen. 'WE CAN LOSE THEM HERE - THE MARA BENI NEBULA.'

Hod winced and shook his head. 'WE *CAN'T* GO IN THAT NEBULA – IT'S HAUNTED,' he replied.

Axel looked at him incredulously. 'WHAT?!'

'THERE ARE DEAD PEOPLE IN THERE -' Hod explained.

Axel frowned. 'WELL, THERE'S GOING TO BE TWO MORE DEAD PEOPLE IN HERE IF WE DON'T.'

Another loud shot shuddered through the Unicorn, forcing Axel off his seat. 'WE NEED COVER. YOU HAVE ANY BETTER IDEAS?' Axel shouted.

Hod scowled.

'AT LEAST LET ME FLY. YOU'RE BETTER WITH THE GUNS.'

Hod grimaced and handed the controls over. 'YOU CAN *FORGET* THE BIKE, AXEL. YOU'RE GOING TO OWE ME A NEW SHIP IF WE *EVER* GET OUT OF THIS NIGHTMARE!'

Axel's poor flight skills spun the ship, managing to avoid getting hit for a few moments.

Hod looked over in shock. 'YOU'RE A TERRIBLE PILOT – BUT KEEP DOING WHATEVER THAT WAS,' But Axel wasn't listening. Behind the remaining fighters, and gaining on the Unicorn with terrifying speed, were two enormous Unity Assault Cruisers.

'ERR, HOD, YOU SEEING THIS?'

'WE'RE TOAST…'

An almighty boom shuddered through the ship as the Assault Cruisers fired at them. A deafening bleeping filled the air as well as smoke from an array of small fires that had popped up around them, that Axel was desperately trying to put out.

'ANOTHER HIT LIKE THAT AND WE'RE GONNERS!' Hod yelled.

The pink clouds of the nebula started to whip past the windows of the Unicorn, growing denser with every passing moment. For a few brief moments, they had a respite from being shot at, and they drifted through the nebula, their eyes wide to the strangely coloured clouds and brightly sparkling stars around them.

Suddenly, the ship's communicator started emitting a strange, rhythmic clicking sound. Hod looked at Axel in alarm. Loud static blared through the communicator. Then, Hod's music started up, all the lights on the control panel lit up in frenetic chaos and the compactors and converters stored in the back all started to rattle violently. They lifted into the air, along with Axel and Hod, who grabbed hold of the tops of their chairs to stop themselves floating to the ceiling. And then, as suddenly as it started, it all stopped.

Axel, Hod and his supplies fell heavily to the floor and there was silence once again. Axel and Hod exchanged glances as they pushed themselves up off the floor.

'Believe me now?' Hod said, dusting himself off. Getting back into his chair, he flicked some switches and turned the steering wheel.

'What are you doing?' Axel asked.

'What do you think I'm doing? I'm getting us *out* of here. You know what *that* was? That was a warning. *They* don't like us being here and, guess what? *I* don't like us being here either.'

'Well, we don't have much of a choice,' Axel said with horror, he noticed the sharp nose of one of the Assault Cruisers pushing through the clouds to their right.

Hod sighed and took them further into the depths of the Nebula, as fast as they could go.

'THEY'RE CATCHING UP!' Axel yelled.

And then, to Axel's amazement, Hod slowed the ship to a stop.

'WHAT ARE YOU DO -' Axel started to say, and then he saw it.

Above them, hundreds upon hundreds of ships of all shapes and sizes were emerging from the clouds, buzzing around a large circular spaceport.

'Think we found your ghosts,' Axel said.

'Insurgents...' Hod breathed.

Stumbling to the back of the ship, Axel and Hod watched as the fighters firing on the Unicorn were destroyed by a fleet of ships travelling out from the base. A couple of massive explosions somewhere else in the nebula suggested that the Assault Cruisers were also gone. For a moment Axel and Hod stared at each other in shock.

'Ha-HA!' they both cried, hugging each other excitedly, before pushing each other away in embarrassment.

'Hod?' a voice suddenly drifted through the ship's communicator. 'You alright in there? It *is* you, right? I'd recognise that heap of junk anywhere,' Hod froze, looking as though he had just heard a ghost.

'I *know* that voice…but it *can't* be…' he said, frowning. 'Chad? Chad Vossloh?' He stuttered, after seating himself down at the helm.

'Yeah, it's me.'

'But, you're dead. The Banren Run, nine years ago. You – you *disappeared*…along with all the others.'

There was silence for a moment.

'Why don't you come up to the base and get some repairs done?' Chad said. 'I'll explain everything then.'

*

'You're *sorry*?' Hod said, his whole face having gone from the palest white, to a furious shade of puce in a very short space of time, whilst Chad Vossloh had explained how he came to be standing before them, very much alive.

'You fake your own deaths, so that you can leave to become insurgents. All *twelve* of you. My *so-called* friends. I mourned for you, man.'

Chad dropped his gaze to the floor. 'We asked you to come with us, Hod.'

'When? I think I would have remembered if all of my friends had told me they were going on a Revolution and asked me to come along.'

217

'I specifically asked you if you wanted to fight against the Regime, free Eleusis from tyranny and bring liberty and justice to the system. *You* said you weren't interested in politics.'

Hod looked up, wide-eyed. 'But that was – *I* was –'

Axel suppressed a smile. Hod sighed heavily. 'Okay, yes, I admit, that does sound like something I would say.'

They were sitting in a small mess room in the spaceport. The walls and ceiling were curved, and the white walls interrupted by large windows that looked out onto the beautiful pink clouds beyond. Far to the right, the Unicorn could be seen, undergoing a few essential repairs in a space dock. A glass wall led out to the corridor beyond, where lots of people bustled through, busily working at this and that.

Axel had nothing but good memories of Chad, most especially of all the times he had given Axel flight tips and stopped Hod from terrorizing Chuck. Despite being a revolutionary, Chad still looked just as clean cut as Axel remembered him, his dark hair smooth and neat, brown eyes bright, face handsome. There was nothing about him that would hint at his living off world for nine years. Everything about him seemed to scream of Eleusis.

'You've sacrificed so much for this,' Axel said.

Chad nodded slowly. 'But I can't tell you how great it is to see you both. To speak to you again,' he said, his eyes glistening. 'You know – you never really appreciate home, until you realise you can't go back.'

A raucous noise in the corridor interrupted their conversation. They all looked towards the glass door as a bunch of pilots suddenly burst into the room and, without hesitation, all jumped on Hod. After a moment of confusion, Hod's face burst into a grin as he recognised more and more of his friends. The missing twelve were all here, all still alive, and all on top of him. Axel smiled. It'd been a long time since he'd seen Hod this happy.

*

'Vossloh, please bring our guests up to V1, the commander wishes to speak to them,' a cold female voice said, through Chad's communicator.

'Sure. I'll bring them right up, Perdot.'

'Don't keep us waiting, funkbreath,' Perdot added.

Chad grinned as he looked at Axel and Hod. 'I'm working my magic on her. She's warming up to me.'

'Sure,' Hod said, nodding. 'Sounds like it's working.'

V1 was the bridge of the spaceport, a vast circular room in the middle of the structure, filled with busy, working people. The curved walls were lined with consoles and control panels with flashing buttons and a domed glass roof arced above them, framing the beauty of the nebula beyond. Perdot was waiting for them, tapping her foot impatiently. She was dark skinned, with a long shaggy main of brown curly hair, and a severe expression on her face.

'Finally,' she said tapping a button on her communicator. 'You made it.'

'Hello, Perdot,' Chad said, grinning. 'Did I tell you how beautiful you are looking today?'

'Shut it, funkbreath,' Perdot said, her eyes narrowing dangerously.

She looked at Axel and Hod, with a weary expression on her face. 'You two follow me, I'll take you up to Commander Lodre.' Axel and Hod exchanged frightened glances as Perdot stomped off across the room and up a ladder.

'You'd err, better go, you don't want to see her angry,' Chad said, pushing them forward.

'HURRY UP!' Perdot yelled.

The Commander was standing by a console, a small group of people clustered around her, talking in hushed tones. She was a woman of around fifty, with black hair that curled around her shoulders and bright, intelligent eyes that exuded a lot of energy. She must have been very beautiful once, as the vestiges of that beauty remained, though worn through the years of war and resistance. She smiled warmly at them both as they entered, but her eye lingered on Axel a little longer. He squirmed a little under her penetrating gaze.

'We know why you are here,' Commander Lodre said, once they had all introduced themselves. 'We have been listening to the radio chatter from the Unity base on Jura. We heard of the escapee...Someone who knows the position of a Völvur artefact hidden on Eleusis. An object of power, that the Regime seeks.'

She shot a penetrating gaze at Axel, as though she was trying to fathom him out. He nodded. 'Our Proxy has been accused of treason – he was seeking Laan so that the co-ordinates of the artefact could be known. I came here to save Laan from the Regime.'

'The Proxy of Eleusis?' Commander Lodre said, a strange expression on her face. She frowned at the floor a moment, a bitterness in her eyes. Then, she smiled a little. 'You are loyal to this Proxy, even though he seeks this object for himself?'

Axel frowned. 'He would never use it for himself. The Proxy is an honourable man. He only wishes to destroy it.'

Commander Lodre nodded, but Axel felt as though she was not in agreement with him. She fixed her penetrating eyes on Axel once more. 'I know that the prisoner is now dead and on board your ship. It is a great shame. Did he tell you where the object was hidden?'

Axel felt his heartbeat rise a little. He could feel every eye in the room fixed upon him. 'No,' he said, shaking his head. 'I'm afraid he...he died before he could tell me anything.'

Commander Lodre was watching him, her eyes sharp. Axel shot a nervous glance at Hod, who seemed to share his concern.

'Thank you for your hospitality Commander, but if the repairs are completed on our ship, I think we'd better be heading back to Eleusis now,' Hod said.

Commander Lodre said nothing for a long moment and then nodded. As Hod followed Perdot back down the ladder to V1, Lodre laid a surprisingly strong hand on Axel's arm, forcing him to stay a moment longer. 'Trust not a soul in your search for the Bright Darkness,' she whispered quickly in his ear. '*Not even yourself.*'

*

'Did that really just happen?' Hod said, when they were almost back to Eleusian space.

'Yeah…right?' Axel said, in agreement.

'Now, we just have to get back through that blockade in one piece and we're home and dry,' Hod said quietly, his mind obviously still on the friends he had left behind.

Axel nodded, looking up at the large variety of Unity ships that loomed ahead. His eyes shifted unwillingly to Scarto, which was also growing closer, wincing in pain as he felt the dull throb of the presence grow successively larger in his head, the closer they got to the moon. He had gotten used to the pain being more of a dull ache. Now it was back to being a full-on bombardment. He got up and walked to the back of the ship, leaning against a wall for support.

As he looked to the still, silent form of Laan, laid out on the floor in front of him, Axel knew it could not be just a headache. It was much, much more than that, he'd just been afraid of admitting it to himself. His gaze drifted down to his fingertips once more.

'Control ship to merchant vessel, identify yourself and state your business,' a voice filtered through the ship's communicator.

'Oh no,' Hod said, tapping something on the console dashboard in a panic. 'The scrambler's not working.' He shot an anxious glance at Axel. 'They're going to know you're here!'

Fighting the pain in his head, Axel hurried over and took a look at the scrambler. 'It's fried!' he groaned, shaking his head. 'Seems like our new friends forgot to fix it.'

'Forgot, or chose not to?' Hod said suspiciously.

They stared at each other for a moment, at a loss for what to do.

'Control ship to merchant vessel, identify yourself and state your business,' the voice said again, this time with less patience.

Hod clicked the ship's communicator on. 'Unicorn to Control ship…Hod Bergo here. Just returning from Kagbeni…' Hod said, trying to sound casual.

'There are two life sign readings coming up on our system from your ship,' the Guard from the control ship said. 'Have you got an unauthorised passenger on your ship?'

'Err…Not that I know of!' Hod said, with a forced laugh.

Axel shook his head silently.

'Your – err – systems m-must be malfunctioning,' Hod added quickly.

For a long moment, there was no response. Axel and Hod held their breath.

'Stop your engines and prepare to be boarded for an inspection.'

Hod clicked the communicator off and put his head in his hands.

'Not that I *know* of? *Not that I know of?* That's basically like saying *yes*!' Axel said.

'Well, what would *you* have said?' Hod replied, defensively.

They watched in mute horror as a small inspection ship approached their position.

'Okay…okay, look, whoever's coming abroad…we'll just *bribe* him…with something…' Hod said.

'*Bribe him*?! Hod, not only am I on this ship without permission, but we have a dead guy in the back, who also happens to be an escaped Unity prisoner. That's going to take one heck of a bribe.'

They looked wearily at Laan for a moment. Hod seemed like he was about to say something and then thought better of it at the last moment. Axel tapped his fingers on the edge of the console in an effort to calm his mind.

'Okay, what were you thinking we could use as a bribe?'

'*I don't know*, what have you got?' Hod said.

'Nothing! I've got absolutely nothing to my name...' Axel replied.

'Spacenuts, Axel...why d'you have to be so poor?' Hod moaned.

A sudden shudder and a low hum made them both freeze.

'Ship docking complete,' the flight computer announced proudly.

Before either of them could say, or do anything else, the airlock opened, and two Unity Guards walked through the open shield door, straight into the Unicorn.

*

It was one of those moments when no one could think of the right thing to say. The Guards looked from Laan to Hod and Axel, and Axel and Hod stared open-mouthed straight back at them. This was because the two Guards were none other than Chuck and Mork.

No one spoke or moved for a good long while.

'What - what's happening here?' Axel said, finally breaking the silence.

'Well, we could ask you the same thing!' Chuck replied. 'Who's under the blanket? And why are you wearing a Guard uniform?' Chuck asked.

Axel frowned and looked down – he'd forgotten he was still wearing FQ-1's uniform. 'Long story. Why are you?' Axel said, still taking in the red of their uniforms.

Chuck's shoulders slumped slightly. He shifted uncomfortably on his feet, looking decidedly green. 'Well...Nine got rid of the Heimdall – and said something about the Proxy not needing a special Guard, so, well...we...we're both Unity Guards now.'

Axel stared at them both, stunned. Chuck winced and stared at the floor.

'Look, I know it's not exactly the best job but...' his voice trailed off. 'So, what happened to you guys?'

Frowning, Axel brought them up to speed. Once he was finished, Chuck exhaled loudly. 'Listen, Axe, I know you said you'd find something else to do, but I didn't think you meant going on some crazy mission to the edge of the system and back,' Chuck said.

'Well, there *was* nothing else to do!' Axel replied. 'And, I didn't think that in the meantime, my best friends would go off to Danulix Port and come back as Unity Guards, but I guess life's funny like that, huh?'

'Hey, don't be a funklebag about this,' Chuck said, defensively.

'Yeah,' Mork added. 'It's not like we had a much of a choice. And anyway, we thought it could be...useful, to you know...know what's happening from the inside. Don't you want to know what's really going on here? With this blockade? With the convict?'

Chuck looked at Mork, shaking his head to stop him talking.

'Wait, are you telling me that you guys wanted this?' Hod piped up. 'You two idiots *chose* to become Unity Guards? Have I not taught you anything?'

Chuck frowned. 'No, not really,' he said.

Axel shook his head. 'I can't believe it! I can't believe that you would choose to become one of those faceless Guards, like the ones who terrorise us on a daily basis, who burnt down our huts. Who *Vanish* people?' Axel said.

Chuck shuddered, resting his hand on a control panel that was still sooty from being on fire. 'I feel like there's a lot of judgment going on here,' he said, looking from Axel to Hod and then back to Axel again.

'If you think that *now*, well wait till our mother dearest hears about this. Boy, are you going to get it!' Hod said, rubbing his hands together with glee.

As Chuck and Hod started bickering, Mork pulled Axel over to one side.

'Listen, Axe, I don't know when I'm going to be back home. But see, I'm worried about Blix.'

'Blix?' Axel said, frowning.

'Yeah. You'll look out for her won't you? I can't, whilst I'm stuck up here. And I think, I think she's in trouble.'

'What's this about, Mork?' Axel said, wondering if this was something to do with whatever Blix was cooking up in her basement. 'I had a feeling she was mixed up in something.'

Mork frowned to himself a moment, staring at the floor, conflicted. 'Now that it comes to it, I don't know if I should say…I wanted to tell you last time I saw you – but, well…I wasn't sure if it was right to tell.'

'Come on Mork, you can trust me.'

Mork relented. 'Well, you remember we were talking about the escaped convict? The Völvur?' he asked quietly. Axel felt his pulse rise slightly. He nodded. 'Well, this is going to sound strange, but ever since he escaped, I've felt, *different.*'

'Different how?' Axel said, his heart starting to thump against his chest.

Mork shook his head. 'I don't know. Can't put a finger on it. Anyway, one night, I woke with a terrible headache and that's when I saw her - Blix – walking around outside.'

Blix lived far out in the ice fields, and Mork's hut was the closest to hers, although it was still at least five kilopars away.

'She was sleepwalking. Heading straight into the bog next to my hut. It took both me and that old Servicebot of hers everything we had to drag her out of the mud before she drowned. And then, she was hysterical, she kept saying, '*He's* here, *he's* here...*he's* come for us...' and when I asked her who she was talking about, she said. 'The convict...the sorcerer...*the Raven...*"

Axel felt everything around him swim.

'*The Raven...*?' he repeated quietly.

'Yeah...Anyway, after that she came round suddenly, you know, woke up, and then she asked me what we were doing out in the ice fields in the middle of the night. Seemed to have no memory of any of it.'

'She definitely said '*the Raven*?' Axel asked, his face ashen.

'Yeah - that mean something to you?' Mork asked.

'Control ship to Guard CB-90, update on status,' a voice through Chuck's communicator interrupted them.

'Do you require back-up?'

Axel exchanged an anxious glance with the others. Chuck clicked the communicator on to reply. 'CB-90 to Control, no, no back-up required. All clear here on the Unicorn, must be a systems malfunction. Clear for landing.'

Axel sighed with relief.

'You're welcome,' Chuck said huffily, smoothing his red Unity bodysuit down and inadvertently smearing it with dirt in the process. 'See you two hosers back on Eleusis.'

*

They laid Laan to rest in an ice tomb, in a peaceful cave behind a frozen waterfall, deep within Loom forest, a wreath of white snow flowers placed over Laan's clasped hands. With a push of a button, the lid of the coffin slid shut with a quiet hiss, its surface as smooth and transparent as glass.

'Do you think we did the right thing?' Axel asked quietly. 'If we hadn't intervened…well, Laan would still be alive.'

They looked upon the tomb in silence for a moment. It glowed a little in the dim light of the cave, illuminating their faces with soft white light. Hod shook his head.

'He'd be alive but being tortured, and the Proxy would be dead. Now, I heard that they're likely to release him and reinstate him - lack of evidence or some such. If you ask me, *that* sounds like a win.'

Axel dropped his gaze to his feet. Hod winced a little and uncertainly placed a steadying hand on Axel's shoulder. 'Listen, Axe, Laan knew what he was getting into when he got on my ship…He *chose* this. That's how much he didn't want the Regime to get him. He must have really believed that things would be better this way.'

Axel nodded. But nothing anyone could say could get Laan's face out of his mind. His dying words ran through Axel's mind, haunting him. *Find the Lys Myrkr, Axel…destroy it…Promise me you will…Your father gave his life to hide it…You must…destroy it…You must not fail…'*

*

'How did this happen?!' Protector-9 snarled.

A red projection of General Cylix flickered in the air, an apologetic expression on his face. Nine was in his study, a room deep within the Palace of Light, where the Protectors resided. The walls were white and smooth and devoid of any windows and anything that would interrupt their purity. A holocrome projector sat in the middle of the room, a console close to it and a chair, mounted on the top of a small raised platform, where Nine was sitting now.

'A full-on rebel assault, sir…We were overrun. They came from nowhere. Two Assault Cruisers were completely destroyed,' General Cylix said.

A murderous expression passed over Nine's face. 'And Laan is dead?'

'We injected him with Venin, as a safeguard, should he escape.'

Nine said nothing for a moment, but just surveyed Cylix as though he was something unpleasant he'd found on the bottom of his shoe.

'Thank you, General. That is all,' Nine said, looking past Cylix to the Guards that stood behind him. 'Take him,' Nine said, and the Guards advanced on Cylix.

'What? Sir? No - no!' Cylix pleaded.

But it was too late. Nine's order had been given. Cylix' screams filled the room, whilst Nine watched with a smile on his face. After a moment, Nine flicked the projection off, tiring of it. He sat in silence for a few moments, staring into the empty space before him. With a low bleep, the door slid open and Berau entered, flanked with Unity Guards, his face flushed with anger. 'Is it true? That you have lost the proof of my father's treason?'

'Yes,' Nine said curtly, as he tapped his communicator.

'Protector?' A voice said as a hologram of Guard XB-1 appeared.

'Release the Proxy,' Nine said.

'Sir?' XB-1 prompted for an explanation.

'Keep him under close watch. I *want* to see what he will do now.'

Berau shook his head. 'No, no, this cannot be. You *told* me he would be executed. That you had the proof…and now you reinstate him?'

'Patience, young Proxy...' Nine said, struggling to keep his temper in check.

'Patience?! You know what he will do, don't you? He will try and find a way to usurp me...He doesn't want me to rule,' Berau whined.

Nine pursed his lips. 'There are greater things at play here, Feovold. Your father *will* fall...and you shall gain your rightful place. In any case he has no real power anymore, only the illusion of it.'

*

'For real?' Hod said, looking around the emergency quarters. 'This is where you, my mother, Chuck and Kolbjorn have been holed up?'

Axel nodded wearily. 'Yep...' he replied, as Servicebot excitedly served them a cup of Frick juice each. 'Except, well, lately it's mostly just been me...and Servicebot.'

'Oh Axel, you need to find yourself a lady friend,' Hod said, grinning.

Axel smiled wryly. 'Yeah, well maybe you should take your own advice on that score.'

'Trust me, I've no problem when it comes to women,' Hod said, smiling smugly.

Axel nodded with a skeptical grin. He was soldering some wires together on an old circuit board he'd acquired from one of Hod's less reputable acquaintances. Now he just needed a droid of some kind... A senile sounding bleep from the other side of the hut caught Axel's attention. Chuck's Servicebot was doddering about, pouring out some Frick juice for Hod and missing the cup by some distance.

'Mmmm...' Axel said to himself, eyebrows raised in thought. 'Come here, buddy, I've got an upgrade for you.'

Servicebot bumbled over excitedly.

'Hold him, would you?' Axel said.

'What are you doing *now*?' Hod whined irritably, reluctantly clamping his arms around the droid as Axel soldered the circuit board into Servicebot's extremely ticklish innards.

'There we go,' Axel said, pressing a grimy button on Servicebot's head.

A small screen next to it powered up.

'Wait a minute - that looks like the Regime's system,' Hod said, stiffly. 'Tell me you're not hacking into the Regimes system?'

'Well, I know the Proxy's apparently a free man and all again, but I'm guessing the Regime's watching him. So, if we're going to find Laan's daughter, we're going to have to get information another way.'

'Laan's daughter?! What are you talking about?'

'He left a bequest, remember? I've got to find her,' Axel said, working away.

Hod rolled his eyes. 'He was a *monk*, noid. Monk's don't have children. Also, you still owe me an airbike.'

Scrolling through the bounty hunter's reports, he found that Laan appeared to have spent time on pretty much every planet in the system. Other than that, the reports were as sparse as Axel had expected them to be for someone who had been in hiding for nineteen years. No children were listed. Well at least the Regime would not be going after Laan's daughter any time soon.

'Find anything useful?' Hod asked.

Axel shook his head thoughtfully. With a loud whirring and the sudden flash of white sparks, a circuit in Servicebot's head exploded, and smoke rose out of him with a faint hiss.

'Ah great, *now* who's going to make dinner?' Hod groaned.

'Trust me – I just did you a favour.'

That night, it was not Hod's snoring, or his frequent murmurings about pickled halitoffs that kept Axel awake, but the splitting pain in his head…the throb of the presence…the RAVEN.

The name spun round and round in Axel's mind. *Dark magic? A darkness he was connected to?* It was nuts. And yet...he thought, staring at the ceiling...he knew it was the answer to everything he had been running from since the day he had first noticed the presence...A chill tingled up his spine. Tossing the blanket off of himself, he opened the shield door to get some air.

As usual, it was raining outside, but the sky was already lightening, the night drawing to a close. Rubbing his eyes wearily, he listened to the sound of the water falling off the lightly sloping roof to the ground below, finding it soothing. Blinking into the dark streets beyond, he noticed something approaching...a dull light glowing dimly through the falling rain. The quiet whirring sound that accompanied it was familiar, Axel realised, just as his airbike emerged from the darkness, smoke billowing from two large gunshot holes in her body.

'Ax-el...' the airbike said brokenly as it approached. 'Re-pair re-qui-red imm-inen-t...'

Axel ran out into the muddy street just as her headlight flickered off. The whirring of her hover mechanism suddenly stopped and the bike crashed into the ground.

'Oh, no...' Axel cried. 'Sandra! Oh, what happened to you?'

Hod was dead to the world, so, with recently repaired Servicebot's help, Axel tried to drag his airbike inside the emergency quarters. He didn't have much luck.

'She's too heavy without her hover function...I'll try and fix it - she must be waterlogged!' Axel said, getting his tools out and waving smoke away from his face. Just then, he noticed the sound of a transport of some kind approaching, through the dark street and Axel found a gun pushing into his back. The creature behind him squeaked orders in another language, that he understood to mean, 'Hands up!'

'Okay, okay…' Axel said, standing slowly, his hands behind his head.

He turned to get a look at his attacker. A dark furry creature about half Axel's height stood facing him, a Stun blaster pointed straight at Axel.

'Oh no…' Axel said, his voice full of dread. 'Knodas again! Of *all* the bad luck. Come on now…you don't need this hunk of junk…' Axel said, kicking his airbike. 'Her parts are fried…You don't want this.'

The Knoda prodded Axel with the blaster, pushing him back so that he could inspect the fallen airbike himself, lowering his gun a little as he did so. Axel took his chance and wrestled the Knoda, trying to get his blaster off him, just as a small transport arrived. A hoard of Knodas tumbled out chaotically, their dark fur slick with rainwater.

'Servicebot…*wake up that useless lump*!' Axel yelled.

Servicebot did Axel's bidding and started prodding Hod in the face. Hod groaned. With a surge of anger and frustration, Axel noticed his fingertips were glowing with white light again, and around him, the wind started to pick up, forcing the Knodas back. The wind swirled around them, growing stronger and stronger, until the Knodas started to lift up off their feet, into the dark night air. Gripping onto the side of their transport, they squeaked to each other in alarm.

Struggling against the wind, one of the Knodas managed to aim his Stun Blaster at Axel and fired. Axel fell backwards into the mud, stunned and the wind immediately calmed into a quiet swirling bluster. Through his eyelashes, he watched as the glow in his fingertips quickly diminished. The world around him grew dim as he watched his beloved airbike being dragged off, into the transport.

'Axel…if that's your bike, you can keep it…' Hod's voice drifted out of the emergency quarters, before he shut the shield door, leaving Axel spread-eagled in the mud.

'Ughhh…' Axel moaned in frustration, before passing out. Hod really was an idiot.

*

On Scarto, the Raven stood, silhouetted in the gloom, in a cave whose mouth looked out into a dark sky full of bright stars. Several cloaked figures stood before him, their faces partially concealed with metallic masks.

The figure closest to the Raven stepped forward, and knelt on the rocky ground. He was an Eleusian Protector known as Protector-10.

'Laan is dead, my lord,' Ten said.

'Are you sure he told the boy nothing?' the Raven hissed.

'We do not believe so.'

'Where is Bodo?'

'Bodo is still missing, my lord. We fear he may have turned against you…As he did once before.'

'*Axel Lennart* is becoming more of a threat,' the Raven mused.

'We could dispose of him on your behalf?' Protector-10 proposed.

'No,' the Raven said. 'Leave the boy to me.'

THE END

Thank you for reading Volume I from the Axel Lennart series! For a sample of Volume II – *Axel Lennart and the Bright Darkness*, please read on. Please visit www.axellennartbooks.com for Volume II and more information on the Axel Lennart series.

AXEL LENNART AND THE BRIGHT DARKNESS

D.M.Z. Liyanage

Powers!

1.

'What the hell happened to you?' Chuck's voice permeated through the fogginess that was Axel's brain.

Axel blinked his eyes open and then immediately squeezed them shut as the dull morning light forced its way in. He was still lying spread-eagled in the middle of the street, outside the emergency quarters. Chuck stood over him, dressed in his new Unity Guard outfit. Axel recoiled instinctively. He was never going to get used to that.

'Bad luck, and your *hoser* of a brother, that's what happened,' Axel moaned, pushing himself up into a sitting position.

Chuck rolled his eyes at the thought of Hod and offered his hand. 'Come on, let's go inside.'

Just then, the shield doors to the quarters opened behind them and Hod appeared, dressed only in his underpants. He sipped at a cup of Frick juice whilst scratching himself. 'Oh, brother Chuck! You're back early. What happened, the Regime raise their intelligence requirement to 'moron'?'

Chuck raised his eyebrows and shot a dark look at Axel. 'One day…I'll prove he was adopted.'

*

'So…you haven't found anything else we could try to wake up that creepy old thing in the hibernator yet? Because he's starting to really freak me out,' Blix said, her hands on her hips.

235

'I've - been a bit busy,' Axel said lamely. S-LO, who had been battling a deep-set stain in a nearby rug, rumbled up to Axel, bleeping irritably.

'I know, I know S-LO...Well, I'm here now, aren't I? And still in one piece.'

S-LO bleeped in annoyed acceptance.

'And where have you been all this time?' Blix continued. 'I was...I *thought*...' her words trailed off and she looked away, pretending to examine a broken machine part. 'Autobot was worried, that's all.'

'*Autobot* was worried?' Axel said, with a slight grin.

'Wait, Bodo's still here?' Chuck said, catching up with the conversation.

He brushed some crumbs off his Unity Guard uniform and threw a space bean in his mouth. 'I'd totally forgotten about that old nutbag. How is he?'

'Not good,' Blix replied, moving over to a cauldron that was bubbling over the fire.

She grabbed a handful of snow out of a bucket at her feet and added it to the mixture, whilst her Servicebot buzzed around her, getting in her way.

'He's started screaming in the night. Stay long enough and you'll hear it for yourselves,' she said, stirring the mixture in the cauldron with a short wooden spoon.

Chuck stopped mid-chew and looked at Axel.

'Okay, that is pretty creepy,' Axel admitted.

S-LO bleeped in agreement.

Axel looked out through the open door of Blix's maintenance hut, into the blustery snow beyond. Although he could not see anyone moving about in the ice fields beyond, he knew there was someone there, a shadow concealed within the inky darkness.

'What is it?' Chuck asked, midway through another space bean.

Axel shook his head. 'I think I'm being followed…' he muttered, pressing a button on a control panel on the wall.

The door of the maintenance hut slid shut with a swift whoosh.

As Blix's concoction started to boil and steam rose from the cauldron, filling the hut with a strange aroma, Chuck sniffed at it and grimaced.

'Ughh. Blix what is that? It smells like something died in there. A long time ago.'

A thunderous look came into Blix's eyes. 'That's my Grandmother's recipe, Funkbreath! It's a healing draught. I thought it might work for Bodo, to wake him up…unless you two have any better ideas?'

Chuck frowned, pulling his cloak tight over his nose in a disgruntled manner.

'Has he said anything, in his sleep? Anything about the convict?' Axel asked, moving over to the window and looking out at the glowing hibernator outside.

Blix stopped stirring the cauldron and looked up. 'No…' she said hesitantly. 'He just keeps muttering about how something's his fault…that something's breaking…'

'Do you know what that means?' Axel asked.

Blix stared at him. 'No, why would I?'

'Because…' Axel started.

He didn't quite know how to say what he wanted to say. 'There's something I came here to ask you about, Blix…about the time Mork saved you, out on the ice fields.'

'Huh?' Chuck said, confused.

Blix paled. 'Mork told you?' she asked, her voice little more than a whisper.

'He was worried about you.'

'Told you what?' Chuck asked.

'Axel, you know what the Unity Guards will do if they find out that I – that I'm a…a *sleepwalker*,' she said, her voice trailing off into silence.

'Relax, Blix, they're not going to find out from Mork, or from us, right Chuck?'

'Sure,' Chuck said, still not entirely sure about what they were talking about anyway.

'Has it happened more than once, then – the sleepwalking?' Axel asked.

Blix nodded. 'I programmed Servicebot to trail me if I do. I hate it.'

Axel shot Blix a troubled look. 'Mork said that you mentioned someone called *'the Raven,'* when he found you sleepwalking.'

'I-I did? It was just a dream, Axel,' Blix said, looking petrified. 'I don't even remember saying that.'

'But you know who he is, don't you?' Axel asked, moving closer to her.

Blix pulled her cloak around herself and sat down. 'Well, it depends if you believe the old stories. They say the Raven was a Völvur. A dark Sorcerer.'

'Will someone please tell me what is going on?' Chuck asked. 'You're asking Blix about someone she dreamt about?'

'Yes,' Axel said hesitantly. 'Because I dreamt of him too. Convict-5257 *is* the Raven.'

Chuck and Blix stared at him.

Axel described the dream as best he could. Blix nodded.

'The black feathered cloak - that's what I saw too – but it wasn't a dream like you describe – there was no lake, no fire. Just flashes of his image. There was mostly darkness. And I could hear a voice. A whisper in my mind, in a language I couldn't understand,' Blix whispered. 'He had the strangest eyes…they were empty…and totally red.'

238

Axel's stomach dropped.

'What is it?' Chuck asked.

'I saw that too – the red eyes.' Axel murmured.

'So, what…the convict's in your minds? Do you guys realise how absolutely nuts this sounds?' Chuck said, looking freaked out.

'Yeah,' Axel replied. 'And what's more, Bodo was his apprentice.'

'What?!' Chuck cried.

Blix paled. 'You can't be serious?'

'I am.'

'Axel. You made me keep him here! How could you?' Blix cried.

'Well he's hardly posing a threat now, is he? What's he going to do, attack you with his snores?' Axel argued.

Blix groaned in frustration. Chuck moved over to the window, as if to check Bodo was still where they had left him.

'Ah, he's still there. Never thought I'd be so happy to see him,' Chuck said, sighing with relief.

'The Raven was the one in the caves that day, wasn't he?' Blix said, after a moment.

'I think so,' Axel said, his heart thumping in his chest. 'I - I can feel his presence when he's near. Do you feel it too?' Axel asked hopefully.

Blix shook her head with a slight frown. 'His presence? No, it's only the dreams - and the sleepwalking.'

Axel nodded, wondering what that meant. 'I felt it strongly that day, at the Bay of Ruins…I'm sure that he was there and he stopped the P-600 from crashing. The convict…*the Raven*…saved our lives that day.'

Chuck said nothing for a moment, then poured himself a cup of Blix's Smoke Gin and downed it whole.

'So, what are you saying here…that we have another Völvur on the loose, and we almost met him?'

Axel nodded. 'Yes. And he's on Scarto right now…'

AUTHOR'S NOTE

I just wanted to say thank you so much for reading *Axel Lennart and the Ice World*. I hope you enjoyed reading it as much as I loved writing it!

I started writing this book in around 2012, when I was working as a researcher on a live morning TV show. At that time, I felt like I was on an endless treadmill of getting up horrendously early for work, putting in long hours and wondering what on earth I was going to do with the rest of my life. I quit my job that year and went back to University. It was during this period of study and a new beginning, when I wrote *Axel Lennart and the Ice World*.

I finished both this book and the second book in the series – *Axel Lennart and the Bright Darkness* in 2016.

The core theme of the book, which I hope comes across, is about accepting yourself – especially if you are different. Growing up in London, I experienced a lot of racism. It happened every day, in almost every class for about four years. It made it hard to feel good about where I came from and what I looked like.

If you are experiencing something similar, it does become easier to deal with as you get older. And a big part of that is accepting yourself and being proud of who you are. You are a scientific and spiritual marvel – and your life can be anything you want it to be. Never forget how wonderful and special you are.

D.M.Z. Liyanage, 2020.

Please visit www.axellennartbooks.com for *Volume II: Axel Lennart and the Bright Darkness,'* and more information on books in the Axel Lennart series. Thank you again – I would very much appreciate it if you would be so kind as to leave a review for this book, as I'd really like to know what you think of it ☺!

Printed in Great Britain
by Amazon

46228896R00144